The Weight
of Death

Nicky Stratton

First Published in 2016
by GWL Publishing
an imprint of Great War Literature Publishing LLP

Produced in United Kingdom

ISBN 978-1-910603-22-2 Paperback Edition

GWL Publishing
Forum House
Stirling Road
Chichester PO19 7DN
www.gwlpublishing.co.uk

Nicky Stratton lives near Stratford on Avon. She completed a degree in Humanities with the Open University aged 55 and began writing shortly after she had graduated. The Weight of Death is her first novel.

Dedication

For Myles.

Acknowledgements

I'd like to thank Valerie Hoskins and Guy Kennaway for their steadfast support.

And for their invaluable criticism and camaraderie, my writing group: Lindsay Stanberry Flynn, Rosemarie Davies, Robin Heaney, Maureen Hall, Diane Colvin, Christine Steenfeldt, Julian Eldridge, Mary Durndell and Paul Budd.

Chapter One

Lady Laura Boxford looked down at the pug as he clattered into the lift beside her. "Parker," she said, "we must have your toenails done."

The lift was one of the many benefits of having her family home converted into a residence for the elderly. The Jacobean mansion, Chipping Wellworth Manor, now renamed Wellworth Lawns, was a successful business with a healthy – well, as healthy as could be expected, under the circumstances – waiting list.

"Toenails, now that's an idea," Laura continued. "I wonder if Hetty would like a pedicure?" Parker gave a small whimper as the doors closed. They stood, legs firmly apart, as they were whisked up to the first floor.

The lift came to a halt and, as the doors opened, Brigadier Stanway stood facing them. He still had the semblance of a military bearing but the jacket of his tweed suit now hung off his once broad shoulders. "Morning, Boxford," he said and marched in beside her. She put out her hand to stop the doors from closing.

"Morning, Brigadier. My floor, I think." Laura walked out, pulling Parker close beside her. The lift doors shut and she was left alone in the corridor. She shook her head. "That man has no manners at all."

Laura deposited the dog in her suite of rooms, throwing him a chew from the old Fortnum's tin she kept on a table beside the coat stand.

"You stay here. I won't be long," she said, shutting him in before taking the few short steps to her old friend Hetty Winterbottom's room next door. Knocking, she called out as she let herself in, "Hetty, are you up yet? I've just been stuck in the lift with that terrible Brigadier. Hetty?" she called again. "It's nearly eleven. I thought I might take you into Woldham. We could have a pedicure at that new fish place."

As the early spring sunlight streamed in the huge bay window, a myriad of brightly coloured lights reflected round the room, darting from wall to wall and over the ceiling. It reminded Laura of the Greek nightclub she'd once been to while island-hopping on a yacht in the Aegean with her late husband, Tony. It was a veritable disco glitter ball of colours.

"Hetty, why have you put those paperweights in the window? They'll cause a fire if you're not careful. I would have thought you'd remember that after your brother's little accident." She turned towards the bed. *That's odd*, she thought, looking at the crumpled heap of blankets, eiderdown and pillows. Hetty was most punctilious about her bedding; she insisted on hospital corners at all times.

The remains of Hetty's breakfast lay on a tray on her bedside table. Crushed egg-shells in their cups – she always liked to let the witches out – and an empty toast rack were now the only evidence of the meal.

The bathroom door was ajar. "Hetty," Laura called again and walked in. The room was empty; Hetty's freshly laundered towels lay folded on the heated rail, unused. She caught a glimpse of herself in the mirror above the basin. Her new contact lenses heightened the startling blue of her eyes, but also revealed only too clearly the lines around them. *Not too bad, all things considered.* She smiled at herself. *And at least they're not from frowning.*

Beside the basin she noticed a little oblong box with the image of a red Chinese dragon stamped on it. Laura picked it up and shook it. *What's Hetty doing with these ridiculous pills? Another of Nurse Creightmore's herbal remedies, I bet.* She put down the box and looked out of the window onto what had once been her kitchen garden. It was now a cluster of newly built bungalows designed for more independent living. She wondered what Tony would have made of the transformation. "Bloody Legoland," he'd probably have said.

She returned to Hetty's bedroom. The sun had disappeared behind a cloud so that the reflections from the small collection of glass paperweights no longer dazzled her. She gazed out at the hills in the distance and then down into the gardens. Since Hetty had broken her ankle, Laura knew she would not see her friend strolling below.

Perhaps she had an appointment with Dr Mellbury? He ran a surgery in the old stable block twice a week for non-urgent cases and Nurse Creightmore sometimes took Hetty down in her wheelchair. But the chair was parked in the corner by the door and the diary on Hetty's desk contained no revelation as to her friend's whereabouts.

Laura crossed the thick Wilton carpet and perched on the end of Hetty's bed. Something hard was digging into her left buttock. Jumping up, she pulled back the bedclothes. It was Hetty's plaster cast and that pedicure could not come too soon. Hetty's big toenail protruded well beyond the end of the purplish toe.

She threw the eiderdown and sheets to one side. "Oh no!" she cried.

Hetty Winterbottom was dead, of that there could be no doubt. Her hair surrounded her head like a halo of spun sugar and her mouth was agape, a deep denture-less cavern. But it was Hetty's eyes that drew Laura's attention. Wide open, they were glazed in an expression of fury. Hetty was prone to shortness of temper, usually concerning any delay in the arrival of food. Laura looked again. No, it wasn't exactly fury – that was wrong. It was more outrage – something between shock and indignation.

"Oh, Hetty." Laura reached into the sleeve of her cardigan for a handkerchief and then sat down beside her friend and held her stiffening hand. "How often did I tell you?" she said, as Hetty stared up at her. "Three eggs for breakfast is too many."

Then she remembered something the undertaker had said when laying out Tony. "It's the rigor mortis, your ladyship. I've done my best with 'im, but as you can see it's not to the standard I should have preferred."

Laura had noted Tony's expression: the eyes ever so slightly open. She rather liked the look. It reminded her of when he pretended to scan the racing pages for a long shot but was, in reality, mentally undressing her.

"Inflation," the undertaker had continued, "and poor pay conditions in the nursing fraternity is what I put it down to," he said, bemoaning the fact that it took all of two coins to do the job of keeping shut the eyelids of the departed.

Laura hunted round for Hetty's bag and then remembered she kept loose change in the small porcelain bowl on her dressing table. She fingered through the coins and, picking out a couple of two pence pieces, hurried back to the bed. She gently pressed down the lid of one eye and placed a coin on top. Hetty stared up at her, Nelsonesque.

"Goodbye dear Hetty," she said, pressing down the other lid. At that moment the first coin fell off onto the carpet and rolled under the bed.

Laura heard the crack of her knees as she hitched up her skirt and bent to kneel down. She was feeling under the valance when there was a knock on the door. She turned and saw the shapely leg of Mimi, the Bulgarian maid.

"Morning, Mrs. Hett," Mimi called, pulling the hoover in behind her. "Ladysheep! What you doing down under, your age and all? But holding horses… What this here?" She looked down at Hetty, the thick lock of her lustrous black ponytail swinging forward over her shoulder so that it brushed Hetty's face. "Oh me." She turned to Laura and tutted. "She no look so good…"

"I'm afraid that Mrs. Winterbottom has met her maker," Laura said.

"I thinking Mrs. Hett no more meetings butcher, baker, how you say." Mimi shook her head. "I thinking Mrs. Hett she going gone."

"Yes, gone. She's gone and we must get her eyes closed before it's too late… Ah, here it is." Laura rose, clutching the coin. "But I think we might need something a bit heavier. See what you can find that's heavy Mimi."

"You want heavy?" The maid looked around the room. "Chair or table maybe. I lifting?"

"No, no, not as heavy as that. Just something to keep her eyes shut." Laura put each of her index fingers on Hetty's eyelids and gently closed them so that Mimi would understand. They watched as the eyelids slid open again.

"Oh dear, this is no good at all," Laura moaned. "Hetty would be livid if she…"

"Livid? I not so sure. We doing past tense in my class. Teacher very bad, but I no think Mrs. Hett is livid. Yesterday she livid, nowaday she dead."

"I know she's dead. I can see that." Laura looked around the room. "Get a couple of those glass paper… ornaments Mimi… Two." She pointed to the window. "Them. There."

Mimi picked up a swirling pink Caithness weight in one hand and a green bubble dump doorstop in the other.

"No, no, not that big."

Mimi returned with two smaller paperweights. One, Laura knew well. It was cut glass with a small blue flower in the centre. Hetty's daughter Gloria had given it to her mother for her eightieth birthday. As Mimi handed it to her, Laura remembered how thrilled Hetty had been. It had come in a matching blue box, 'The Diamond Cut' in gold writing on the front. It was etched in Laura's memory because she herself had won it in a tombola and had given it away. "We might get a couple of quid for it," the lady in the charity shop had said.

"Here, Mimi, put them on Mrs. Winterbottom's eyes while I hold down the lids… Carefully now." Laura looked down at Hetty. Something definitely wasn't right. "No, wait," she said. "Put them back. We must not move her… But hold on, Mimi, didn't you bring in Mrs. Winterbottom's breakfast earlier?" Laura pointed to the tray. "How was she then?"

"I no bringing Mrs. Hett her breakfast. That from last night. Her wanting late-time snack. She no calling kitchen for her breakfast morning time."

"What? She didn't have breakfast? That must mean… Is Doctor Mellbury here this morning?"

"I no thinking, but Nurse Creight, I seen her doing thing with Mr. Thorn. His bedroom I cleaning early."

"Good. Do you think you could go and find her? I'll sit here with Mrs. Winterbottom until you get back. I wouldn't want to leave her on her own."

Mimi pattered from the room and Laura went to find a comb from the bathroom in order to tidy Hetty's hair. She remembered that Hetty had only had her hair done earlier that week. Dudley, of 'Dudley's Hair Designs,' came in once a fortnight to attend to those of his clients who could not get in to the salon in Woldham. Hetty had made an awful fuss when he asked her to bend her head over the basin. But she'd seemed so well. Tetchy maybe, but strong and tetchy. Not weak, as if she were about to drop off her... pass away. Even Dudley had commented on it as he wrestled her under the portable dryer.

"You get back under there if you want some curls, Mrs. W," he'd joked, as he turned up the heat control, leaving Hetty looking like an irate space invader.

Laura sighed and continued combing as if she were disentangling a cobweb. How cross Hetty would have been if she had pulled a knot.

"Bugger it, Laura, mind out. There's precious little left!"

Yes, she'd certainly have cursed. Laura looked again at her friend's pained expression. But why was her mouth open as if some half-formed word was escaping from her lips? Laura remembered the previous evening. She had returned from playing bridge and thought she'd say goodnight to Hetty. Parker had sniffed and snuffled at the bottom of the door but there was no light coming from under it, so she had assumed Hetty was asleep. But then she had seen a small glimmer — Hetty kept a torch beside her bed — so Laura had called out to her. Hetty had answered, her voice sounding frail when she said she was "all right". That was not unusual but what was out of character was that Hetty had then said, "Night night dearie," and Hetty never called her 'dearie'. It seemed odd at the time and now it seemed even odder.

Nurse Creightmore unwrapped the clean starched sheet. "Thank you, Lady Boxford, I'll take over now." She positioned her feet in their flat brown lace ups and shook the sheet. It flapped and unfurled, covering Hetty.

"I've got an uncomfortable feeling," Laura said.

"Tired yourself out, I should think. It must have been a nasty shock finding Mrs. Winterbottom, but it's nearly lunchtime now…" The nurse squinted at the watch pinned to her chest. "Well, nearly. Alfredo's sure to have made something nice. Then you can have a rest before tea."

"But that's not what I mean," Laura said.

Nurse Creightmore ignored her and began studying her clipboard notes, thin lips puckered in concentration.

"Shouldn't we get Dr. Mellbury?" Laura asked.

"Dr. Mellbury won't be back until this afternoon." The nurse put down her notes and adjusted the grips in her short mousy hair. "It's not as if she's going anywhere, is it?"

Laura winced as Nurse Creightmore put the clipboard under her arm and made towards the door. She could understand the nurse's brusqueness. Naturally, Wellworth Lawns had a high turnover of residents – but this was Hetty. She tried to voice her concerns again. "I just thought Mrs. Winterbottom looked…"

"Yes?" The nurse straightened her white coat with authority and held the door open.

"Oh dear. I'm sure it's nothing really…"

Nurse Creightmore sighed and her almost lash-less eyes narrowed. "What is it?"

"Never mind. It doesn't matter now."

Laura returned to her apartment. Parker was asleep in his basket in the sitting room next to her bedroom. She sat down on the sofa and listened to his rhythmic snore. *But it* does *matter*, she thought. And the more she thought about it, the more disturbing it was, Hetty's sudden demise. She couldn't get her dear friend's expression or the sound of those last fateful words out of her mind. There was something unquestionably not right about it. Even chronic indigestion after three boiled eggs would not have resulted in that look of… What was it? Agonised astonishment.

Then something else from the previous day came back to her. It was as she had sat with Hetty before going to the Bridge Club at Strudel Black's, she drinking her chamomile tea sitting in Hetty's worn out satin tub chair, Hetty eating Wagon Wheels in bed. They were talking about Brigadier Stanway. He had recently arrived at Wellworth Lawns and was in a room further down the corridor.

"I hope he's not at bridge. Last time he frightened Strudel into bidding four no trumps," Laura had said.

"I can't say I miss Bridge Club. Sometimes this ankle's a blessing in disguise," Hetty said. "But I told you the old sod barged in yesterday while Nurse Creightmore was giving me my Chinese tea infusion. Pretended he'd gone to the wrong room. Ridiculous idea, he's much further down the landing, isn't he?"

They'd huffed and Hetty had continued, "He came right in. Said what a large room it was. 'This is a bloody big room,' that's what he said. I found him quite threatening, looming down at me like an ancient Vincent Price."

Laura remembered him getting into the lift. What was it about him? She'd seen him bidding at the charity auction the previous week. He'd rather got in people's way waving his arms around, and all for a box of After Eights. She had thought him absurd at the time. His head jostling above the crowd like a barren hilltop, the few strands of hair clinging to the summit defended by a battalion of grey around the back of his neck and ears while another squadron kept look out above his top lip. Laura had never been overly fond of moustaches.

But he was right about the room. Hetty's was by far the nicest, well, after hers of course. It had been the main guest bedroom with its own en suite bathroom and had not been touched, unlike some other rooms that had been chopped and changed in the conversion.

Laura toyed with the Navajo bracelet on her wrist, concentrating hard now. She turned the heavy silver band feeling the three uncut turquoise stones. Had the Brigadier been in Hetty's room a second time? Asked her to swap? Intimidated her? Laura sat bolt upright. Last night. That flicker of light under the door... Parker's insistent sniffing... The voice... "Dearie."

It was clear as Hetty's crystal paperweight. The Brigadier had murdered Hetty.

Chapter Two

L aura clipped the pug's lead to his collar. "We must speak to John Fincham immediately," she said. With her thumb on the brake button, she checked the lead was secure by giving it a yank. "But how did the Brigadier do it?" Parker looked up at her, his great saucer eyes bulging. *Strangulation?*

On her way out, she locked the door. "But I didn't see any marks around Hetty's neck," she said dropping the key into her handbag. *Perhaps he hit her over the head?* She hurried down to find the manager of Wellworth Lawns. *But I'd have felt a bump when I combed her hair.* Laura knocked on John Fincham's door.

A stiletto? He was not in his office.

Smothered with a pillow? There was no one at the reception desk.

Poison? Ideas swirled around in her head, but there was nothing for it. *I may as well go and have an early lunch*, she thought.

In the middle of the dining room the original chandelier still sparkled overhead but the twelve-leafed mahogany table and chairs had been replaced by modern sets made of formica and chrome. The room was buzzing with activity and Laura waved briefly as she passed Sandra Abelson and some other ladies from the Horticultural Society. Then she spotted Brigadier Stanway. He was sitting with Venetia Hobbs at a table laid for four. She decided to join them to see if she could find out where he'd been last night. As she neared, Venetia waved her spoon. "Hurry, hurry Laura," she said. "Alfredo's made us mince." It was obvious that the news of Hetty's death had not leaked out.

The Brigadier stood up and Parker, straining at the lead, sniffed his leg and growled. Laura pushed the pug under the table and sat down beside the Brigadier. "You weren't at bridge last night?" she said, staring up at him.

"No." He glanced at her with steel grey eyes and sat down again.

Mimi placed a plate of steaming lamb macedoine, mashed potato and peas in front of Laura. "Here you going, Ladysheep," she said.

Laura thanked her and returned her attention to the Brigadier. "Did you stay in? How is your room?" she asked.

The brigadier looked up from his plate. "My room?"

"Yes, is it to your liking?"

"You are such a wonderful hostess, Laura," Venetia said, from the opposite side of the table. "You know that this is Lady Boxford's home, don't you, Brigadier?"

"It *was* my home. It's not any longer. I was making a general enquiry, that's all. Some people find moving house difficult, especially if they've been accustomed to more spacious accommodation. Down-sizing can be a problem, you know."

"My room is perfectly adequate, thank you. A lifetime in the military has taught me to keep things in an orderly fashion. That's what matters. Discipline."

The Brigadier's hearing aid let out a high-pitched whine. Laura looked at him. The hairs sprouting out of his ear reminded her of a miniature clematis seed head. *No wonder it doesn't work properly, fighting through all that undergrowth, the murderous old fool,* she thought.

"Fuck," he said.

Laura wondered if he'd come up through the ranks, as he ripped the device from his ear and left the table.

She put her knife and fork together. "Really, that man's language."

Venetia cleaned the last of the gravy on her plate with one finger. "What did he say?" she asked, licking it off.

"Never mind, dear. D'you mind awfully if I leave you now? I must take Parker for his walk."

She meandered around the gardens, passing the carp pond and the herbaceous border, green shoots appearing through the brown earth. Eventually, Parker cocked his leg on the plinth of an urn in the rose garden and Laura hurried back in through the hall to see if John Fincham had returned.

The door to the manager's office was ajar. She pushed it open, "Hello, John?" she called, looking round the room.

"Afternoon, Lady B." John Fincham was on his knees beneath his desk. Parker rushed up and licked his mottled face.

"Dogs on leads at all times, Lady B," he said, looking up and banging his head.

"Come here, Parker." Laura called.

John rubbed his head. "Sad news about Mrs. Winterbottom." He smoothed his hair back into place. "I gather you found her... I am sorry. I know you were very close. My, but you're looking nicely plump about the cheekbones today, if I may say so."

"Am I?"

John Fincham often passed personal comments such as this; it came from his years as a plastic surgeon. Laura patted her face. Perhaps the night cream wasn't such a waste of money after all?

"Lunch good I hope?" John said.

"Yes, lunch was delicious. I must thank Alfredo. But what are you doing down there?"

"I'm looking for the DVD for this evening – *Ice Cold in Alex*. It's here somewhere I'm sure."

"*Ice Cold in Alex?* Didn't we have that last week?"

"The Brigadier has asked for it again. He says we've had too many costume dramas recently." He rose from under the desk brandishing the DVD. "Here we are." He flicked some dust from the knees of his worn grey suit and sat down on his swivel chair. "So what was it you wanted to see me about? Do you need more bath towels? I'll call Mimi."

"No…"

"Or is it the heating? I'll get young Tom the handyman to crank it up. He's bleeding the radiators. Perhaps that has something to do with it." He reached for the phone.

"No no, I've plenty of bath towels and please don't turn the heating up any more. It's already like an… well I suppose it is an old people's home… But no hotter, please. Anyway it's Hetty I've come about."

"Quite a shock I must admit and Dr. Mellbury had only seen her last night."

"Dr. Mellbury had been to see her?"

"Yes. He and Mrs. Hemper."

"Hetty's daughter Gloria was here last night?"

"Yes, she had some forms for her mother to sign. Had to be witnessed. Dr. Mellbury was doing his rounds, so obliged." John Fincham looked at his watch and gave it a tap. "The undertakers will be here later this afternoon," he said.

"So Hetty's still here?"

"Yes."

"Oh dear me, that is good news."

"Good news? Why's that, Lady B?"

"Well, you see, I'm most concerned. I wonder if you would come with me and we could have a look at her together?"

"Have a look at Mrs. Winterbottom? Why would you want to do that? You mustn't upset yourself further."

"I need to be sure of something. You see, Hetty looked… well there was something in the expression on her face I wasn't happy about."

"Death is never a pretty sight but I suppose if you think it is important. Hold on and I'll find the key. Nurse Creightmore thought it best to lock her in."

They went upstairs and unlocked Hetty's door. Parker sniffed the air.

"I think I'll put him in my room," Laura said.

When she returned, John was standing by the window, his complexion, while still uneven, was now considerably paler.

13

"Have you…?" Laura motioned in the direction of the bed.

"I did take a peek, I must admit."

"So you see what I'm talking about?"

"I have every confidence in the undertakers' abilities."

Laura walked over to the bed. The pillows had been removed and she could see the outline of Hetty's body under the sheet. She hesitated and then pulled it back.

Hetty's jaw had been bandaged shut and her eyes elastoplasted over. She looked like the prototype for a B movie of *The Mummy*. The expression that had so disturbed Laura had been obliterated.

"Oh no. We're too late," she cried, and sat down on the end of the bed.

"I don't think so," John said. "Mr. Bone did a splendid job on Sheila Mowbray after she fell out of the minibus."

"No, I mean too late to see the evidence."

"The evidence of what?"

"I believe there may have been foul play."

John's brow rose in furrowed lines like seagulls in flight across his forehead. "Foul play?"

"Yes," Laura said. "I think we should call the police."

"I know you're upset, but I don't think it's a matter for the police. She was a good age after all." The manager looked at his watch. He raised his wrist to his mouth and exhaled onto the watch face. Then he rubbed it with his sleeve.

Laura looked on in exasperation. "What's her age got to do with it? We're all old here. It doesn't mean we can't be murdered."

"Murdered?" John's hands froze mid polish. "Hold on now, Lady B…"

"And I think I know who did it."

"What?" Finally he had stopped fixating on the timepiece.

"It was Brigadier Stanway."

"Good God. Whatever gave you that idea?"

"Her room. He wanted her room and was prepared to kill for it."

"That's a serious accusation, Lady B. Mind you, I've heard of these petty rivalries."

"Exactly."

John smoothed his hair with one hand. "And he does have a certain streak... of... I'm not quite sure how to put it..."

"What do you mean 'a certain streak'?"

"Well, he cut through the wires of the sound system with a sabre last Tuesday afternoon. Tom had to spend the rest of the day repairing it. That reminds me, we must re-word the list of 'treasured possessions' prospective clients can bring with them to Wellworth Lawns."

"Why did the Brigadier do that?"

"Said 'Lara's Theme' was driving him mad."

"I'm inclined to agree. Why do we have to have music in the afternoons?"

"Calming ambience." John waved his arms about as if conducting an orchestra.

"We're getting distracted," Laura said. "I know I'm right."

"If you are serious..."

"Deadly."

"Well then, I shall have to call Inspector Sandfield at Woldham Police station."

Laura returned to her rooms. She sat down on the sofa and pointed the remote control at the TV. The action in itself reminded her of a lunge from the Brigadier's sabre. She recalled the day he had moved in. She and Hetty had watched out of the window as he barked orders at the removal men. More and more strangely shaped objects tied up in hessian bags had been unloaded. They had laughed, as he began yelling when they manhandled a life-sized stuffed black grizzly bear out of the van, head first. Laura remembered remarking on the fact that his quarters were going to be pretty cramped.

"Perhaps he bunks up with the bear," Hetty had suggested.

Laura turned up the volume and watched the last race from Wincanton. She had called her bookmaker earlier and put a fiver each way on a horse that was now trailing in seventh place. It didn't stand a chance and she was silently berating it, when she heard a knock on the door. She turned down the volume and called out, "Yes? Who is it?"

"I've got the inspector here," John Fincham said. "Can we come in?"

Laura was well acquainted with Phil Sandfield. He had played golf with her son, Henry and had remained loyal to the family when Henry's body had been discovered in the brothel in Woldham.

"Good afternoon, Lady Boxford." The inspector took off his greasy checked cap.

His obsequious tone made her shudder as she recalled Henry's mental decline after the catastrophic collapse of the family business.

"Hello, Phil," she replied, pulling herself together. "Do sit down. You too John." She gestured to the two dark blue velvet button-back chairs that stood either side of the sofa.

The inspector looked at the chair with suspicion, as if it might not accommodate his stocky thighs. He took the plunge and sat down, then leant forward to his briefcase, his belly nestling on his knees, and fished out a notebook and pencil. "I gather from Mr. Fincham here that you have some concerns over the circumstances surrounding the death of... " He opened the notebook. "Mrs. Henrietta Winterbottom."

"Yes, I do. You see I knew her better than almost anyone, and while she may not have been in the best of health, I know she wasn't at death's door." Laura went on to describe Hetty's tormented expression. "And when I was returning from playing bridge last night − it must have been about ten thirty − I saw a light under Hetty's door and when I called out to ask if she was all right, she answered in a strange voice that I'm convinced wasn't hers."

"A strange voice?" The inspector turned to John. "You didn't tell me this."

"It's the first I've heard of it. But perhaps because she was feeling unwell her voice sounded unfamiliar."

"How do you know she was feeling ill?" Laura said. "And anyway, it wasn't just the uncanny tone of the voice it was the fact that she, or he, called me 'dearie' and Hetty would never call me 'dearie'. If she had been feeling ill, she'd have more than likely told me to bugger off."

The inspector looked up from the notebook. "It's a delicate one this. She may have been somewhat confused," he said.

"Why is it always assumed that old people are confused?"

"Well you see, after Mr. Fincham informed me of what you had told him about Mrs. Winterbottom's visual appearance, I had a chat with Dr. Mellbury. He seems to think that the look to which you are referring is consistent with a heart attack. He suggested she may even have had a series of them."

"Yes, a series of minor heart attacks. Followed by one massive fatal one," John said.

"I've heard that in the early stages they can lead, in some cases, to the patient actually speaking in a foreign language." The inspector scratched one armpit. "Spanish, for example."

"That's a revelation." John said. "Perhaps what she was actually saying wasn't 'dearie' but, 'Meerie'. Hail Meerie?"

"'Meerie'; 'Dearie'." The inspector nodded in agreement and jotted it down. "Good point, John."

"Are you saying you don't believe me?"

"By no means, Lady Boxford. But without any evidence, we don't really have cause for an autopsy." Phil Sandfield shut his notebook. "But, I believe you think that a certain Brigadier Stanway may have had a motive?"

Laura explained about the Brigadier coming into Hetty's room. She did not want to lose the inspector's attention so she tempered her accusation. "I'm not necessarily saying he murdered her. But what if he had intruded? He might have frightened her... Accidentally caused her death. It would still be foul play, would it not?"

"I'll look into it, see if I can ascertain his whereabouts last night," the Inspector said. "But I'm afraid it's not much to go on."

Laura was pouring herself a gin and tonic when there was another knock on the door. It was Charles Mellbury. He put down his medical bag and smiled. "Good evening, Lady Boxford."

The doctor's physical appearance had always mildly revolted Laura and she was at pains to avoid him, choosing to see any of the other doctors in the practice. Normally under the circumstances she would have removed her glasses but with her new contact lenses his disconcerting baby face with flaccid lips and lack of chin was all to clear. She took a sip from her drink.

His beady eyes homed in on it like a well-trained Clumber spaniel.

"Don't mind if I do," he said. "It's been one of those days."

"You don't have to tell me, Doctor. I've just lost my oldest friend." She walked back to the drinks tray and handed him a glass. "But you know that."

The doctor pushed up the sleeves of his dark blue suit and picked up the bottle, glugging in the gin followed by a dash of tonic.

In his basket, Parker began to yowl in his sleep. His feet twitched as he chased some phantom rabbit.

Dr. Mellbury stared down at him. "That dog looks ill. Sometimes it's better not to leave it too long. Can be a messy business."

"There is nothing wrong with Parker, thank you, Doctor."

"You've got to think ahead. Quality of life and all that. Now, I've had a word with John and the inspector," he said. "And I thought I'd come and reassure you that everything is in hand over the matter of Mrs. Winterbottom's death."

"What do you mean, 'in hand'?"

"What I mean to say is that you need have no concerns. You know I saw her earlier last evening?" Dr. Mellbury took a slurp from the glass and sank into the chair that Inspector Sandfield had recently vacated.

"Yes, John told me you were with her daughter, Gloria; but Hetty was perfectly all right then, wasn't she? It was only a broken ankle, after all."

"I can't comment: patient confidentiality and all that, but suffice to say I am unequivocal in my assertion that Mrs. Winterbottom died of natural causes. Her heart was weakened by her lack of exercise and, as you will I'm sure agree, she was not helped by her weight."

Patient confidentiality? Laura thought. *What a lot of nonsense.*

"Now, as for your own health, Lady Boxford, I think we might run some minor tests."

"Tests? Whatever for? There's nothing the matter with me."

"Finding Mrs.Winterbottom has given you a nasty shock. Nerve endings in the brain are easily susceptible. It may well have affected your mind."

"Affected my mind? Are you implying that I'm losing my marbles?"

"Just to be on the safe side, you understand. We need to be sure there's no permanent damage. There's a very good new counsellor in the practice: Miss. Crane. She may want to refer you on. You have insurance, don't you?"

Laura was incensed, but before she had time to formulate a reply, the doctor had changed the subject to the evening's Bingo.

"John's got me reading out the numbers again." He laughed. "He does it so he can play the game himself. He's easily pleased."

Laura was reminded of John Fincham's obsession with games of chance. Not the same as her own punditry, which was based on years of experience – well, most of the time. She remembered happy afternoons watching the racing with Hetty sitting beside her, a large bag of chocolate éclairs in her lap. She had to smile to herself as she recalled the time that Hetty was rendered speechless and failed to place her telephone bet, her false teeth glued shut by a mass of toffee.

"You should come," the doctor was saying. He put down his glass and got up to leave. "Make the effort. A little light entertainment might take your mind off things."

As the door closed behind him, the vision of Hetty's deathly visage came back to Laura. *That man's a brute,* she thought.

Chapter Three

Bingo was one of many activities provided at Wellworth Lawns. It was not one of Laura's favourites and, as the doctor had insinuated, she would not normally have gone, but she didn't relish the idea of being alone all evening, sitting right next door to Hetty's empty room.

Perhaps tonight's game would provide an opportunity of checking out the Brigadier again? There was also the troubling matter of the doctor's belligerent attitude. She could use the occasion to observe him in a non-professional setting.

And what of Dr. Charles Mellbury? It was almost as if he blamed Hetty. He had mentioned her weight, but Hetty wasn't really fat. *BMI? What a lot of nonsense that was.* But it was as if he was saying she had brought it on herself. Perhaps he even saw it as his duty to hasten the natural process of decline? Perhaps he had returned after witnessing Gloria and Hetty signing the papers? Laura shook her head. "Oh Parker," she said. "Listen to me, I'm getting distracted from the main purpose. The doctor may be ugly but it's the Brigadier we're after."

Venetia Hobbs was sitting at a small table by the doorway of the old ballroom – now the 'Recreation Room'. In front of her were the stack of cards and a small metal box containing coins and notes.

"Hello Laura," she said. "How many would you like?"

"I'll take two. How much is that?"

"Um… I should remember, I've just sold eight to Mr. Fincham, but now Gladys Freemantle has left me on my own, I'm at a bit of a loss. She had me folding the numbers this afternoon. All those bits of paper made me feel quite dizzy."

"Oh look, it says they're a pound." Laura pointed to the sign that had fallen on the floor. She took out her purse and popped the money into the box.

"Here you are, dear." Venetia handed her a fistful of cards. Laura took two and put the others back.

Looking round the room she noticed Strudel Black. She was dressed in scarlet, a matching Tyrolean hat with a spray of pheasant feathers sticking out of it was a typically exuberant reminder of her Austrian roots. Standing next to her, and holding her arm, was her recent co-habitee, Jervis Willingdale, his dyed brown hair combed back neatly. This amorous development had taken everybody by surprise. Jervis had only come down from London to visit his sister who had moved to Wellworth Lawns. They had met Strudel while taking a stroll in the gardens one winter's afternoon.

Laura contemplated the unlikely pair as Strudel dusted the lapel of Jervis' racy blue and white checked jacket.

Instead of going back to London, Jervis had moved into a hotel in Woldham from where he'd conducted a short but effective campaign to win Strudel's heart. There ensued a lot of idle gossip about living in sin. Hetty had been quite vexed and threatened to go to John Fincham to demand a moral code be introduced to all the residents. But Jervis and Strudel were in love, and thus oblivious to the wagging tongues.

Now, from Strudel's bungalow in the old kitchen garden they ran, along with the Bridge Club and Old Time Dancing classes, a dating agency named Ancient Eros.

Strudel beckoned Laura over with one brightly painted fingernail. "I am so sorry to be hearing the news of Hetty," she said, embracing Laura. "So sad, and I had for her a new date all lined up."

Despite her misgivings about Strudel and Jervis' marital status, Hetty had been an early conscript to the dating agency but had not managed to form any lasting relationship.

"I thought she'd been through all the men here?" Laura said.

"Ah, but since Jervis is making the website, Ancient Eros has expanded. Such a nice man, from Burford. He is antiques dealing and will be most upset. I don't suppose…?"

"That's enough, Strudel my love." Jervis turned to Laura. "I should think you've come out tonight to take your mind off things. A little light entertainment might cheer us all up."

"That's exactly what Dr. Mellbury said. I hope you're right." Laura gave a wan smile.

They wove their way across the room and chose a table by one of the matching pair of Robert Adam marble fireplaces that adorned either end of the room. The tables and chairs were of the same design as those in the dining room but the rubber feet on the base of the chrome chair legs made them hard to push in and out on the parquet floor. As Laura tussled with one now, she scanned the room. John Fincham was sitting nearby, his pen already poised in his hand, cards laid out neatly in front of him. But there was no sign of the Brigadier.

Soon Doctor Mellbury arrived. He walked over to the caller's table that had been placed on a makeshift dais in front of the French windows, and picked up the basket containing the numbers. He gave it a shake. "Who's going to get lucky tonight?" he said.

"Not me, with my luck," came a husky voice from the back of the room.

"Was that you, Gladys Freemantle? I wouldn't be so sure. I saw you giving Bob Whale the eye. No wonder Dora won't let him out of her sight."

Shrieks of laughter filled the room and heads turned in the direction of the abattoir moghul – the King of Render, as Bob Whale had been known – and Dora, his wife. Then the doctor called everybody to order and the proceedings began.

"Eyes down." He put his hand into the basket and began rustling the little pieces of folded paper.

"Get on with it," John shouted.

"In your lucky seat, I see," the doctor quipped. Laura turned to see the manager's lips were compressed tight shut – no sign of the seagulls now as a frown of concentration crossed his brow.

"Don't forget, it's 'straight line horizontal'. Horizontal. Like this, Mrs. Hobbs," the doctor said, waving his finger at Venetia.

He began to read out the numbers. "Avian Flu, forty two." It was one of his little jokes. He often referred to illnesses and drugs. Some that no one had ever heard of, and even occasionally in Latin. His joviality was, on the whole, taken in good spirit but on this particular evening, it seemed to be in doubly poor taste.

"Swiss Clinics, sixty six," the doctor called, grinning over the top of the half moon glasses he had put on.

Laura turned to Strudel. "That's a step too far," she said.

Strudel shook her head. "No sense of decorum."

Laura checked her card. Very few of her numbers had come up, but she observed that John was becoming animated, his mottled complexion now positively blotchy.

"Yesss!" The manager punched the air at 'curvature of the spine'.

The numbers kept coming. "Rising heart rate, eighty eight."

"Bingo!" Jervis called out.

The doctor walked down from the dais to check the card. "First winner of the night, and its Wellworth Lawns' answer to Fred Astaire, Jervis Willingdale."

Strudel's complexion had gone the colour of her hat but Jervis smiled as Dr. Mellbury clapped him on the back and gave him his five-pound prize.

They took new cards and started again.

"Bingo," called Henry Gordon.

"Don't be silly, you batty old thing." Ex-forty-a-day Gladys Freemantle, sitting next to him, leant over, her ample bosom swaying, and tore up his card. "This is a new round."

"Pay attention, Henry," Dr. Mellbury said, and carried on calling numbers. "Two anorexics number eleven." He paused. He was stuck and called out irritably, "Twenty six." There followed another series of numbers that he was unable to find rhymes for, but he perked up after a while and called out, "Ruptured spleen, seventeen."

Laura was watching a bead of sweat on John's temple when she heard a gurgling sound close by. She looked round and saw Bob Whale as he coughed weakly and fell to the floor. John put down his pen and rushed over. "Doctor Mellbury," he called. "Could you come here a minute?"

The doctor joined them. Dora Whale was loosening her husband's tie and unbuttoning his shirt.

"Let's have a look at him." The doctor eased Dora aside. "John, fetch Nurse Creightmore. On second thoughts, call an ambulance. I think he's had a stroke."

John hurried out and soon Nurse Creightmore appeared. Together, she and the doctor administered vigorous and, Laura thought, possibly unnecessary, mouth-to-mouth. But Bob Whale's constricted gasps were muffled as the strains of *Lara's Theme* could be heard coming through the sound system.

By the time the ambulance arrived, it was deemed too late to continue with the Bingo, as the refreshments trolley had appeared and everybody was much too busy jostling for lemon squash and a Garibaldi biscuit.

"That was simply appalling timing," John said.

Laura thought she saw a tear of frustration appear in the corner of the manager's eye.

"Jolly bad luck," she said.

"Damnable. I only had one to go."

"On Bob Whale, I mean." She was suddenly tired of it all. She picked up her bag and edged her way out of the room, hoping nobody would notice. There was nothing good about the day. From finding Hetty, to Phil Sandfield's reluctance to believe that there was anything amiss, to the doctor's casual, even insulting approach, and now John's bon homie and infantile obsession.

And what of John? She took the lift upstairs to collect Parker. Could he have been instrumental in Hetty's death? Turning a blind eye to the Brigadier? She was reminded of the small matter of Hetty's room rate.

Laura had acquired the room for Hetty for a reduced sum for her lifetime. She and her granddaughter Victoria had been discussing the fee structure with John and Victoria's husband, Vince Outhwaite, who had paid off the family's debts and saved Chipping Wellworth from the clutches of the bank. What a piece of luck that had been. Heaven knows what might have happened if Victoria hadn't taken the job with the self made Leeds underwear magnate. And then the sheer good fortune of him falling in love with her… It had been nothing short of a miracle, but dear as he was, Vince was first and foremost a businessman.

"Hetty will never afford that amount of rent," Laura had said.

Vince crossed his arms, the cloth of his Savile Row suit moulding into the change in posture. "That old crow?" he said. "She's nothing but trouble. Remember the year we had her to stay for Christmas. She ate everything in the hamper I'd had sent up from town, including me Anguilles en Gelee and the mucky fat I'd specially ordered."

"Vince, darling, that's a bit harsh, Hetty is Granny's oldest friend. She wasn't to know about your penchant for eels and dripping and 'London' please, not 'town'," Victoria corrected.

"Oh, have it yer own way."

"But we can't have one rule for one and another for the rest," John piped up.

"Victoria," Laura pleaded.

Victoria had whispered something in Vince's ear and he had given a little shudder of pleasure. "Oh go on then," he'd said, and the matter was concluded.

Now, as Laura walked with Parker through the garden, her thoughts were still on the manager of Wellworth Lawns. It must be a thorn in John Fincham's side, having one of the best rooms taken by someone not paying the full whack.

No, that's ridiculous. But still she felt overcome by suspicions. *Damn it, maybe the doctor's right, perhaps I am losing my marbles. Charles Mellbury, John Fincham, next I'll be thinking Bob Whale had something to do with it.*

Parker snuffled through a bank of overgrown box bushes, their dark leaves rustling in the moonlight. She needed to concentrate on Brigadier Stanway. He was the most likely suspect and, anyway, where had he been during the evening? She was sure that Bingo would be just his sort of thing, but he was probably far too busy planning where to mount his sabre on one of Hetty's walls. Hetty… She could almost see him leaning over her… "Now Mrs. Winterbottom, why don't you see sense. This room is wasted on you. You can't even get out of bed… What's the point of a view like this if you can't see it?" And then him getting a bit too close and poor Hetty paralysed with fear… or anger? Her refusing. And then, him taking matters into his own hands… Laura felt her breath shortening. "Parker!" she called. The extendable lead was straining at its maximum length. Finally he shuffled out from behind a bush and came puffing back to her.

When she returned, the hall was empty but she could hear the sound of a raised voice coming from the bar.

"Bloody outrage, the prices that crook Fincham charges." Maurice Dickinson, red faced, belched as he reeled out clutching a bottle of port. He blundered past Laura with the grace of a bison and out of the front door in the direction of the bungalows where he lived.

"What a bore that man is," Laura said.

She was about to call the lift when its low hum indicated that it was in use, so she took the stairs, Parker struggling behind her as he negotiated the polished oak steps.

Back in her room, Laura drew the curtains and began pacing up and down. Seeing Maurice Dickinson had been one grim occurrence too many and she knew she would not be able to rest. She went to the bathroom to find her sleeping tablets. Unscrewing the lid she tipped the bottle. *Blast!* It was empty. She wondered if Nurse Creightmore was on night duty. Putting Parker back on his lead, she headed down the corridor to the set of stairs that led up to the staff wing.

The staff quarters were situated in much the same place as they had always been. At the top of the narrow staircase was a door. In her husband's day it had been padded green baize, studded with brass tacks. Now, it was a half glazed aluminium fire door. It swooshed mechanically closed behind her.

Not wanting to wake anybody unnecessarily, she was relieved to find that the old linoleum had been replaced by carpet that muffled her footsteps. She crept along past Mimi and the other girls' rooms, until she got to the door with Nurse Creightmore's name on it.

The door was ajar but there was no light coming from within. Thinking that perhaps Nurse Creightmore was on duty but resting, she knocked gently. The door swung open further. Parker sniffed and pushed ahead. She pulled him back. The lights in the corridor dimly illuminated the room. She peeked in. As her eyes began to focus, she heard a thud. It seemed to have come from the bathroom. She heard a voice. One word, but she couldn't make it out. At that moment the door opened and she saw the figure of a man. He was wearing striped pyjamas, and on his head was a torch. The figure turned in her direction flashing the beam straight at her. She raised one hand to shield her eyes and opened the door further to let in more light from the corridor. And then she recognised him.

The Brigadier.

Laura gasped. "I beg your pardon." She took a step back, shutting the door behind her and returned hurriedly along the passage, through the glass door and down the stairs. At the bottom she bumped into Venetia Hobbs, her stick in one hand.

"Hello, Laura," she said. "I fell asleep after the Bingo. It must have been the tension. Actually, I think I may have had a little doze during the game. Who won, by the way? Mr. Fincham, I shouldn't wonder. He always seems to have good luck. Anyway, when I woke up, everybody had vanished… And now here I am. Well, good night, dear." She hobbled away to her room at the less expensive end of the corridor.

Laura let herself in to her own rooms. She poured herself a tot of brandy as Parker lapped water from his bowl, spilling it all around him.

"Don't you worry, Hetty. I'm on the case," Laura said, directing her words to a silver framed photograph of them both that was sitting on the mantelpiece. It had been taken during one of the Horticultural Society's visits to Highgrove. "Mind you, what that Brigadier was doing in Nurse Creightmore's room, I do not know. Most suspicious, I'd say." She wandered over to Parker's treat tin and threw him a bone-shaped chew. On bandy legs, he waddled after it and Laura returned to the photograph.

"Tell me, Hetty, is he bribing the nurse with favours of an intimate nature? An older man with a younger woman... Surely not... But what was he doing in his pyjamas...?" She continued addressing the photograph "...With a torch on his head? It can only mean one of two things. Either they were playing 'Doctors and Nurses', or they were meeting secretly to discuss your room." Laura took another sip of brandy and sat down on the sofa to think about her next move. Feeling somewhat confused, she flicked on the TV remote control.

Some minutes later, over the noise of the TV and Parker's snoring, she thought she heard a tapping noise and again wondered if perhaps the doctor was right and she was going off her head.

She heard the noise again and realised it was someone at the door. Tiptoeing over, she listened at the keyhole. The tapping came again and then a short cough. She flung open the door and Brigadier Stanway stumbled, gangly-limbed, into the room.

"Ah, Boxford," he said righting himself.

He had changed from his pyjamas into the tweed suit and tie she'd seen him in earlier that day. There was no sign of the head torch.

"I thought I'd better make sure there was no misunderstanding, d'you see?" As he straightened his already perfectly positioned tie, his head moved from side to side, his narrow beaky nose pointing this way and that like an over sized directional arrow. "D'you think I could come in?" he said.

Hell, he's changed his mind. "You seem to be in already," Laura said. *Now he wants my apartment. I've got a killer standing right here in front of me.* She backed towards her desk and felt for the paper knife.

"I'll be brief," he said.

"If you must." She concealed the knife behind her back.

The Brigadier peered down at the sleeping Parker. "Fine set of adenoids," he said, adjusting his hearing aid.

"Pugs always snore. What is it you want?"

"I think I should explain why I was in Nurse Creightmore's room."

Laura stared at him. "I'm sure it's none of my business. I myself had gone to see if she could find me a sleeping tablet."

"Of course." The Brigadier appeared to be at a loss for words.

"I expect you were doing something of a similar nature," Laura offered.

"Well, no. Actually I was there because of Mrs. Winterbottom."

"Hetty?" Laura felt the weapon in her hand. "What do you mean?" She picked up her glass and saw that it was empty. She badly needed a top-up, but it meant she'd have to offer him a drink. Still, it might slow his murderous intent if she could get him drunk.

"Can I offer you a brandy?" she said.

He nodded. "I could do with one."

Laura turned, sliding the blade down the side of the sofa as she did so, and walked over to the drinks tray. She poured him a glass, refilled her own and took a slug. She felt her resolve return and handed him his glass. *Perhaps the brandy will loosen his tongue. Make him give something away.* "You'd better take a seat." She motioned to the chair, it's third incumbent that day, and took her place on the sofa, feeling for the security of the knife.

The Brigadier looked at the chair but chose instead to balance himself on a somewhat rickety upholstered stool at the side of the room. As he sat, his tweed trousers rose, revealing a pair of pink spotted socks. There was an awkward silence during which Laura heard the delicate antique creak.

"So, what is it you wanted to say about Hetty?" she asked.

He took a gulp from his glass.

Laura felt the seconds tick by.

He took another swig. It seemed to give him the impetus he needed. "It's like this." He cleared his throat. "I've had my eye on Nurse

Creightmore for a week or two. Did you know, she's been peddling a line of Far Eastern herbal pills and potions to the residents here at Wellworth Lawns?" The Brigadier was gaining momentum.

"And so?"

"She tried her sales pitch out on me. Laxatives -- but that's by the by. I refused, of course. I happen to know a thing or two about these Chindit remedies, and believe you me, they can be damn dangerous. Bloody strong stuff some of 'em. Shrunken heads and viper's bladder. They can do some serious damage." He was in full flow now. Eyes sharp. "I've seen it for myself. Lost a bloody good sergeant in Burma. Simple case of gippy tummy. The fool went to a local man in downtown Rangoon. Would've been right as rain in a day or two if he'd stuck to boiled rice. Quack poisoned him fair and square." The Brigadier shook his head and took another gulp from his glass. "Nothing we could do about it. We'd no proof and my man was dead. No such thing as a post-mortem out there, back in those days. Humidity'd make the whole thing far too damn slippery. Bloody outrage it was."

"I'm sorry but what has this got to do with Hetty?"

"That's just it. I overheard the nurse talking with Mrs. Winterbottom a couple of days ago. The door to Mrs. Winterbottom's room was open, you see. Nurse Creightmore was offering her hair-restorer."

"But Hetty had no need for hair restorer."

"My point exactly." The Brigadier touched the top of his scant pate. "But I thought I should offer my services on the matter. Give her the benefit of my experience. I mean, have you seen Mrs. Northbridge?"

"Francesca? But she's been having chemotherapy."

"Yes. But have you seen any improvement? You see, I for one know that she's been buying Nurse Creightmore's remedy, and she's still as bald as a coot. And what about Mrs. Hobbs's wind?"

"Venetia?"

"Venetia Hobbs. Yes. She was telling me at lunch that she's been supplementing Dr. Mellbury's Gaveson with seaweed and monkey gland tea, and that, by the sound of things, is plainly doing her more harm than good."

Tea? Laura remembered Hetty's herbal infusion.

"And then there's Sandra Abelson…"

"Sandra Abelson?"

"Yes. She's been taking Creightmore's pills for arthritis. As a matter of fact, most of the residents of Wellworth Lawns are on those, as far as I can tell."

Pills… Laura remembered the box with the dragon on it in Hetty's bathroom.

"Anyway, she's no better; have you watched her eating soup recently? But that aside, I thought it only right that I should try and get to the bottom of the thing… In a manner of speaking. I mean, the hair restorer could have been the tip of an iceberg of drugs in Mrs. Winterbottom's case."

Laura took a sip of brandy. Could she have been wrong about the Brigadier?

"A veritable submerged frozen mountain of poisons," the Brigadier continued. "That's why I was in Nurse Creightmore's room. I knew she was in the sanatorium wing. There was an incident at dinner. Did you not see?"

"I had supper in my room."

"Jock Frazer's false eye fell into his custard and he swallowed it. I heard Creightmore telling young Fincham she'd keep him in overnight to monitor the situation, as it were. So I thought I'd take the opportunity of seeing what I could discover."

Laura loosed her grip on the knife. "So did you find anything?"

"Nothing. She must keep her stocks elsewhere. And that's why I've come to you."

"What can I do?"

"I thought you should know, that's all. Nurse Creightmore's vile concoctions may well have been instrumental in Mrs. Winterbottom's sudden death and I don't think the matter should be allowed to rest."

Laura was torn by her suspicions, but what he had said sounded plausible. His concern seemed real. He couldn't have killed Hetty after all. It had to be Nurse Creightmore.

Laura recalled how Hetty and the nurse had developed a close relationship since Hetty had broken her ankle. In fact, now she thought about it, she had quite often come in to visit Hetty and found her chattering away to the nurse at odd hours. Laura had even asked her why she liked the Nurse at all.

"I mean she's so humourless."

"You mustn't say that, Laura," Hetty had said. "She's had a very hard life. She was married to an acupuncturist. He used to practice his techniques on her and, by all accounts, he wasn't very competent. Have you seen her arms? Then the bastard left her for a yoga teacher."

Laura turned to the Brigadier. "So what are you suggesting we should do?"

The Brigadier lowered his voice. "A spot of breaking and entering, I thought might be in order. While we've still got the chance. I saw the undertakers arriving this afternoon, but to my knowledge Mrs. Winterbottom's possessions are still in situ. We might find some evidence, something that would point the finger, fair and square in the nurse's direction."

"I did see something in Hetty's bathroom." Laura told him about the box.

The Brigadier leant forward on the stool. "This is more like it," he whispered. "What do you say?"

Still dazed; her preconceptions about the Brigadier were up in smoke. His genuine indignation at the possibility that there had been some nefarious act perpetrated against Hetty by Nurse Creightmore echoed her own misgivings at the sudden loss of her friend. "All right, I'm with you," she said.

"Excellent, Boxford. The tiger sleeps but the Lemur is alert! I thought we could climb out of your window and somehow…"

"Don't be ridiculous and do stop calling me Boxford. My name is Laura and I've always kept a key to Hetty's room."

Chapter Four

All was silent in the dimly lit corridor. Laura and the Brigadier hurried to Hetty's room and let themselves in. As they stood in the doorway, Laura felt a sepulchral cold hang in the air. The room already felt un-lived in. Even though she knew Hetty was gone, Laura was still shocked by the sight of the empty bed. She wavered by the door.

"Man up, Boxford." The Brigadier patted her on the shoulder. "We must remember what we are about here. Justice for Mrs. Winterbottom."

His intimacy was irritating but she put it to one side. "You're right. Let's see if we can find the box of pills."

The Brigadier marched in and turned on the light.

"Wait," Laura said. "Should we not close the curtains? Someone might see from outside."

"Good plan." The Brigadier went to close the bathroom blind while Laura drew the heavy damask curtains in the bedroom. She returned to find the Brigadier pulling out drawers in Hetty's bathroom cabinet. He held up a tube of ointment. Laura recognised the logo and was about to admonish him – these were Hetty's personal things after all, her very private things. She saw Hetty's worn out toothbrush in a mug. *Oh hell, it's got to be done.* She went over to the basin and then checked in Hetty's shower. She opened the door but all that was there was the empty chair that Hetty had used following her broken ankle and a bar of soap on the floor.

"It's not here," she said.

"What's that?" the Brigadier asked, removing the top of a lipstick.

"Stop." Laura gasped. This was too much… Hetty's 'Arabian Nights', the shimmering red hue that had been so much a part of her. A picture formed in Laura's mind of Hetty holding up her compact and applying the lipstick, often between the courses of a meal, if she felt the act of mastication might have caused it to fade.

"Something wrong?" the Brigadier asked.

"It's just… That was her favourite. She had to order it specially from the chemist's in Woldham."

"I'm sorry." The Brigadier returned it to the drawer. "I've nearly finished. There's nothing here."

"And the box with the dragon on it has gone."

"Are you sure it was in here?"

"Yes. I remember it clearly."

"That is indeed a pity. Creightmore must have been in and removed it, along with anything else she was supplying to Mrs. Winterbottom. Looks like we'll never know." The Brigadier replaced Hetty's pink floral plastic bath cap. "But let's check the bedroom all the same."

They hunted through Hetty's bedside table, her chest of drawers and desk. In the cupboard, her clothes hung neatly. Below them, her shoes, paired up, waited for an outing that would never happen. Laura shut the door and turned to see the Brigadier on his hands and knees lifting the valance of Hetty's bed. There was something altogether unseemly about this. "That's enough," she said. "Let's go. There's nothing here."

She went back to the bathroom and turned out the light before raising the blind. The moonshine created an eerie gloom. Laura shuddered and returned to the bedroom.

The Brigadier turned off the main light and was making his way towards the window. He brushed past Hetty's dressing table. Laura felt a sort of déjà vu and called out, "Careful," but it was too late. The porcelain bowl with the change in it tumbled to the floor. They stood stock still. Laura could feel her pulse hammering in her ears.

"That's done it," the Brigadier whispered. "What a bloody clumsy oaf I am." As he got back down on his knees to gather up the coins, Laura tiptoed to the window to open the curtains. She pulled one aside revealing the night sky sprinkled with stars. She recalled the bright sunshine that had heralded this sad day and the innumerable flickering colours created by Hetty's paperweights. She looked down at the collection. Why were they on the window ledge? In all the commotion, Laura had forgotten they had been moved from Hetty's desk. *But who had moved them, and when?*

"Hold on," she said. As she touched them, one by one, she felt her temples begin to throb.

"What is it?" said the Brigadier, still on his knees.

"It's Hetty's Bacchus."

"Her what?"

"Her Bacchus paperweight; the only one she had of any value. It's not here."

"Value?" The Brigadier pulled himself up from the floor with the aid of a chair.

"Yes, it was very valuable as a matter of fact. At least that's what Hetty always told me. And now it's not here with the others."

"Are you sure? Check again, Boxford."

"I have. It's definitely missing."

"Stolen, more like. Poisoning innocent people in order to steal their valuables, that's what she's up to. I knew it wouldn't be long before we found a motive."

The Brigadier asked Laura if any others were missing.

"I don't think so, I can't be sure," she said.

"Try, Boxford. How many were there? This is vital." The Brigadier took a step towards her. He was standing too close.

"Please." She took a step back. "I can't think right now. I'm too tired."

"What?" The Brigadier's hearing aid began to whine. In the stillness of the night, it was as if a siren had gone off.

"Turn it down," Laura whispered.

"What?"

"Turn it off before the whole house wakes up."

"I can't hear what you are saying. Hold on I'll have to turn it off."

Laura drew the remaining curtain open and hurried to the door. She checked for the sound of footsteps but all was quiet. Shutting the door behind them and locking it, they made their way back to Laura's apartment. In the sitting room, she found a pen and a sheet of paper on which she wrote: 'Too late now. Tomorrow in the lounge at 10.'

The Brigadier nodded and padded out.

Chapter Five

"Morning Ladysheep," Mimi called as she let herself in. "Breakfast here."

Laura put down the book she had been trying to read and got out of bed as Parker heaved himself up from under the bedclothes. Mimi placed the tray on the table by the window and unfolded Laura's copy of *The Racing Post*.

"You go somewhere nice today?"

"What?"

"Nice day for it. Sun he shining." The maid gestured out of the window. "I thinking no rain cats or logs our teacher say."

"*Dogs*, it's cats and dogs." Laura thought that the girl must have amnesia if she thought she was going to have a nice day so soon after Hetty had died.

"My country we saying frogs," Mimi continued. "Our teacher she saying people in glass house throwing stones." She shook her head. "I not getting this one."

Really, why confuse young people with all these ridiculous idioms, Laura thought. *Glass houses, I ask you.* But then she remembered the Bacchus. "Mimi, you remember Mrs. Winterbottom's glass paperweights?"

"Mrs. Winter?"

"Her glass ornaments. In the room. From yesterday." Laura cupped her hands together as if she were holding a day old chick.

"Oh, those things, how you say?"

"Paperweights. They were on the window ledge in her bedroom." Laura pointed to the window.

"Oh yes. I putting them when I dusting."

"You mean you moved them from her desk?"

"I forgetting to return. Silly me!"

"I see."

"That all you wanting me?"

"Thank you, Mimi."

"I seeing you later alligator." Mimi waved and let herself out. The door clicked shut.

Clicked shut...

"The door!" Laura said. "How did the Brigadier open the door to Nurse Creightmore's room?"

Parker looked up at her.

"It must have been locked if she wasn't in." She fed him one crunchy end of a croissant. "They could be in it together."

Parker gobbled it down then licked his lips. He stared at her for more, his impertinent eyes dark as the water of a Cumbrian tarn.

"He could still be lying." She ate a piece of croissant.

Parker barked for more.

"That's quite enough," she said. "We don't want you getting any fatter than you are." This reminded her of Hetty again. "Mind you," she said. "Hetty always preferred a Danish pastry; she said you got more for your money in the Low Countries." She took a sip of orange juice and shuddered at the acidity. "He's pulling the wool over our eyes, Parker, that's what he's doing. All that Chindit nonsense is a smoke screen. We must flush him out." Remembering that she had arranged to meet him downstairs at ten o'clock, she finished her breakfast and got dressed, before taking Parker for a quick tour of the garden.

"You must go straight to the police," the Brigadier said, taking a sip of coffee. They were sitting at a table in the window of Laura's old drawing room – now the 'lounge'.

Laura looked at him suspiciously. *He's very sure of himself. But why is he so keen for me to go to the police? I might incriminate him.*

"You must tell them how valuable the missing paperweight is," he continued. "Remind me, what was it called?"

"A Bacchus."

"And you said it was of considerable worth."

"About ten thousand pounds, I think. I don't know, maybe more."

"That's certainly a fair amount." The Brigadier put his cup back in its saucer, spilling coffee as he did so. As he dabbed the table with a napkin, they heard the crunch of gravel in the drive outside and turned to watch as a car came to a halt outside the front door. "But is it enough to murder for?"

"If you're old and frail and someone thinks your life is of little value," Laura said, "then, yes, it probably is."

The car door opened and a tall, dark haired woman in a tight black skirt and jacket got out.

"You're right. We're not worth the paper we're written on. Bloody stupid pair of shoes that woman's wearing," the Brigadier said, as the woman tottered to the front door, her high heels catching in the pebbles.

"That's Gloria Hemper. Hetty's daughter," Laura said.

"She'll have come to take away Mrs. Winterbottom's things, I should think?"

"Yes, I suppose so."

"So she'll see the paperweight is missing. I presume she knew about it?"

"I don't know if she did. Hetty was careful what she told her daughter. But now I remember, John Fincham said Gloria went to see Hetty…" Laura began to wonder if she was telling him too much. But then again, the missing paperweight might have nothing whatever to do with Hetty's murder.

"When did she visit her mother?"

"The day before yesterday. Early in the evening. She had papers for Hetty to sign and needed a witness. She took Dr. Mellbury with her."

"So Creightmore must have gone in after that; administered the poison and stolen the paperweight. If she thinks she can get away with it, she's in for a nasty surprise." The Brigadier pulled out a large green paisley handkerchief and snorted into it.

Laura felt her head begin to spin again. Was the Brigadier framing the nurse? She remembered visiting Hetty one afternoon a few days previously. She had been into Woldham to collect the library book that Hetty had ordered. She breezed in with the book. Hetty was in her wheelchair sitting at her desk, the paperweights in their usual position in front of her. Nurse Creightmore was hovering at her side. And what was Hetty saying? "…An expert eye." And what had Nurse Creightmore replied? "…Of course I have, it's my job." And then they had begun to laugh.

Laura turned to the Brigadier. "But how would someone like Nurse Creightmore know the paperweight was valuable?"

"Anything is possible. She might be a leading expert in the field of glass manufacture as well as toxic Chinese medicine. Alternatively Mrs. Winterbottom could simply have told her. But that's for the police to find out."

"I suppose it could have been her voice I heard…" Laura hadn't meant to say it but it was too late now.

"What's this, Boxford? A voice?"

Laura told him about the light under the door and the voice she was sure wasn't Hetty's on the night of her death. She tried to work out what he was thinking, but he merely looked puzzled.

"'Dearie', you heard? And you say Mrs. Winterbottom would never have said 'dearie'?"

"Yes, It's a bit like loo and toilet. Hetty would never have said toilet."

"Ah, I see where you're coming from. But how damnably close you were. Think of it, Boxford. If you'd gone in…You are lucky to be alive! You must tell this to the police. Don't go into too many details. Sow a seed in their minds. You know how the police hate to be told how to do their job. Mention Creightmore casually. The monkey's banana attracts the buzzing anteater." He tapped the side of his nose.

*

With Parker sitting alert on the passenger seat beside her, Laura drove the few miles to the market town of Woldham. She picked up a tuna sandwich from the garage at the top of the hill on the outskirts of the town and they shared it in the police station car park.

"The Brigadier is either very clever or very stupid," she said, as Parker snuffled, his nose pressed into the crevice at the back of the seat, searching for crumbs. "I'll tell you more once I've seen the inspector." She left the pug in the car standing up at the window yapping at her, his brow furrowed in indignation.

Phil Sandfield showed her into his office. She sat down opposite him at his desk. Sitting the other side, next to the inspector's chair was a young woman in uniform. Laura was surprised by the amount of mascara she was wearing on duty. Phil Sandfield introduced her.

"This is my new assistant, PC Lizzie Bishop," Phil Sandfield said. "Lizzie this is Lady Boxford."

Lizzie stood up and held out a hand. "DI Sandfield tells me you're a resident at the care facility in Chipping Wellworth," she said. "Can we get you a cup of tea?"

Laura declined but Phil said he'd like one.

"Would you?" Lizzie stayed put. "I'm parched too."

"No, Lizzie, it doesn't work like that."

While Lizzie went to make the tea, the inspector tidied some papers on his desk. "Look at this," he said showing Laura a picture of a man in full combat gear. "I mean, when am I going to need a Taser or incapacitant spray in Woldham?"

"Open the door for me, can you," Lizzie shouted from the other side of the frosted pane. Phil jumped up and let her in. She handed one of the mugs she was carrying to the inspector.

"Now then, Lady Boxford…" He took a sip "… Hellfire that's hot."

"What did you expect?" Lizzie blew on her mug. "Steam's a bit of a giveaway."

Phil turned to Laura. "Ooh, she's sharp as anything," he laughed. "Now, let's get down to business, shall we? What was it you wanted to see me about?"

Laura told him about the missing paperweight.

"This is an important development," Phil said. "Lizzie, take some notes."

Lizzie put down her mug, sighed and took a pad of paper from a drawer in the desk.

"So let's get this straight. Mrs. Winterbottom had a collection of paperweights..." Phil tapped the desk with a pencil. "Got that Lizzie?"

"How d'you spell 'weight' sir, is it a-t-e, or a-i- t?"

Phil sighed. "Neither, it's e-i-g-h-t. I seem to recall they were kept on the window ledge, were they not?"

"Yes, but they didn't normally live there."

Lizzie looked up from her notes. "That's eight."

"No there were more than eight," Laura said.

"Yes," Phil said. "No." He turned to Lizzie. "You've forgotten the 'w' Paper-w-eight."

A look of revelation crossed Lizzie's face. "My bad. I get it, sir," she said, crossing it out and starting again.

"So, you're saying they were moved. D'you happen to know when?" The inspector took another sip of tea and flinched.

"Yes, Mimi the maid moved them to do the dusting."

"Ah, ha. The maid," Phil said.

"But that's not the point. The point is the one that's missing was very valuable."

"Valuable? This could be significant." Lizzie looked up from her notes. "Any idea how much it's worth?"

"No... not exactly, but they can fetch thousands."

"Thousands, you say? Could you describe it for us?" Phil asked.

"It's called a Bacchus concentric. Bacchus is the maker and concentric is the pattern. They arranged minute canes of multi-coloured glass in circles round a central motif. Hetty's had a tiny silhouette of a woman in the middle and was surrounded by blue and pink flowers."

"So how many more of these paperweights were there?" Lizzie asked.

"I'm not sure, ten or so. But they weren't valuable like the Bacchus."

"And when did you realise this particular one was missing?" Phil said.

"Last night with Brigadier Stanway..." Laura saw her mistake.

"You were in Mrs. Winterbottom's room with Brigadier Stanway? But hold on a sec..." Phil rolled up the sleeves of his shirt exposing his chunky forearms. "I thought yesterday you said..."

"I may have changed my mind about the Brigadier."

"Right... So he didn't murder Mrs. Winterbottom?"

"I'm not sure. He may have had an accomplice. Nurse Creightmore, for example. That's why I'm here."

"Nurse Creightmore?" Phil ran his hand over his chin.

"Exactly how late last night were you in the room with this man, who may or may not be a murderer?" The young PC was paying keen attention now.

"I don't know... possibly midnight."

"Midnight?" Lizzie looked at Phil and put down her pen. "Been out on the town, had we?" She gave Laura an exaggerated wink, the mascaraed lashes shutting like a miniature iron grille. "And how did you get in?"

"I have a key."

Lizzie leant forward. "You are in possession of a key to Mrs Winterbottom's room?"

"Steady, Lizzie. I'll ask the questions."

"Yes, I've always kept a key," Laura continued. "Hetty kept one to my room too. In case of emergency."

"Nothing untoward there, Lizzie. Nice to see you're paying attention to detail, though. First class. So, I think we've got all the information we need to know, Lady Boxford." The inspector rose from the desk as Lizzie closed her notebook. "We'll be looking into this as a matter of some urgency," he continued. "I may have to contact you again after we have made some preliminary enquiries."

"Thank you Ph... Inspector Sandfield." Laura stood up and the inspector held the door open for her.

As she walked down the passage to the main entrance, she felt uneasy about the interview. Phil had been his usual affable self, but the young policewoman, Lizzie… What was it about her? Was she being dismissive? It was annoying she had mentioned the Brigadier. An unnecessary complication. Still, as he himself had said, it was the police's job to find out.

As Laura pushed open the door to the street she remembered she had forgotten to mention Nurse Creightmore's pills. *But that's such a vital part of the story.* She felt a hint of nausea creep over her. *They'll think I'm dotty forgetting to tell them that.* She smiled at the desk sergeant and retraced her steps to Phil Sandfield's office.

She could see Phil and Lizzie's outlines through the frosted glass of the door and was about to knock when she heard the two of them in conversation. She stood to one side and listened.

"…Bless her, she means well," the inspector said.

"But she told you she thought it was murder yesterday. Said she'd heard a voice. Convinced herself it was this Brigadier bloke and now she's on about the nurse and some paperweight and, from what you said about Mrs. Winterbottom, it doesn't sound like she was the kind of person to be in possession of a highly valuable object of any kind."

"It's a problem, dealing with these old people."

"Midnight, she said. I mean, what's she on?"

"And all that stuff about hearing voices. I ask you."

Laura heard laughter.

"She likes a tipple," Phil said.

Laura stifled a gasp. *How disloyal of him.* She remembered the time he had been investigating the theft of the weather vane from the roof of the stable block one winter. It was freezing outside and he had been having trouble with the ladder. She'd felt sorry for him and, much against her daughter-in-law's wishes, had invited the inspector in to join them for a glass of sherry.

"Off her trolley, I'd say," Lizzie said.

"Dr. Mellbury did say something to that effect."

Laura's jaw dropped.

"I think we can safely draw a line under it, sir. She'll have forgotten all about it by tomorrow and we've got all those 'effing fixed penalty notices from market day to deal with."

"Well, Lizzie, *you* have."

"Oh, please…"

Laura tiptoed back down the passage. Charming. She smiled again at the desk sergeant. *It's a fine state of affairs when the police don't believe you just because you're on the wrinkled end of the human spectrum.*

As she walked up the steps to Wellworth Lawns, Laura could see the Brigadier, still sitting in the chair by the window of the lounge where she had left him earlier. He put down his paper and waved. Had he been waiting for her all this time? She went in and found him doing the crossword, a pot of tea on the table beside him. He looked up.

"Ah, Boxford. Thought you might be back. I ordered two cups in case." He put down the paper and took off his misshapen horn rimmed glasses. They fell onto his chest, dangling on the thin plaited string around his neck. "Did you have it out with 'em?" He slopped tea from the pot into a cup for her.

Laura sat down on the window seat. "It was a complete waste of time."

"How so? It seemed pretty clear cut to me."

She told him what she had overheard, omitting the part about her accusation of him. She also glossed over the inspector's comment about her liking a drink. "Basically, what they were saying was that I was over the hill and consequently, unreliable."

"But that's a bloody outrage," the Brigadier huffed. "How dare they assume that because we have a few grey hairs, we have no grey matter?"

"Exactly the same conclusion I came to. I couldn't believe it and heaven knows what that wretched Charles Mellbury's been saying about me behind my back."

"That doctor… hasn't he heard of the Hippocratic oath? But never fear, Boxford, we'll prove 'em wrong. We'll get to the bottom of this ourselves. It can't be that hard. After all, I've seen enough detective programmes on daytime TV to last a lifetime. I must have picked up a few pointers along the way. So, for starters, we need to get some of those pills of Creightmore's. Have 'em analysed. Find out what she gave Mrs. Winterbottom and what she did with that paperweight."

Laura looked over the rim of her teacup to see if she could discern anything in his expression that might give her a clue as to his involvement or innocence, but all he did was scratch his ear. The high pitched whine that ensued set Parker off. He sat up, held his head in the air and howled.

"Job's a good 'un," the Brigadier shouted.

"Turn it down, or up. One or the other!"

"Sorry." He fiddled with his hearing aid. "Is that better?"

Laura nodded and Parker lay back down again.

"Getting back to the paperweight," the Brigadier continued, "I'm curious to know how Mrs. Winterbottom happened to have one that was worth so much, when all the rest of her collection are, as you say, to all intents, valueless?"

"It belonged to Hetty's brother, Stanley. He won it in a card game in Las Vegas. When he died, he left it to her." Laura felt herself getting hot as she recalled the woeful tale. "I need some fresh air," she said. "And Parker needs some exercise."

"Good plan. I'll join you, if I may?"

The last thing Laura wanted was her walk disturbed by him and his defective hearing apparatus, but she was beginning to realise that she needed to keep him on side if she was to find out what had happened to Hetty. And if he was involved, he was bound to put his foot in it sooner or later and give something away.

She agreed. "We'll go up to the pet cemetery," she said.

"The pet cemetery?"

"Yes, Parker and I like to visit our old friends."

They set out at a brisk pace, Parker's lead reeling out like the line of a salmon rod as he cantered ahead. They passed round the side of the bungalows before climbing the small hill that led to a larch spinney where the dogs and horses of Chipping Wellworth Manor, as it had been, were commemorated. Each animal had its own carved stone plaque.

The Brigadier bent down and studied the names as Laura sat on the fallen tree trunk that had been hollowed out to form a rudimentary bench. She remembered how her late husband Tony had had it pulled up there with the tractor, so many years ago, and how much they used to enjoy having a glass of champagne there on a sunny summer evening, laughing about how naughty the dogs had been and how badly this or that horse had behaved out riding. And then Tony would haul her to the ground and they'd have a jolly good romp in the long grass.

Now she looked down beside her and saw that someone else had been up there and had carved something into the wood. 'Wayne is a fucker,' it said. *What a lot of work*, she thought and wondered how long it had taken the person who found Wayne so distasteful.

The Brigadier straightened up and rubbed his lower back. "I should like to be buried in a place like this."

"I used to think that." Laura sighed. "It's quite magical later in May. These trees have the most wonderful purple flowers that give the place an almost papal charm."

"You're not one of *them* are you, Boxford?"

"No, but why should it matter?"

"Had a run-in once with the Archbishop of Nairobi. Never could get on with the smell of incense after that."

The Brigadier did not appear to want to elucidate further. He picked up a twig, tried to interest Parker in it, then threw it. The pug followed its trajectory with scant interest and did not move from Laura's side.

"He's never been much of a retriever; it's his stubborn nature," she said.

The Brigadier turned to her. "Bit like me. I'm not a quitter, you know. It's not my style. The good people of Muranga would testify to that, if they were here today."

She looked at him, his tall, thin old body erect but swaying slightly. His craggy features reminded her of one of the ancient knotted trees surrounding them. He seemed so honourable and…honest, but she had to know for sure.

"How did you get in to Nurse Creightmore's room?" she asked.

Without hesitation he answered, "Took the spare key from Fincham's office during the Bingo. All the keys are labeled and numbered, including staff. He's got them in a cabinet behind his desk. Showed me the day I lost mine. Man's a fool. Mind you I had a nasty moment when he came to call the ambulance."

There was something of a boy-scout twinkle in his eye. "What were you saying about Muranga?" she asked.

"Long story. Seige. Bad business. Two months on a diet of elephant dung, but we got through it. We saw 'em off. Oh yes." The Brigadier took out his handkerchief and wiped his eyes. "Damn wind plays havoc with the tear ducts. But as I was saying, we'll get to the bottom of this, whatever it takes."

He'd fight and even kill for Queen and Country but Laura knew then and there, that he was no more capable of murdering Hetty than she was. "That's very heartening," she said. "I'm so sure something wicked happened to Hetty." Laura told the Brigadier about Hetty's final expression.

"Sound's exactly like my lad in Burma. I can remember that as if it was yesterday." He shook his head. "Shall we walk on?"

They headed down the other side of the hill towards the river.

"But do you think it could have something to do with Dr. Mellbury?" Laura asked.

"Mellbury?" The Brigadier looked thoughtful.

"I know it sounds absurd and perhaps I'm over-reacting, but I get the feeling he doesn't actually like old people." She told the Brigadier about her interview with him.

"I must say he's been damnably unhelpful about my hearing aid."

"He wants me to be referred to a counsellor. But he kept making remarks about old people and death…"

"I suppose it's not beyond the realms of possibility they were in it together."

"Charles Mellbury and Nurse Creightmore? Oh dear, this is exhausting."

"No point discounting possibilities. We must consider anyone who was in contact with Mrs. Winterbottom. But I still think we should focus on Creightmore first. She is our prime suspect. We must have a full disclosure of all the facts at our fingertips. I'd suggest a briefing over dinner, but I'm expected somewhere this evening, so why not sleep on it. You will feel refreshed by morning, I'm sure."

"Yes, I don't think I can face the dining room – I'll have my supper sent up again and get an early night."

"And you may find you remember other hints or clues. We'll meet tomorrow morning and plan our strategy."

"But we don't want to arouse suspicion. I'm sure the waiter gave me an odd look when he brought us coffee this morning and people are bound to have seen us out walking. I tell you what, I have another suggestion, we could meet tomorrow in Woldham. Do you drive?" she said.

"I'll take my bike."

"But its five miles."

"That's nothing when you've cycled 160 kilometres through the Abedares with a pack of raging Mau Mau on your heels."

"But that was years ago. Not that I'm questioning your bravery, of course."

"I still like to think of myself as a fit man." The Brigadier patted his stomach.

"I have a Horticultural Club meeting in the morning. It's the annual plant sale coming up, so shall we say three o'clock in the Garden Tearooms?"

Chapter Six

Laura passed the Brigadier cycling hard up hill, bicycle clips around the ankles of his tweed trousers and a florescent yellow safety tabard over the top of his jacket. He was bent low over the handlebars and on his head, a bright blue helmet almost covered his eyes. From her mirror, she saw a fellow cyclist overtake him. He glanced up. The helmet caught in the wind and jerked back. Laura could see the headline. 'Old man garrotted by cycling helmet'. *He'll be hours, if he ever makes it,* she thought.

She didn't like to use the disabled parking badge that Doctor Mellbury had organised for her when she'd had her hip done and instead parked down a side street. "I won't be long," she said, patting Parker and attempting to wrap him in his pink crocheted blanket.

After her third cup of tea, Laura was of a mind to leave the Garden Tearooms. She was about to call the waitress for the bill, when the Brigadier staggered through the door, helmet in hand.

"Ah, Boxford," he said. "Didn't think I'd get here, did you?"

"I have every confidence in your cycling ability," Laura assured him.

"Glad to hear it. Now let me order you some tea."

"I'm awash with the stuff."

"Cream bun?"

Laura looked down at the green leather belt she had put on over her dark grey wool dress. "Oh go on then," she said, easing the buckle out a hole.

He waved his arm about until he caught the attention of a waitress.

"You should get your cycle helmet fitted properly," Laura said.

"What?"

"I passed you on my way here. Your helmet's far too loose."

"Trouble is, the straps interfere with my hearing aid. Frightful racket when a lorry passes."

The tea and buns arrived. The Brigadier was about to take a mouthful, when he put the bun back down on his plate. "Before I forget," he said, "I must tell you about Venetia Hobbs."

"Venetia? What about her?"

"I sat with her at dinner last night."

"I thought you had a prior engagement?"

"Slight change of plan. Blackballed from the Dart's Club at *The Swan* when I turned up with my blowpipe. Anyway, Venetia had what I can only describe as 'a turn'. After the asparagus, it was. She went into a kind of trance. Silly grin on her face."

"You know she can be rather absent minded."

"It was more than that. More like the children's game of Statues. She came round before I had to ask for assistance, but it was a rum do. Didn't like the look of it. I asked her if she was all right and she said that it had happened on more than one occasion and that she saw things."

"What kind of things?"

"She wouldn't say, but from her expression, I reckon it was something pretty disturbing. I've seen that kind of look before. Chap on Boulder's beach, Cape Town. Shark took his wife right in front of him. Powerless he was. Bloody fool."

"How horrible, but Venetia wasn't anywhere near the sea. And why was it the husband's fault?"

"You're quite right. The thing about Venetia's case was that I was under the strong impression that she may have been hallucinating."

"Hallucinating?"

"A side effect of Creightmore's ministering…" The Brigadier took a great mouthful of his bun. "…Is what occurred to me."

"Oh my goodness." Laura held her breath as a dollop of cream lodged in his moustache. Automatically, she felt her upper lip, and made a mental note to make an appointment with Karen at the beauty salon in Sheep Street.

He pulled out the paper napkin from under the remains of the bun and wiped his mouth. "You must have a word with Venetia. See what else she's been getting from Creightmore. I know she had the herbal tea but I'll eat my…" He looked at his cycle helmet. "Perhaps not, but I'll bet you anything she's been buying some of those pills as well. They may not be the same as those the nurse gave to Mrs. Winterbottom, but it could prove useful evidence. I thought I would make some enquiries with Dr. Mellbury; find out his opinion of Creightmore; see if he knows what she's been up to. I've got a certain knack with this kind of thing, sort of sixth sense. Years in the bush… I have to see him again about my hearing aid."

."But where is this going to get us?" Laura said.

"The twitching ears of the antelope hear the cheetah."

"What?"

"We must look and listen, remain alert at all times. Any snippet of information could be vital. And now I think we should discuss the paperweight. A full description. D'you think we might find a picture of one anywhere?"

"We could look in the Antiquarian bookshop in Bear Court; Ernie Batterham has a very eclectic range. Mostly my late husband's, it has to be said." Laura remembered the rows of well-thumbed *Wisden's* and the *Playboy* magazines – Ernie had given her a good price for them.

They left the Brigadier's bike chained to a lamppost outside the tearooms and collected Parker from Laura's car.

"So, tell me some more about Mrs. Winterbottom's brother," the Brigadier said, as he attempted to guide Laura across the road. "He won the paperweight in a game of roulette?"

"No, not roulette." She shrugged off his hand from her elbow and then thought perhaps she had been a little ungracious.

"Oh, it's all history now. I don't suppose it matters telling you."

They crossed the road and carried on along the High Street.

"Stanley Beaumont was Hetty's only sibling," Laura said. "He was a successful banker in the city, but then, not for the first time, things started going downhill."

"Downhill. Stock market crash?"

"More his personal life. I think it began with a pillow fight at prep school. But whatever it was, as he grew up his preoccupation with feathers took control. And then he was away from home such a lot. Nights spent alone in hotels…" As the Brigadier walked on beside her, Laura thought again of Tony's *Playboy* magazines, but they were harmless fun, more of an art form. "I don't know how it took hold," she continued. "But the need became all consuming. Any which way, apparently."

The Brigadier stopped in his tracks.

Well, if the old buffer's prudish that'll give him something to put in his pipe and smoke, Laura thought. But his next reaction was quite unexpected; he shoved her into the open doorway of the newsagents.

"What did you do that for?" she asked.

"John Fincham. Coming out of the bookmakers. Didn't want him to see us." He tapped the side of his nose with his finger. "Fetishism… yes I've come across it once or twice. Fellow in the officer's mess had a thing about the regimental goat. Shall we get a Milky Way?" The Brigadier fumbled in his pockets for loose change.

"No, thank you." Laura followed him to the till and then they waited by the magazine rack – Laura kept her eyes firmly on the row of home interior publications as the Brigadier ate his chocolate bar.

"Carry on about Stanley Beaumont," he said.

"His wife Sally found out. Poor Sally." Laura looked around her. There were no other customers but she kept her voice low. "She sent him to a rehab clinic in Las Vegas. There was an American industrialist on the programme who was in for compulsive gambling, but he can't have been very committed: he started organising gaming sessions in his room in the evenings after therapy. That's how Stanley got the Bacchus. He won it at a game of poker."

"And did the treatment cure Stanley?" The Brigadier threw Parker a corner of chocolate. His lead uncoiled before Laura had time to press the brake button, and Parker gobbled the chocolate down.

"Please don't feed him," she said. "I have enough trouble with his weight as it is."

"Sorry. So did it?"

"What?"

"Cure Stanley?"

"For a while it did. Shall we go on, I don't think they like dogs in here."

"Hold on," the Brigadier said, crumpling the blue wrapper in his hand. He walked to the door and looked from side to side down the street. "All clear." He tossed the packaging in a bin outside the shop. "So what happened next?"

Laura followed him out and they carried on towards the bookshop. "Stanley got back home, gave up banking – he was nearing retirement anyway. He started collecting paperweights as a panacea, I suppose. It became his new obsession. He had so many by the end that he had to build an extension to house them all."

They stepped to one side to let a woman pushing a buggy pass them.

"Carry on." The Brigadier said.

"Stanley began to get bored, took to the bottle. Then Sally found something on his computer and, believe me, it wasn't anything to do with quill pens or fishing flies. Here we are." Laura stopped outside the shop.

"So what did she do?" The Brigadier held open the door for her.

"She left him." Laura looked around the familiar scene. Row upon row of dusty shelves heaved with ancient volumes. Typically, there was no sign of Ernie and a library-quiet filled the air. As they waited by the counter, Parker lay down at Laura's feet and closed his eyes.

"So then what happened to Stanley?" the Brigadier whispered.

"The paperweights started a fire. The sun refracted onto one of them; it was sitting on his wooden desk underneath the window," Laura whispered back. "They think he'd fallen asleep because it must have happened very slowly. He was killed by smoke inhalation, still sitting at his computer. The fire brigade put out the fire and the police took the computer away. They couldn't press charges, obviously, because he was dead. Really it was a blessing in disguise for Sally, except of course, by that time he had rewritten his will and left everything to Hetty."

"So Mrs. Winterbottom, Hetty, got them all?" The Brigadier leaned against a shelf, stacked floor to ceiling with orange Penguin Classics, and folded his arms. "Does anybody work here?"

"It's a bit of a maze. He'll be here in a minute." Laura pressed the bell on the counter. "Yes, Hetty got them all, but not for long. She started selling them; spent the money on cruises. That's when I met her – in the Caribbean. She was nearly broke by then – I had no idea of course."

Parker began to snore at her feet. Laura pressed the bell again.

"The next I knew of her," she continued, "she wrote to me from a terrible place her daughter Gloria had found for her. She couldn't have stayed there, so that's when I got her the room at Wellworth Lawns."

"A good friend indeed."

"She sold what remained of the collection to help pay for the room, but she kept the Bacchus as a sort of insurance policy. Then she started collecting them herself. Not on Stanley's scale of course."

Laura heard a cough and looked round. Ernie Batterham appeared in the doorway of one of the adjoining rooms, a duster in his hand. "Oh its you, Lady Boxford, what a pleasant surprise. Have you been here long? I've been trying to sort out Zoology; terrible mess."

"In the back of beyond too, no doubt, but don't worry, the Brigadier and I have had plenty to talk about." Laura introduced them. "We're looking for a book about glass paperweights."

"Surprising how many people collect them," Ernie said, and disappeared again. He returned with a glossy volume entitled *Paperweights of The World*. "Seven hundred colour illustrations. This the sort of thing you meant?" He placed it on the counter. "I'll leave you to take a look. I'll be next door in the poetry section. No one ever goes in there and dust only ever does one thing and that's settle."

Laura went to the back of the book and flicked through the index. "Here we are, George Bacchus and Sons: Concentrics." She turned to the page and scrutinised the reproductions. "That's it." She pointed. "Look. That's exactly like Hetty's. D'you see the silhouette?"

"Great Scott, and that's what Mrs. Winterbottom had?"

"I'd say it was, yes."

"If that's the case, we're half way there. Creightmore's our murderer and here's the motive clear as daylight. Now all we have to do is link the two together."

Laura didn't see why finding the picture brought them any nearer to solving the crime but she called out to Ernie and bought the book.

They returned to where the Brigadier had parked his bike.

"Will you be all right?" she asked, as he unlocked the chain. "We could fit it into the back of my car if we left the boot open."

"I'll be fine." He produced the head torch from one jacket pocket and from the other he took out a compass. "If I get lost, I've got this. But I like to pride myself on my sense of direction. I'll be back before dark. Shall I see you in the dining room later?"

"I think I might give it a miss, if you don't mind."

"But you'll go and see Venetia Hobbs?"

"Yes, I'll try. Call me tomorrow. Here, I'll give you my number." She rifled through her bag and found a piece of paper and a pen, and wrote it down. Then she watched as he mounted his cycle and wobbled off down the road in the opposite direction of Chipping Wellworth.

As she drove back, she felt guilty that she could have thought the Brigadier had been involved in Hetty's death. "He's really trying to help," she said, patting Parker and automatically turning down the back drive to Wellworth Lawns. It was the way they always went before the new car park was built and the old garages had been converted. "He's really not such a bad old stick," she continued. "Heaven knows where he'll be now. We should have shouted to him." She had a vision of the Brigadier cycling blindly down the Banbury Road into the middle of Oxford, the feeble light from his head torch glowing in the darkness.

As she rounded the corner, Tom Scott Hopkinson sped towards her in his old green Vauxhall. She was never quite sure about the handyman. He was very competent at his job but it was an odd occupation for an Old Etonian. Laura was reminded of the time that Vince had interviewed him for the job of manager before John Fincham. He had turned up in his old school tie. Of course Vince had no idea what it was and, either way, it had not impressed him. "He's too young. Too much floppy yellow hair. And where is a first in Mathematics from Christchurch going to come in useful running a care home?" Vince had said.

Then John had come along but Tom had reappeared in answer to the advert for a handyman. Vince told him the salary was far less than that of the previous post he had applied for, but Tom said he was desperate and had a practical streak that most would find surprising for someone his age.

Now Laura noticed Mimi was sitting beside him in the passenger seat, her large white teeth flashing in an elated smile.

How nice, Laura thought. *Young love!* Mimi waved to her and Laura smiled as she remembered how she had loved to drive fast when she was that age. But then she was reminded of how Hetty used to moan and cling to the seat belt if Laura went over forty miles per hour.

Chapter Seven

Laura was of the opinion that the Brigadier was exaggerating when he said he thought Venetia had been experiencing hallucinations. She was probably suffering from little more than the effects of over-doing the pre-dinner sherry, and so it was not until the next afternoon that she went in search of her.

Venetia was not in her room, so Laura went downstairs to see if she could find her there. In the hall she heard the strains of a Viennese waltz coming from the Recreation Room.

Strudel Black's old time dancing class was in full swing. Strudel herself was being swept around the room in the arms of Jervis Willingdale, a sea of fuchsia organdie swirling out around her. Her eyes were closed in a reverie of romance. It was this passion for dance that had cemented their union.

Strudel's husband Ronnie had left her in somewhat mysterious circumstances the previous year and everybody knew that she had started up her dating agency, Ancient Eros, primarily to find herself a replacement for him. In the event, Ancient Eros had not been necessary, as Jervis had appeared on the scene.

Laura wondered if any of the various couples dancing around them now, and being careful not to intrude into their sacred space, were the product of Ancient Eros' endeavours.

Not the Miltons; George and Sylvie, both once foreign office mandarins, had been married for centuries. They danced mechanically like a pair of penguins, their chests jutting out; George, a look of intense anxiety on his face as he concentrated on not stepping on Sylvie's large flat feet.

Nor Lance and Carol Paterson for that matter. Air Commodore Lance Paterson, the suave sophisticate of the skies had married dimple cheeked air-hostess Carol during his years as a pilot of Concorde back in the eighties. Laura spotted Olive Fitzherbert partnering a rotund little fellow she was sure she had never seen before. Was he perhaps part of the Ancient Eros new website bandwagon?

Quite a few of the couples were both female. Emma Lucas, a woman of considerable height and Sandra Abelson, who despite her arthritis was still well muscled from her latest bid to swim the channel, were both attempting to take the man's role. Each fighting to lead the other, and ending up in an impasse, whereby they remained turning in ever decreasing circles.

"See how we float, " Strudel exclaimed over the music.

Half a dozen other women sat in chairs around the side of the room, supposedly making mental notes on footwork. Amongst them, Laura could see Venetia in the corner in her old green jumper. Her head seemed to have slipped between her shoulder blades leaving only a small mound of tightly curled white hair protruding like a cloud passing between two grassy knolls. She went over and tapped her on the shoulder. "Wake up, dear."

The cloud sprang up revealing Venetia's sweet round face and blinking eyes. She gazed at Laura. "Where am I?"

"Do you feel like dancing?" Laura asked. "You won't need your stick, I'll hold you up."

"What a jolly idea."

They took to the floor, Laura guiding Venetia slowly round the room.

"Bravo!" Jervis called out, as they passed by.

After a few more turns, Laura could feel her partner waning. "Are you all right?" she asked.

"I'm feeling rather dizzy." Venetia gave a little moan.

"We'll go and sit down in the lounge." Laura danced her slowly back to her chair to collect her stick.

She left Venetia on a sofa by the fire and went to ring the bell on the bar. Mimi appeared looking cross.

"What you... Oh, sorry Ladysheep. I thinking some other old thing. How I helping you?"

"I wonder if Mrs. Hobbs and I could have a cup of tea. She's feeling a little faint after the dancing and I think she needs reviving."

"Doctor Mell, he not keen. He always saying Nurse Creight not to do reviving."

Laura raised an eyebrow. "Really?"

"I getting tea now. Mrs. Hobb not quite all dead beat yet," Mimi said, and wandered off down to the kitchen.

She returned with the tea a little while later. Laura poured and Venetia took a sip and sighed.

"Are you feeling better?" Laura asked.

"Thank goodness, yes. I thought I was about to have one of my funny turns."

"Funny turns?" *Perhaps the Brigadier was right?* "That's not like you. Has Doctor Mellbury changed your medication?"

"That old quack? His pills are useless. I know I shouldn't complain, I mean everybody's got it, but my arthritis was getting positively worse with his useless prescriptions." Venetia hiccupped. "D'you know, he asked me if I was afraid of death the other day. I'd only gone to get some cream for my dry patches. No, I'm trying out something Nurse Creightmore recommended. One of her natural products, I'm sure they're helping, only..."

"Only what?"

"Well it's happened recently that, after I've taken them, I feel quite woozy and sometimes I have..." Venetia leaned closer and whispered, "The most peculiar thoughts."

"That doesn't sound right at all. What kind of peculiar thoughts?"

"Last time, it was when I was having lunch, or was it dinner? Anyway I was with Brigadier Stanway…"

"And?"

"I began to imagine him with no clothes on. Eating carrot puree from a trough, quite naked. It was most disconcerting. And then he asked me if I wanted to take his piglets for a walk and there were half a dozen snorting Gloucester Old Spots right there under the table. And then I came round and it was perfectly normal. Him in his tweed suit, not a piglet in sight. I've had a few such occurrences. What do you think I should do?"

"Stop taking the… what is it? Pills?"

"Yes."

"Well, stop taking them, whatever they are. Have you many left?"

"A few."

"I'd like to see them."

"But you don't suffer from arthritis. You must be the only person here who doesn't."

"No, I'm very lucky, but I'd like to see them all the same."

"They're in my room and, actually, I think I'd like to go up there now and have a little lie down."

They went to Venetia's room. Laura could not remember what it had been before the conversion, but it was so small and pokey that she could only imagine it had been some sort of laundry or ironing room. A reclining orthopaedic chair covered in beige velour occupied most of the spare floor space that was not taken up by Venetia's single bed and battered chest of drawers. Venetia opened the top drawer and started to rummage through the contents. As she waited, Laura's eye was drawn to a small Victorian oil painting of a girl in a pale blue dress, a starched white bonnet framing her face.

"That's most charming," she said.

Venetia looked up at it. "It's the only thing I've got left," she said, and continued throwing knickers and other sundry items out onto the floor. "They're in here somewhere, I know."

Laura wandered over to the window. Drawing the net curtain to one side, she peered out. The view was obscured by rising steam. Through it she could see a mass of cast iron guttering and drainpipes like a map of the Northern Line. Below was a small courtyard where she spotted Alfredo, the chef, carrying what looked like a large sack of potatoes that he deposited on top of a wheelie bin. She thought of her own view and felt a pang of guilt. *Venetia must be even poorer than I realised...*

"Here they are!" Venetia handed her a flimsy little box.

Laura looked at the unintelligible writing on it. She turned it over and there it was. The dragon. Exactly like the red one on the box that Laura had seen in Hetty's room. The only difference was that this one was green.

"Could I borrow these for a while?" she asked.

"Of course. I can always get some more next time I see...But you said I shouldn't. Oh dear..."

"I'll drive you into Woldham. We'll get an appointment with another of the doctors there."

"That's an idea. But there's no need to go out of your way. I'll take the bus with Sandra, we like to go in on a Tuesday. They've such lovely knickers at the market."

"That sounds a good idea. Now you have a nice lie down and I'll pop in and see you later."

Laura returned to her room. "I'm doing this for Hetty," she said to Parker as she filled a glass of water in the bathroom. "I need to know if there is any truth in what Venetia's saying and I'm afraid there's only one way to find out." She tipped out the contents of the packet. Three off-white pills landed in her hand. That was all that was left, mind you Laura had no idea how many Venetia had had in the first place. Thinking of Venetia's petite frame, she put one back in the box and downed the other two.

"I've borrowed an earring."

Laura stared intently at Parker sitting in his basket. "An earring?"

"Yes," said the pug. "I hope you don't mind?"

The handsome baroque pearl dangled from the diamond hoop as he flapped one ear with a paw. "It offsets my coat magnificently; taupe and that slight apricot iridescence – it's a must. You haven't forgotten I'm going out tonight?" He started to lick his feet. "It's the Kennel Club Ball."

"You're a cheeky one," Laura said, as his blue furry-lined basket rose slowly off the floor with Parker, now standing up inside it.

"All aboard," he yapped. "I can feel my nose is gloriously shiny this evening. Black as jet in the moonlight. The Pomeranians will go mad for it." His wide nostrils quivered. "Now I must hurry, I don't want to miss the Dog Bone Shuffle."

His bed accelerated. Up and down and round and round it went like a fairground attraction with the pug at the helm, legs apart, tail curled like one of Alfredo's French pastries, his ears pinned back in the current of air. "Crack open the bubbly, I'm on my way," he howled as the basket flew past the window. "I can hear the band playing. It's Sinatra. My favourite song." His fat neck straightened as he lifted his head and crooned the lyrics of, 'Fly me to the Moon.'

When Laura came to, she was lying flat out on the sofa one leg dangling over the edge. She turned her head to the carriage clock on the mantelpiece. It was ten past seven. She had been out cold for nearly an hour. She rolled onto her side. Below her on the floor she saw her red patent brogues and a mess of chewed up bits of paper. It was the remains of the packaging of the pills Nurse Creightmore had given Venetia. Through the rice pudding of her brain, she recalled there had been one pill left in the box...

Parker lay on his back snoring heavily in the middle of the room. Laura fell off the sofa with a thump and crawled over to him. He was out for the count. She scooped him up and put him in his basket in what she calculated to be the recovery position for dogs. Picking up the scraps of paper, she moaned and lay back down on the sofa.

Half an hour later, feeling a little better, she pulled herself up and went to the bathroom for a glass of water. "And those were just for arthritis!" she said to herself, as she stood in front of the basin mirror.

What if they were the same as the ones the nurse had given Hetty? She stared at her reflection. *But Hetty didn't have arthritis...* The sight was pretty devastating... *Unless her ankle was giving her pain? Or what if Hetty's pills were something different... Something say, for her insomnia? Something even stronger?*

Laura smoothed a finger over her delicately arched eyebrows – at least they were holding up – and resolved to go and find Nurse Creightmore. She must pretend that she too, needed some of the nurse's medications. Get her hands on some more, hard evidence. Then she really would have something to report back to the Brigadier.

She returned to the sitting room where Parker lay asleep on his side, his tongue hanging out of his mouth like a pink slug. Laura thought she saw it begin to crawl across the carpet. She slapped herself on the cheeks with both hands until it stopped.

The sanatorium wing consisted of a small cluster of rooms that had been added on to the old boot room beyond the kitchen. It now had its own entrance down a passage beyond the reception. Laura found Nurse Creightmore sitting behind her desk at the nurse's station.

She looked up from her book. "Is there something the matter, Lady Boxford?"

"Oh nurse, I'm so glad I've found you."

"You're lucky you have. I should have been off an hour ago but the agency nurse from Woldham hasn't turned up yet."

"Poor you. You must be tired out. Perhaps you have a special pick-me-up to keep you going?"

"That's not a bad idea. I think I'll make myself a coffee. But what was it you wanted?"

"I've been feeling a little jaded, and I can't seem to get to sleep..."

"Hot chocolate. I thoroughly recommend it. Anything stronger and you'll have to see Dr. Mellbury in the morning. I'm afraid it's no longer possible to hand out sleeping tablets. The doctor's put a stop to it since he found out Mrs. Huxley had been hoarding them."

"You don't have anything of an alternative nature that might help?"

"Alternative?"

"Yes. Mrs. Hobbs says you do a very good herbal tea."

"But that's for wind. Do you suffer from an accumulation of gas in the alimentary canal?"

"You're sure it's only for that?"

"Of course I'm sure. Now if you don't mind…"

Laura let out a sigh and leant on the desk. "Goodness my knees are painful. It must have been that shower of rain I got caught in this afternoon. Still, that's arthritis for you."

"Now there I can help you, but not tonight. Come and see me in the morning and I'll sort you out."

Laura tried to remember what else it was the Brigadier had said she had cures for. Hair-restorer was the only other thing that came to mind, but of that she patently had no need. Granted it was short and white and, according to Dudley, shockingly untidy, but there was plenty of it. No, hair-restorer was out of the question, unless she developed raging alopecia in the next fifteen seconds. In the end all she could do was thank the nurse and say she'd see her in the morning.

She walked back to the main house and, looking up at the grandfather clock in the hall, realised she was late for supper.

In the dining room, knives and forks clattered as the hungry residents tucked in. She saw the Brigadier sitting with Strudel and Jervis.

"You've missed the soup," Jervis said.

"We've only just started the main course though." The Brigadier waved his arm in Mimi's direction. "Over here Mimi, one more sole for Lady Boxford, please."

"I must say, Laura, I was most impressed. The waltzing you were achieving was most commendable," Strudel said, re-arranging the lime green chiffon scarf around her shoulders. "But I fear you may have exhausted Venetia. I don't see her here tonight."

Mimi placed a plate of fish in a creamy sauce in front of Laura, who thanked her and turned to Strudel. "I expect she's having something in her room. But it's not often we see you over here for dinner. To what do we owe the pleasure?"

"The cooking Jervis and myself could not be bothered with and Jervis is having his bellyful of my sauerkraut."

"Oh come, come, my love." Jervis took her hand, his heavy gold signet ring gleaming against the white damask tablecloth. "How could I ever tire of your sauerkraut? No, we thought we'd have a change, that's all."

When they had finished, Laura suggested they join her in the drawing room for coffee. It came so naturally to her that she had temporarily forgotten that it was no longer known as the drawing room.

"In the lounge, you mean," the Brigadier corrected her. "Capital idea."

Strudel and Jervis excused themselves and said they had paperwork for Ancient Eros to catch up on.

"We left some leaflets in the chiropodist's in Woldham. Bit of a result," Jervis said.

Strudel nodded in assent. "There have been many responses. We are hopeful not all are suffering with the verrucas."

"Christ, athlete's foot." Jervis jumped up.

"An epidemic of this nature would be unfortunate" Strudel stood and took his arm. "Shall we be adding fungal infections to the registration form?"

They said goodnight and Laura followed the Brigadier into the lounge. They chose a table by the fire and waited as Mimi poured them coffee.

After a while, John Fincham came in to announce that the film would be starting in the Recreation Room.

"What is it tonight?" someone asked.

"*Pride and Prejudice.*"

There was a general moaning.

"The 1940 version with Laurence Olivier."

There followed a clattering, this time of coffee cups and Zimmer frames and soon Laura and the Brigadier were left alone.

She told him about her experience with Venetia's pills and the encounter with Nurse Creightmore.

"That was a damn risky thing to do, Boxford. On no account must you take any more of that evil woman's concoctions." The Brigadier was emphatic. "Make sure she writes down instructions for anything she gives you and then we will take the loathsome stuff to be analysed."

"Where would we get that done?"

"Nephew in the regiment. Rupert – must be a colonel by now. Mind you, they're all colonels these days. He's done a tour or two in Afghanistan. Same neck of the woods as China regarding illegal substances, I'd say. He's bound to know someone in the medical corps who'll have come across this sort of thing."

"But don't you think we should confront Nurse Creightmore?"

"We must wait. Bide our time. But mark my words, it's the eye that has travelled that is clever!"

"What do you mean?"

"Old Masai saying." The Brigadier tapped the side of his nose.

"But what does it mean?"

"Eyes sharp as a hoopoe...carrier pigeon...owl? I don't know, but in the meantime, collect the drugs from Creightmore. Ring me when you have them. Here..." He handed her a card, on which were printed his name, the address at Wellworth Lawns and his telephone number. "I'll alert that young nephew of mine in the morning. And I've had an idea about the Dionysus."

"What?"

"The paperweight."

"The Bacchus, you mean."

"My mistake. Always was better at Greek than Latin. The thing is, I have an acquaintance who works at Christie's who might be able to throw some light on it. He'll know if anything's coming up at auction."

"But why would Nurse Creightmore think to sell it at Christie's."

"She may well have an accomplice. She could even be stealing to order. You never can tell how the criminal mind works and, for all we know, she may have contacts in the game."

"Nurse Creightmore? Contacts in the art world?"

"Have faith, Boxford. The Lake Naivasha Largemouth Bass will, on occasion, surface."

Chapter Eight

Parker turned his head away when Laura offered him some of her breakfast croissant, plainly still suffering from the side effects of his inadvertent drug experience. She left him in bed and went down to the sanatorium.

Nurse Creightmore was standing behind her medication trolley counting out pills and referring to her notes. "Olive Fitzherbert... Two, four times a day," she muttered, rattling a small bottle.

"Good morning," Laura said.

Nurse Creightmore looked up, startled. "Please, Lady Boxford, don't interrupt me now. I'm sorting out Dr Mellbury's prescriptions." She returned to her notes as Laura hovered by the trolley.

"Two spoonfuls twice a day..." She looked up again. "Oh, what is it?" she sighed.

Laura reminded her about the arthritis remedy she had promised her.

"Ah yes, I'd forgotten." Nurse Creightmore brightened visibly. "I'll go and get some. You wait there." She disappeared, leaving the medication trolley unattended.

Laura picked up a packet and read the label. They were for Sandra Abelson. *Swimming the channel with a complaint like that?* Laura winced at the thought. *But really, Nurse Creightmore is so intent upon her wicked endeavours, that she has entirely forgotten her professional etiquette.*

The nurse returned clutching a brown paper bag. She checked the contents, pulling out a box and eying it before returning it to the bag. She handed it to Laura. "Take one tablet before mealtimes and two at bedtime if you still feel the pain. That'll be fifteen pounds."

Laura rootled about in her purse and handed over a jumble of coins and a ten-pound note. She thanked the nurse and hurried back upstairs to open the package.

There it was, the same box with the dragon on it, only this time the dragon was yellow, not green like Venetia's or red like Hetty's, but otherwise identical as far as she could tell. She turned it over. The base was covered in the same unintelligible characters – she assumed it must be Chinese. She opened it up and tipped out the contents into her hand. They looked the same as the one she had taken. She sniffed them. There seemed no difference, but how could she tell for sure? She decided to call the Brigadier.

As she waited for him to reply, she studied the card he had given her. 'Brigadier A.G.M. Stanway' it read. *What an odd sense of humour his parents must have had,* she thought and was wondering what the initials stood for when he answered.

"It's me," she said. "I've got the evidence."

"Wait there, I'll come straight round."

A few minutes later, Laura heard him knocking on the door. She let him in and handed him the package.

"You don't think we should tell John Fincham?" Laura asked, looking up at him.

"Your trusting nature is a natural charm," the Brigadier said. "But from our experiences with the doctor and the police, both of whom we are fully aware have the ear of Fincham, I think we are better advised to tackle this alone. At least until we know exactly what we are dealing with. I've spoken with young Rupert – turns out he's a General. Promotion these days, I ask you? Says he'll send the stuff to the army medical laboratory. Once they receive the goods, it shouldn't take long for them to identify the contents."

"Do you think the colour of the dragon matters?"

"Two sticks in the bush. One gnarled. Both facing west." The Brigadier gave a purposeful nod. "Oh and talking of gnarled sticks, I caught Mellbury before breakfast at early morning surgery. At last he's agreed to send me to the ENT man at Woldham for my hearing. But only after he'd asked me if I thought my quality of life would be improved by it. The impudence. And all the time, he was toying with a very expensive looking gold pen that I've not seen on him before. I'm coming round to the idea of him and Creightmore being in it together."

As the Brigadier pushed his hearing aid further into his ear, the silver hairs splayed out, reminding Laura on this occasion of tiny frosted tentacles. "Mellbury and Creightmore?" she said. "I think I'll go and see the doctor myself."

"But you're not ill."

"I'll pretend something. I'm getting quite good at it."

Laura's consultation with Dr. Mellbury at Woldham Medical Centre, did not go according to plan.

"Lucky I could fit you in," he said, looking up from behind his desk where he was writing notes. "Normally I'm chockablock, but they're dropping like flies with this latest flu epidemic. You'd have thought it would be over by this time of year but one of 'em pegged it shortly before lunch. Meant I missed my sandwich at the pub." He sighed, took a lump of wobbly neck flesh between two fingers and massaged it. "Still, at least he didn't need his appointment this afternoon. So, while it wasn't great for him, it turned out to be most fortuitous for you. What seems to be the matter?"

"I'm tired of life," Laura said, easing the silk scarf around her neck.

"I'm not surprised at your age. What do you expect? I'll give you a prescription." He put down his pen and turned to the computer. "Anti-depressants should do the trick."

It looks real, Laura thought, weighing up in her mind if the pen might even be eighteen carat gold. "But it's more than that, Doctor. I sometimes see little point in living anymore," she said, straining to decipher the initials engraved on it.

"Exactly. I couldn't agree more. It's as I said, the shock of losing Mrs. Winterbottom has befuddled you. Let's hope it's temporary. Start taking the pills and come back and see me in a couple of weeks. That is, if you haven't managed to contract flu in the meantime. Then all your worries will be over." He got up from his chair. "Have you had a jab? Make an appointment with the nurse." He held the door open for her as she folded the prescription and put it in her bag.

"Really," she said, as she pushed Parker out of the driving seat. "That man has no bedside manner whatsoever." She put the car in gear. "Befuddled. I mean what kind of medical term is that?" She was still feeling irked about his insulting behaviour as they turned into the drive to Wellworth Lawns.

Behind the reception desk, Mimi was dancing in her pink tracksuit, a pair of white headphones in her ears. Her eyes were shut as her lithe young body moved rhythmically to the unheard tune.

"Do, does, did. Done, doing, dong. Have, has, had. Hod, hoeing, bong," she sang merrily, her hips swaying from side to side. Laura went round and tapped her on the shoulder. She jumped backwards pulling out the earphones.

"Ladysheep!" Her large mascara-lashed eyes flashed wide. "You giving Mimi fright."

"Sorry, I was curious to know what that song was?"

"Oh. They no song you say. I practicing my irreg'lar verbs. You know. Went, goss, going, gong. We got test next week, my class."

"Irregular verbs? That's very difficult."

"Don't you tell me. I never remembering. Oh but I remembering something now. Is Mr. Finch. He say me he wanting see you. He in his office now time I think."

"Thank you, Mimi. I'll go and find him."

Laura knocked on the manager's door before walking in. He was on the telephone.

He put one hand over the mouthpiece. "One sec," he whispered and gestured to a chair. "All right, Jim... Yes, yes. The full amount. You know me. Goodbye." He put the phone down.

"Lady Boxford, the very person. Good look that, scarf around the neck area. Double chin always a tricky op."

Laura was momentarily distracted as she remembered Dr. Mellbury's saggy encumbrance.

"Now, a couple of bits of news," the manager continued. "Firstly, Mrs. Winterbottom's funeral is at Woldham crematorium on Monday at two-fifteen. I wondered if you would like me to accompany you?"

Laura thought about the proposition and decided it would do no harm. The Brigadier had reminded her that, even the most unlikely situations should be seen as an opportunity to throw some light on their investigation. "Thank you, John," she said.

"Good. I'll drive us there. Now the second thing is, that we have a new tenant for Mrs. Winterbottom's room. He'll be moving in next week."

"What?" Laura gripped the arms of the chair. *A man? In the next door room?* She knew the room couldn't remain empty, but it had not occurred to her that John would want it filled so soon and, far worse, with a man. It was tantamount to a mixed ward.

"A man is going to be in Hetty's room, right next door to me?" she said.

"The walls are good and thick in that part of the house and, anyway, it's Sir Maurice Dickinson. You know Sir Maurice, don't you?"

"Everybody knows Maurice." *Maurice Dickinson... In Hetty's room?* It was unthinkable.

"Yes, he's sold his bungalow. It was getting too much for him to manage on his own. I'd have thought you two would get on well as neighbours, what with him having been in the racing game."

The telephone rang on John's desk. "Excuse me." He picked it up. "Kevin, now what was it? Oh yes, the latest invoice. Paper napkins. They've gone through the roof. We need a better rate..."

Laura listened as he talked to the supplier. By the time he got to renegotiating toilet roll prices, she lost patience. She waved airily at him and walked out.

Back in her sitting room, she picked up the telephone. Wishing that Victoria and Vince didn't live so far away in Yorkshire, she rang her granddaughter.

"Darling, it's too awful. Vince must speak to John Fincham immediately."

"But Granny dearest, I'm so sorry about Hetty and of course I will speak to Vince, but you must remember Wellworth Lawns is a business and he can't really go riding roughshod over John's decisions. Don't forget, it was you who wanted him as manager in the first place…"

Laura remembered with a degree of irritation the occasion of her first meeting with John Fincham, when he arrived for the interview with Vince. At the time she had thought him most agreeable but Vince said he was far too old at fifty-five.

"On top of being over the hill and addicted to minor forms of gambling, he used to be a plastic surgeon. It's not a field of expertise that's likely to be of much benefit to the running of a care home."

"But Vince dearest, that means he has medical knowledge and Dr. Mellbury can't be here all the time."

"Someone from the hospitality sector is who we need. Not a man with an obsession for Bingo."

"But Bingo is perfect for us old things. Plenty of mindless pastimes is exactly what we want." She had turned to Victoria. "Make him see," she implored. Victoria gave Vince one of her little nuzzles on his neck that she said sent all his business sense flying out of the window. Vince capitulated and John had got the job.

Now Victoria asked, "Who is the man taking Hetty's room anyway?"

"Maurice Dickinson."

"Not…"

"Yes."

"Of the horse doping scandal? He got thrown off the board of Cheltenham racecourse didn't he?"

"Amongst other things, yes. And he's a drunkard."

"I'll see what I can do. Have you a friend who could move into Hetty's room, if Vince were to agree?"

Laura thought of Venetia. Her need was greater than Vince's profit margin. "She's called Venetia Hobbs," she said, "and I'm afraid you'll have to persuade Vince that the room can be retained on the same terms as Hetty."

Venetia was thrilled at the prospect of moving rooms, although Laura was not sure she fully understood the financial magnitude of the largesse that was being bestowed upon her. Still, it mattered little as long as the dreadful Maurice Dickinson was not next-door.

"And anyway," she said to Parker, as she walked back from seeing Venetia. "What's the point of Victoria being married to the owner of Wellworth Lawns, if not to make our dotage a little more comfortable?"

She could hear her phone ringing as she opened the door to her apartment and ran to pick it up. It was the Brigadier. She told him about Maurice Dickinson.

"I mean if it had been you in the next room, |" she lied. "It would have been quite another matter."

"Sir Maurice is not everyone's cup of tea that's for certain," he said. "And I'm not sure he could actually afford the room anyway. I know for a fact that he had a mortgage on that bungalow. He told me so himself, when we were having a glass of port in the bar. Well, he was. I don't touch the stuff. I find port can play havoc with the… Perhaps I won't go down that route, but he didn't say anything about moving. I'll see what I can find out and report back."

"And I said I'd go to Hetty's funeral with John. Oh dear, I can't think why."

"No, no. Damn good plan. Remember the antelope."

"The antelope?"

"Exactly. It might prove useful. I remember being in the back of a Land Rover in Botswana. Discovered my batman was a cross-dresser."

"I'm sorry?"

"I'd never have known if I'd taken the staff car. I've sent the pills to London by the way. We should hear back in a day or so."

Chapter Nine

Laura took her black 'Crem Coat' out of the dry cleaner's bag, but decided Hetty would not have wanted her to look so funereal at the service. It was a difficult time of year for clothing. The mayflowers were out but on some days, winter coats were still in order. She determined to look for something more colourful in Woldham when she went to have her hair done.

Dudley flicked off the dryer and put it down on the shelf below the mirror, in front of Laura. "Were you thinking of wearing a hat for the crematorium?" he asked, as he nudged a newly created curl into place behind her ear.

"I don't think it's necessary these days, do you?"

"I haven't worn one since I had my transplant." Dudley patted the top of his blond head. "I don't know what it is about Scandinavian hair. But I'm glad I took advice. Scottish was half the price but you can never get away from that reddish tinge."

"It's very convincing, I must say," Laura said, looking up at him in the mirror. She glanced at the photograph hanging on the wall of Dudley as he received his prize for the Independent Hairdresser's Regional Finals in 1996, tall and lanky, his prematurely bald head shining under the glare of the cameraman's lights. Then she remembered what the Brigadier had said about Francesca Northbridge using Nurse Creightmore's remedy.

"Did you ever try hair-restorer, Dudley?" she asked.

"All a lot of rubbish. Sea salt from Ireland; Volcanic ash from Vesuvius; thyroid extract from Indonesian pygmies; believe me I tried the lot. None of it works. Having said that, I do keep a small herbal range for the girls who've kept their extensions in too long." Dudley explained how this could cause hair loss.

"It does no harm and it keeps them happy till the hair grows back. Knotweed extract, I think it is. Funny thing that, my sister in Milton Keynes has got an epidemic of it."

"What?"

"Japanese Knotweed. Can't get rid of it. Roots get under the house and you're a goner with estate agents."

"Could I see some of this knotweed remedy?" Laura asked.

"What d'you want with hair restorer, Lady B? You're not considering extensions are you?" He laughed.

"It's for a friend."

"Tell her to come and see me. I've got a new selection of wigs coming in."

"She wouldn't want to go that far." Laura was feeling the strain of the deception. "She's thinning a bit on top, that's all. It's only natural, she's ninety-six, but she still likes to mess around with beauty products."

"Say no more." Dudley winked at her in the mirror and went out to his stock room.

He returned and handed her a small brown bottle. She recognised the logo with a sense of mounting excitement. On the label was a blue dragon. Laura stared at it as Dudley sprayed her hair with a thick miasma of lacquer. "There you go," he said standing back. "Not even a balaclava'll shift that lot."

"Thank you Dudley, very nice." Laura was never sure about curls and she mostly managed to brush them out when she got home – "But could you tell me where this comes from?"

"You take that one. Have it on me for your friend."

"That's very kind, but I was interested to know who your supplier is."

"Not thinking of going into competition with me, are you, Lady B?"

"Of course not, Dudley…" Laura had to think fast. "Its just that my friend is very interested in Chinese calligraphy, particularly in the field of advertising. She once had a job with Saatchi and Saatchi."

"Blimey, it takes all sorts." He picked up the bottle. "Hang on, I'll get you one of his business cards."

Dudley disappeared again but returned empty handed. "I've told those girls not to tidy up but they just can't help themselves." He called out to one of the juniors who was sweeping hair off the floor.

"Steph, what've you done with my filing system? I can't find the card of that man who brings the chinky-chonkey lotion."

"Dunno what you're on about?" the girl said.

Dudley turned back to Laura. "He's called Barry Wong, but that's not much help. I'll have another look when we're quiet later on. There'll be one in there somewhere."

"I… my friend would very much appreciate it."

"I tell you what; I'll drop the card in at Wellworth. I'm there next Tuesday morning. New client."

"Who's that?"

"Mrs. Duck something… Huck… Huckley? She's come out of hospital. Mr. Fincham said her people thought it might cheer her up having her hair done."

"Huxley. Harriet Huxley. That must be who it is. Goodness, she's been away for ages. I must find out how she is."

Laura thanked Dudley and, with the bottle of hair-restorer safely stashed in her bag, she hurried to the dress shop and absentmindedly searched through the rack of coats. She chanced upon a red one with brass buttons. Putting it on, she looked at herself in the mirror. She gave a half turn and studied herself in profile. OK, it wasn't the figure of her youth, but still, it wasn't bad…less elegant but more…what was it? Comely? No, Homely, that was the word. She was sure Hetty would have approved, so she bought it and returned to Wellworth Lawns to tell the Brigadier of her discovery.

Behind the reception desk, a young girl with a towering pile of blonde hair was sitting filing her nails.

"Hello ladysheep," she called.

Laura took a second look. "Goodness, Mimi? Is that you?"

"What you thinking?" she said, patting the precarious arrangement on top of her head. "I getting sick of all that black hair. Is like every other Bulgarian you seeing all over the place."

"It's… It's very different. But it suits you. Yes, it's lovely Mimi. Where did you have it done?"

"My friend, he making very good price, not like English rip-off. How much you paying yours?"

"I…" Laura clutched her bag containing Dudley's receipt. "I can't remember. But Mimi…"

"Yes?"

"Have you seen Brigadier Stanway this morning?"

"Brig? He taking train to London. I call him taxi. Coming, ooh, how you say…" She tapped the big pink watch on her wrist. "Eleven quarter time."

"Did he say when he would return?"

"He taking suitcase. Here today going tomorrow, how you say? I thinking he staying sister. Something like that maybe?"

As Laura took the lift upstairs, she wondered if Mimi said things because she thought it would please her, or if the Brigadier really had gone to stay with a sister. *Oh well,* she thought, *I suppose I haven't actually got anything to report, it's just a bottle after all, but I need that business card from Dudley.*

John Fincham confirmed that the Brigadier had gone to stay with his sister in London when Laura met him after church the next day.

"He'll be back on Monday evening, I believe," John said. "Are we still on for the Crematorium tomorrow?"

"If that's all right with you?"

"Couldn't be easier. I'll meet you in the hall at… shall we say one forty-five? That should give us plenty of time. Good look there, by the way, Lady B. A hint of blue eye shadow is as good as a nip and tuck any day. Mind you, my clients would have thought I was mad if I'd suggested it." He laughed.

Mad? Laura was reminded of Harriet Huxley. She asked him if it was true that Harriet had returned from the psychiatric unit in Woldham.

"Came back two days ago," John said. "Sad really, they don't seem to have been able to do much for her. I don't think she's left her room since she got back here."

"I'll go and visit her. Is she still in the same room?"

"We've put her in number 38," John informed her.

"Where's that?" Laura asked.

"Old nursery wing. You remember? Instead of going right out of the lift, you go left. Right at the end is the staircase up to the second floor."

The old nursery… Laura walked down the corridor. She could remember visiting Henry there when he was a young boy. It was a large, long room with a fireplace at one end. They always had wood on the fires downstairs but Nanny insisted on coal in the nursery. She said it kept the heat in so much better and what with young Henry's weak chest, she needed to be sure of constant warmth. When Laura made occasional forays, she often found Nanny and Henry rushing around the room pretending to be ponies, Nanny neighing wildly as Henry chased her with a stick.

Laura knocked on the door.

"It's open," Harriet said.

Laura let herself in.

Harriet was lying on her bed staring at the ceiling. She had suffered from depression since her husband, the theatrical impresario Blake Huxley had left her five years earlier. She had been seventy-five at the time – not an age to find oneself alone. Blake was about the same age as Harriet but Davindra Singh, his secretary was a youthful fifty-six. After the divorce, Blake and Davindra took a honeymoon in Cap d'Antibes. Blake had fallen down a cliff and fatally broken his neck. The children said it served him right for leaving their mother, but Harriet was thrown into an ever-deeper slough of despond. It soon became apparent she could no longer cope, so the children sold her house and put her in Wellworth Lawns.

Now, as Laura sat at her bedside, Harriet reached for her box of tissues.

"What's the point of it all?" she said. "I'm good for nothing. I'd be better off dead."

Laura tried to encourage her. "It's nearly that time of the year for the Horticultural Society annual plant sale. That's something to look forward to," she said.

"Lot of ghastly women fighting over begonias. I'd rather asphyxiate myself in a bag of manure." Harriet turned to face the wall. "Or cut off my head with a pair of secateurs."

Laura spent a gloomy Sunday evening watching Antiques Roadshow. Normally she would have sat with Hetty enjoying seeing the items on display, Hetty gasping at the prices, but it was no fun on one's own. She yearned for someone to share it with and found herself wondering what the Brigadier was up to.

Chapter Ten

On the morning of the funeral, Laura got up early. She went downstairs and ordered a full English breakfast as she had decided to skip lunch in order to be ready in time to meet John Fincham. She left Parker in her room – he was inclined to become vociferous when confronted with the smell of bacon.

When she had finished, she went and collected him and took him for a walk. She dropped into the kitchen on her way back. Alfredo was pouring a bottle of vermouth into a large vat of steaming liquid.

"Morning, Alfredo," Laura called over the noise of clanking pots and pans coming from the direction of the scullery.

Alfredo looked up from the pot and wiped his brow with one heavily muscled forearm.

"Eh, Lady B, How ya doin'?"

"Very well, thank you. And you?"

"No so bad." The chef nodded and then turned and shouted in the direction of the noise, "Oy, you in there, shut the fak up. I got her ladyship here." He turned back to Laura and took a swig from the bottle of vermouth. "I could do without fish stew this morning, mind you. Smell reminds me of Genoa harbour. Warm squid in the afternoon sun. Sweet baby Nero, I'm going soft in the head."

"Mmm, the smell is quite pungent, but I'm sure it will be delicious."

"I heard 'bout Mrs. W. Too bad. No more Eggs Benedict, eh?" Alfredo took off his chef's hat, ran his fingers through his glossy black hair and stared at the floor.

"Your recipe was always one of her favourites." Laura put her hand on his arm and they both stood in silence for a moment. Then Alfredo took another swig from the bottle.

"Fak," he said and banged his fist on the worktop. "So, what I do for you? Hit me, Lady B," he said, tipping the remains of the bottle into the fish stew. "We got some nice pastries in at the moment."

"Not for me, thank you Alfredo." Laura patted her stomach. "You feed us far too well as it is. No, what I was wondering was if you had a small bone for Parker. I have to leave him on his own while I go to Mrs. Winterbottom's cremation."

"Holy smoke, don't get me going again." Alfredo wiped his eyes with a tea towel. "I got knuckles roasting in the oven for the stock pot if you want?"

The idea made Laura feel a little queasy. "A chicken winglet would be plenty for him."

"Flame grilled? I do it in a flash."

Laura grabbed the side of the worktop with one hand. "The vet says he should have them raw."

Alfredo picked up a skewer and went out to the refrigerator. He returned holding a chicken impaled on the end of the point and flicked it down onto the work surface. He chose a knife and tested its sharpness with his thumb. "Fak me!" He dropped the knife and put his thumb in his mouth before wrapping it in the tea towel. Picking up the knife again, he severed through the chicken wing. "There you go, Lady B," he said, dropping it into a plastic bag and handing it to her.

Laura put the winglet on her desk as Parker sniffed the air expectantly.

"Later," she said. "Now go and sit in your basket while I get my jewels out."

She pinned a substantial diamond brooch onto the lapel of her new red coat and placed a triple strand of pearls around her neck. She looked at herself in the mirror. The sight reminded her of a Chelsea Pensioner. *Too much bling*, she thought looking at the row of brass buttons. *What a mistake.* Either the brooch, or the coat had to go.

In the end, she thought Hetty would have preferred the jewels, so she got out the old black 'crem coat' and replaced the brooch.

John was waiting for her in the hall. He was wearing a dark suit that Laura thought had seen better days.

"Truly magnificent," he said, eyeing the diamonds. "I've always thought a stunning sparkler's as good as a boob job any day."

"Are you forgetting yourself John?"

"Begging your pardon, Lady B." He laughed nervously. "I only meant a jewel placed judiciously, such as yours, diverts the eye. Far be it from me to imply you need a breast enhancement."

They walked to John's car and he opened the door for her. As they drove to the crematorium, sitting beside him, Laura couldn't help but notice a greasy sheen on his trouser legs.

"I spoke to Mr...Vince this morning," he said, rubbing his left thigh between gear changes. Laura wished he would keep both hands on the wheel.

She turned and looked out of the window. "What did he have to say?"

"You will be pleased to hear, that we think it's in your best interests to have Mrs. Hobbs in Mrs. Winterbottom's old room next to you."

"Really? That is good news."

"Same rental conditions, you understand. I've spoken with Mrs. Hobbs this morning. I'll arrange the transfer as soon as I can get hold of Tom to help move her furniture. He's been doing some plumbing work in Mulberry Close."

"Mulberry Close?"

"The old kitchen garden. You remember, we had to have a naming session when – well actually it was Sir Maurice who complained 'Old Kitchen Garden,' wasn't an address befitting his station."

"Of course, silly me. So where's he going?"

"Sir Maurice will go in Mrs. Hobbs's old room."

"Isn't that a bit of a comedown?"

John turned to her. "Nothing is a comedown at Wellworth Lawns!"

"Look out," Laura said, as they veered into the middle of the road.

"It's all right," he said. "We're here now."

As they drove down the avenue of Leylandii and drew up outside the crematorium, Laura saw a small group of mourners waiting outside. She couldn't miss Strudel standing with Jervis – she was wearing a huge dark sombrero with a row of yellow raffia donkeys attached around the brim. They were talking to the Patersons who, like she and Hetty, were members of the Horticultural Society, and another couple Laura recognised from the bungalows. Standing aloof a short distance away, Laura made out the tall raven haired figure of Gloria Hemper, dressed in a scarlet coat. She breathed a sigh of relief that she had not worn hers.

They parked and went to join the gathering. The small crowd parted as Gloria Hemper, followed by a young man and woman came over to greet them.

"John, Laura," she said. "We're running slightly late; something about a wicker basket getting stuck in the furnace doors. Honestly, how cheap can you get? You know my son Charlie and my daughter Abigail." She turned to the young people. "You remember Lady Boxford, don't you?" she said, ignoring John.

Laura had only ever briefly met Hetty's grandchildren. She did not even know Gloria very well. They had rarely visited Hetty.

"Hello, Lady Boxford, how nice to see you." Abigail held out her hand.

Charlie grunted and turned away to read the inscription on a display of flowers in the form of a football from a previous service. *What a charmless young man; takes after his mother,* Laura thought.

Gloria left them, followed by Abigail and Charlie to attend to another couple who had just arrived.

"Relatives, I imagine," Laura said to John who was still standing beside her, fiddling with his tie.

There were only about thirty people present, but Laura realised how little she knew of Hetty's family. Gloria's husband had left her, so he wasn't there. Hetty had fallen out with her only son, Frank, when he had moved to Australia and then refused to attend his father, Algie Winterbottom's funeral. And, of course, Hetty's brother, Stanley Beaumont, was also dead.

She felt a tap on her shoulder.

"Laura?"

She turned and was surprised to find herself looking down at Stanley's ex-wife, Sally. Always immaculately turned out, Sally was the picture of perfection in miniature. She could only have been five foot two.

"Goodness!" Laura said. "How nice to see you. I didn't expect you'd be here."

Sally smiled. "I know, but I always kept in contact with Hetty and Gloria. We talked on the telephone off and on. I'd been meaning to come and see Hetty but somehow I never got round to it, what with one thing and another. I do feel bad, especially as I'm only down the road now."

"I thought you were in London?"

"I moved up here a couple of months ago. Sold my flat and bought a cottage; Gloria helped me find it."

From the entrance to the crematorium they heard Gloria call out: "They're ready for us now."

"Shall we sit together?" Sally asked.

The room was plain; rows of wooden benches giving it an air of the Scottish Presbyterian. Ahead, Laura could see Hetty's coffin. It looked smaller than she'd expected and she felt a pang of apprehension that Hetty might be cramped inside it. The organist started playing and they stood. Laura looked down at the words in the hymnbook and she realised she did not know whether Hetty had a favourite hymn or not. But she'd had a favourite song. Laura remembered her old friend dancing round the room at the Wellworth Christmas party when she'd asked the DJ to play *Oh Carol* by Neil Sedaka. The lyrics reverberated in Laura's mind as the vicar began to speak… But Hetty was no fool and yet she had been tricked out of life. And who had treated her so cruelly?

Laura was still mulling this over when, to her amazement, John got up and gave a short eulogy to Hetty as if he had been her long lost son.

"Oh yes," Laura heard him say. "Hetty was always the first to embrace the new. She made full use of the extensive facilities of Wellworth Lawns, often joining in the free activities laid on by the staff. She greatly enjoyed the fine dining experience of our newly refurbished bistro-style dining room. Menus can be tailored to meet special dietary needs…"

As John blundered on, Laura was baffled – why had he not said anything in the car about this?

"Despite the tragedy that resulted from her broken ankle, Hetty was always content in her elegantly appointed room – all our rooms are en suite –And I'm sure you will all agree that she will be sorely missed." At last he finished and returned to his seat.

The vicar entreated the congregation to join in the short prayers before it was time for him to press the button. The organist struck up again and, as the curtains drew back, Hetty's coffin was slowly removed from view. The curtains closed behind it and Hetty was gone. The congregation sat in contemplative silence before filing out into a small garden of remembrance.

"I must say hello to my friends," Laura said to Sally, pointing to Strudel and Jervis who were standing reading a plaque on the wall. "Come and meet them."

They walked over and Laura made the introductions.

"That was a lovely service, are you not agreeing?" Strudel said.

"Yes, I think Hetty would have enjoyed it. Interesting speech from John, didn't you think?" Laura said.

"His usual," Jervis muttered.

Sally looked up at him. "What do you mean?"

"He's the manager of Wellworth Lawns," Laura explained.

"I've heard it before. He's got a nice little sideline in eulogies." Jervis gave a knowing nod.

"You mean he charges for them?" Laura said.

"Jervis! How could you be so much cynical." Strudel smacked his hand. "I'm sure it's quite untrue."

Gloria appeared in the doorway. "People," she called. "I should like you all to join us for tea at the Railway Hotel in Woldham. We could have gone to my home, but I thought the hotel would be more convenient... For those returning to London." she added.

Laura raised her eyebrows.

"I quite agree," Jervis said.

"What?" Sally asked.

"Well, the Railway Hotel..." Laura left the sentence incomplete. "What about it?"

"Put it like this, I don't think Hetty would be best pleased. And I can't see many of this lot going to London."

The Railway Hotel was one of those cumbersome Victorian gothic buildings, best described as an eyesore in any situation, but in the picturesque setting of Woldham, it was a travesty. There had been countless petitions to have it demolished over the years but then bats had been discovered in the roof and that was the end of that.

The room Gloria had taken for the tea was cold and dark. In the large mock Tudor inglenook fireplace a wood-burning stove emitted a pitiful glow as the damp logs hissed. On the floor, the threadbare Axminster was stained through years of drunken spillages. At one end of the room stood a Formica table on which there was a chrome catering-sized urn, a large jar of coffee granules and a box of tea bags. A bowl of sugar and a mass of thick white china cups and saucers lay stacked beside two serving plates of white sliced sandwiches that were flattened under tightly wrapped cling film.

"Help yourselves," Gloria told them. She removed the film, squashed it into a ball and dropped it on the floor.

On closer inspection of the sandwiches Laura discovered they were egg, or egg. Granted, Hetty had a penchant for eggs, but Florentine, or Benedict or en cocotte. This was a poor do, to be sure. John poured her out a cup of tea and she put one sandwich on a saucer as there appeared to be no side plates. The saucer was still damp, from the dishwasher, Laura hoped. She felt sad. If only she had known that this was all Hetty's only daughter could muster, she would have organised for the party to be held at Wellworth Lawns. She took a bite of the sandwich. It stuck to the roof of her mouth and she inhaled an aroma reminiscent of her days at boarding school.

Sally nudged her, pointing to the sandwich on her own saucer. "I didn't know they still made this. What's it called? Something cream..."

"Reminds me of that greenish stuff we used to get. 'Sandwich spread'. Do you remember? Rather delicious in its way."

"Salad cream, that's what it is." They began to giggle.

Laura noticed Gloria staring at them. "I feel like a guilty schoolgirl. Let's go and sit down," she suggested.

They found a window seat and looked out at the wasteland of buddleia and stalks of last year's rosebay willowherb that divided them from the railway track.

"Gloria really is a shocker," Sally said.

"Is she very short of money?" Laura asked.

"Not this short. She can still afford a cleaner. Mind you, with a son like Charlie, money is always going to be an issue. She told me he's in debt again."

"Debt?"

"He's incapable of keeping out of trouble. If it's not one addiction it's another. Drink she says, but probably drugs as well. Runs in the family, obviously. I blame Stanley."

"You're very sanguine," Laura said.

"Stanley? Oh, I got over him years ago. But Gloria's forever bailing Charlie out." Sally indicated banknotes as she rubbed her thumb and two forefingers together.

"How do you know all this?"

"Theresa. The cleaner. I share her with Gloria. We only live five miles apart. Gloria recommended her to me, but she doesn't give Theresa a cup of tea and biscuits mid-morning, like I do. Nothing like a chocolate Hobnob for loosening the tongue."

"So you know everything that Gloria gets up to?"

"Not everything. But a fair bit. Theresa likes a natter."

"Shh, she's coming over…" Laura whispered and held up her teacup as Gloria approached.

"Hello again, Laura. I see you've found Aunt Sally." Gloria let one wrist dangle as if her rings were too heavy on her fingers.

"This is a… spread," Laura said.

"I felt I had to do something for Mother."

"Yes, yes you have."

"I think she would have been pleased by the turn out. Well, lovely to see you both. I must be getting off or Abigail will miss her train." Gloria gave a little "huhh" and turned to go. They watched as she sauntered across the room.

"She doesn't get on with her daughter either," Sally said. "Although there's nothing wrong with Abigail, as far as I can tell."

"Well, at least the venue's convenient for her," Laura said. "But listen, Gloria turned up at Wellworth Lawns the evening Hetty died, with papers for Hetty to sign. I've no idea what that was all about. I wonder if your cleaner might know – what was her name again?"

"Theresa. I'll ask her if you like. I'll give you a ring. Or I could come over?"

"Perfect, I'll give you my number but I tell you what, they do quite a good lunch at Woldham Farmshop. Have you been? We could meet there."

By the time Laura was ready to leave, John Fincham was still busy doing his sales pitch for Wellworth Lawns to the couple they had seen earlier. She told him she would get a lift back with Strudel and Jervis.

Jervis put his old Mercedes into third gear and they lurched out of the car park.

"I am feeling whiplash," Strudel cried out from the back seat.

"Sorry, my love." Jervis rounded the corner onto the main road in fourth.

"Did you mean what you said about John taking money to do the eulogy?" Laura asked.

"Hand in glove with the undertakers, Bone and Bone, I'd say. They'll be doing a deal. Decent eulogy makes for a professional looking job. All adds to the smooth running of the operation. Like my driving, eh Strudel?"

"You are making the very bad joke."

"But John doesn't need money, does he?" Laura asked.

"You tell me? He likes a bet. I've seen him in the bookie's."

"Jervis, you must not be letting your imagination run ahead of you. The placing of the bet is not a crime. And how is it you are knowing so much about the bookie shop?" Strudel smacked him on the shoulder. "Now, please to change the subject. Laura, I am very much liking your friend Sally."

"She's Hetty's ex sister-in-law," Laura said.

"And now single?"

"I can see where this is going…" Jervis clipped the pavement as he turned a corner. "Strudel, you're incorrigible!"

"I don't know what you mean."

"Think you can get her on a date. Do we have any jockeys on the books?"

"Oh, Ancient Eros. Actually jockeys often go for taller women," Laura said. "But are you very busy?"

"Flooded," Strudel said. "Actually, I was wondering… I have a very nice gentleman near Woodstock who I think would be suiting you, Laura."

"It's very kind of you to think of me but I'll stick to bridge and the occasional ballroom dancing session, if you don't mind."

"Well, take a few of these all the same." Strudel handed Laura half a dozen printed business cards. "We had them done in Woldham. Aren't you loving the wrinkly cherub in his bifocals? Adorable, Do you not agree?"

Laura was losing concentration. The Ancient Eros logo was of little importance when the list of people who could have had a good reason to want the Bacchus paperweight and might be prepared to kill for it, had suddenly escalated.

Chapter Eleven

When Laura managed to track down the Brigadier the next day, she found he was not entirely on her wavelength.

"Steady, Boxford."

He was shouting again. Laura held the phone from her ear.

"The awful solemnity of the occasion must have heightened your sensitivities," he continued. "Just because Gloria and her son, and for that matter John Fincham, appear to be short of a bob or two, doesn't automatically make them murderers."

"That's as maybe, but you weren't there, and where have you been anyway?"

"I went to visit my sister in London. Got back last night."

"Well you're here now, and I've something important to show you. I'll meet you in the rose garden."

"When?"

Laura looked at the clock on her mantlepiece. It was half past ten. "Now."

She put Parker on his lead and hurried downstairs. Outside a light breeze was blowing, the sky filled with scudding grey clouds. It was one of those days that could go either way, and Laura was glad she had put her puffy jacket on. She found the Brigadier sitting on one of the commemorative benches kicking out with his foot at a wood pigeon that was strutting about on the ground beside him.

"Worse than Trafalgar Square," he said. "It's that damn old biddy with the bobble hat that keeps feeding them."

Parker barked and the pigeon flew away.

"And I can't think why I chose to meet here when there's not a flower to be seen." Laura noticed a few green buds clinging like caterpillars to the thorny rose bushes. "But talking of Trafalgar Square, you didn't tell me you were going to London," she said, sitting down beside him.

"Spur of the moment. Panther leaps when the frying pan's hot... no, that's not quite right... Still, I thought I'd go and see my man at Christie's."

"Was he helpful?"

"No."

The pigeon had returned and was pecking the ground a few feet from where Parker lay.

"Really? That's a pity," Laura said, as Parker began to growl softly.

"He was dead."

"That *is* a pity." With each breath, Parker's growl grew louder.

"Irritating, I know." The Brigadier jabbed his leg out. The bird flew off and Parker relaxed once more. "Still it couldn't be helped and I hadn't seen the man for years. But what was it you wanted to show me?"

Laura delved into her bag. "Look." She handed him the bottle of hair-restorer. "I got it from my hairdresser, Dudley. D'you see the label? It's the same dragon and everything as on Nurse Creightmore's. Dudley's finding me the name of the supplier."

"Excellent, Boxford. This is progress. Creightmore may be a small pawn, one of an extended group of criminals." He turned the bottle over in his hand. "Nursing homes up and down the country infiltrated by bogus members of the medical profession. Oh yes, there's many a weevil in the tiger's dung." He handed her back the bottle. "You must chase up this hairdresser of yours. The magnitude of this unfolding web of depravity is quite mind-boggling."

"Dudley said he'd drop the man's business card in on me when he came to do Harriet Huxley's hair, but I haven't seen him. I imagine she was too ill; she probably cancelled her appointment. I can see him tomorrow when I go to Woldham for mine."

"Harriet Huxley? Is she new?"

"No, but she's been in hospital for some time, suffering from depression. I went to see her when she got back, very sad. And that's another thing I had to tell you about, because her predicament slightly puts the kibosh on the idea that Dr. Mellbury is involved."

"Hold on, hold on. I thought we were pinning down nurse Creightmore." The brigadier looked up at the sky. "Was that a spot of rain?"

Laura held out her hand. "I don't think so. We are, but you said yourself, don't discount any possibilities. Dr. Mellbury could be part of this ring of yours."

"A *ring?* I said that?" The Brigadier felt the top of his head.

"Are you sure that wasn't rain?"

"Yes."

"So why are you now saying he's not involved?" He looked at the palm of his hand, smeared with white.

"Because Harriet wants to die."

"So?" He took out his handkerchief and wiped his hand and then the top of his head.

"You'd have thought it would be the perfect opportunity for Mellbury."

"Ah, but has she anything of value?"

"I don't think so," Laura said.

"That must be the reason why then. But you're right, we should dig deeper into his possible motivations." The Brigadier put his handkerchief away.

"It's good luck, of course."

The Brigadier looked perplexed.

"The shit of the bird upon the head." It sounded like one of his sayings but he didn't notice, so Laura continued, "I'm supposed to report back to him in a couple of weeks on how I'm getting on with the anti-depressants he prescribed me."

"You're not…"

"Of course I'm not taking them."

"Good, and I see that could prove an opportunity… Of course, what we need to know is who of his other patients died unexpectedly. That is more tricky."

As they sat pondering this dilemma, the breeze dropped and the sun came out. Real warm spring sunshine filled the garden. Laura could almost imagine the roses blooming and the thought of deep blush pink hues reminded her of something else.

"Of course there was Nanny."

"Nanny?"

"Yes. We never expected her to go so suddenly." Laura remembered Nanny's glorious rosy cheeks. "But her death can't be connected."

"Why's that?"

"She had a heart attack in the kitchen. She was very fond of Alfredo the chef. He was in the middle of making cheese soufflé and we thought it must have over-excited her."

"Why didn't you think about this earlier? It needn't necessarily have been a heart attack. When did she pass away? This could be vital, Boxford." The Brigadier fumbled with the wooly scarf around his neck and managed to unravel it. He put it down beside him on the bench. "Was she rich, this Nanny person?"

"Nanny, rich?"

"No? Well, she may have discovered something, heard a rumour, you know, being amongst the staff."

"Good point. Alfredo might remember." Laura stood up. "This bench is too uncomfortable to sit on any longer," she said. "I'll go and see if I can find him now."

They returned together but the Brigadier left her at the car park. "Chain on the bicycle needs attention," he said, taking a small can of oil from his pocket.

Nurse Creightmore was manning the reception desk, so Laura pretended to look for something in her bag as she walked past. She was pulling Parker on his lead, her eyes lowered, when the nurse called out, "How's the arthritis?"

"Oh, Nurse Creightmore, I didn't see you. My arthritis? Greatly improved, thank you. But why are you there? Shouldn't you be doing your rounds?"

"Mimi's gone to Paris with that handyman Tom, would you believe it? And who gets collared by Mr. Fincham? So I'm stuck here waiting for that girl from the agency in Woldham, who's late. Why Mr. Fincham couldn't staff the desk himself, I do not know. It's not a situation someone of my professional standing cares to find themself in." She fingered the watch on her chest and sighed.

"Talking of professionals," Laura said. "Do you know if Alfredo is in yet?"

"That foul mouthed man? Yes he's here."

Alfredo was standing in front of the large stainless steel island unit in the middle of the kitchen. He stabbed his knife down into the chopping board beside a pile of onions and removed the spoon from his mouth.

"Hello, Alfredo. Onions are a nuisance, aren't they," Laura said.

Alfredo raised the ski goggles from his eyes and a tidal wave of tears poured down his swarthy cheeks. "Fak this for a lark. Sous chef's done a bunk." He wiped his face with the dishcloth on his shoulder. "I don't suppose you fancy giving us a hand, Lady B?"

"No thank you. Phew, its hot in here, I don't know how you do it. But what is that marvellous smell?"

Alfredo's dark eyes widened in terror. "Madonna. Tomorrow's meatloaf..." He rushed to the oven.

"How delicious. You always manage to get it so smooth. Never any nasty lumpy bits."

Alfredo pulled out the smoky roasting tin and put it on top of the cooker, flapping the dishcloth at it. He inserted a knife and inspected the meatloaf as the juices flowed out. "Close shave there, Lady B," he said. "I like to think all my recipes are designed with delicate bridgework in mind. See this?" The chef opened his mouth and pointed down his throat. A ray of gold glinted amongst the snaggle of his teeth. "Pork ball in Messina."

"Gracious!"

"Lazy faking dago used some cheap mincer. Missed a piece of bone."

"How terrible. You would never allow that."

"Don't worry, he paid for it."

"Yes I'm sure he did. Dentistry is expensive. But Alfredo I was wondering..."

"Hit me, Lady B."

"Do you remember how long you've been here?"

"One of the first, I was. Señor Outhwaite sent for me. Him and Mrs. Outhwaite, Vittoria. Ahh, belissima." Alfredo sighed. "They fetch me out of that Trattoria in the bloody nick'a time I tell you." The chef made a gesture of slitting his throat with the knife with one hand and then crossed himself.

"Careful Alfredo."

"I remember my first days here. Nanny under my feet. Like my old Mama back home."

"Funny you should say that, Alfredo. Do you remember when Nanny died?"

Alfredo crossed himself again and a fresh gush of tears rolled down his cheeks.

"Did it strike you as rather...sudden?"

"Pocco Dio! Don't remind me."

"I didn't mean to upset you, Alfredo, but can you remember any other cases, I mean residents who went the same way without any warning?"

"Holy burning bush, Lady B, you think anybody here getting any younger?" Alfredo wiped his face with his hands. "Pass the cheddar, would you?"

"I'm so sorry. Here you are." She passed him the slab of cheese. "I'd better be getting out of your way."

"No problemo. Here, hold on a sec and I'll get Parker a winglet. We got Chicken Cacciatora on for dinner."

He went to the refrigerator and returned waving the morsel. Parker sniffed the air and began yapping wildly.

"Thank you so much," Laura said as Alfredo wrapped it in a piece of foil. "But there is one more little thing…"

"Hit me."

"Can you remember if Nurse Creightmore had started working here when Nanny passed away?"

"Holy Vatican City, Lady B? You sounding like Detective Morse. Sure she was here with Nanny. I had to tell 'em off for keeping them old witchy pills in my larder. Her and Nanny was in there for hours and they weren't at the panna cotta."

Had Nanny died at the nurse's hand as well? Laura took the lift upstairs. It couldn't be true. Alfredo must have got it wrong.

She was fumbling in her bag for her key, not helped by Parker who kept jumping up at her leg and barking in anticipation of the winglet, when Venetia came out of Hetty's old room.

"There you are," she said, waving her stick. "I've moved in. Come and see. Mr. Fincham helped me." She turned back to the room and pushed the door wide open. "He said it was looking rather bare, so he sent Tom down to the storeroom to borrow a few bits and pieces. Such a nice young man, Tom. So well spoken, and so sad to be disinherited at his age. Such a pity he had to rush off. Said he was going to Paris. Rather a long way to go to mend a sink."

"Tom, disinherited?"

"He told me the story while he was hanging the pictures."

"What story?"

"I didn't really get the whole gist of it. He was up the ladder and he's got the most lovely botty. I think he began to smell a rat when his mother sent him on a plumbing course while all his friends were on gap year expeditions to Thailand. Come in and see what he's done."

John Fincham had furnished Venetia with, amongst other things, and to Laura's astonishment, the collection of prints by the artist Russell Flint that Laura's late husband Tony had kept in the confines of his dressing room. She gazed at one of a bathing beauty stepping into a Roman bath. Perhaps it was Venetia mentioning Tom's posterior, but Laura was suddenly reminded of Istanbul, and the time when she and Tony and the rug salesman had had such fun in the hotel hot tub. *How long ago that must have been*, she thought, as she remembered her own and Tony's pale young bodies as they played around in the bubbling water with the delightful, dark-skinned Turk.

"Gracious," she said. "I thought we'd sold those years ago."

"I think they look very well, don't you?" Venetia walked about the room peering at them.

"But where's your nice painting?" Laura asked.

"What painting?"

"You know, the one of the young girl."

"Oh yes; now I remember. Mr. Fincham took it."

"John took the painting? Why?"

"Now that's a very good question. Perhaps he needs it for someone else. Or has he given it back to you?"

"No of course not. It's not mine, it's yours. Do try to remember. Why did you give your painting of the young girl to John Fincham? Think, Venetia."

Venetia sat down on the reclining chair that had been transferred from her old room. It looked even tattier in its new, grander surroundings. It was also malfunctioning and Venetia was jerked backwards so that her feet left the ground. The effect of this change on her circulation appeared to have a beneficial effect on her memory.

"I remember now," she said, staring at the ceiling. "He very kindly said he'd have it valued for me."

"But why? You're not thinking of selling it, are you? Hasn't he made it clear about your rent… This is too bad. I'll speak to Vince immediately."

"No, no. The rent was all sorted out. I can't thank you enough, Laura. It's even less than my old room. So I'm richer than I thought and, what with these new pictures, I really don't need the one of the girl. I know it's worth something, I've no idea how much, but I thought I'd like to give some money to my daughter, Angela. She's sixty-five and has nothing."

"Poor thing, really?"

"Stony broke and I feel bad about tobogganing through her inheritance."

"Skiing. Where is she living now?"

"I've no idea, but she turns up sometimes with her begging bowl. I normally give her what I've got in my purse and she's always terribly grateful."

Venetia had been fiddling down the side of the chair. She must have located the correct button because the chair righted itself with a jolt and she was propelled into an upright position. "I must try to remember to get a seatbelt for this," she said.

"And we mustn't let John forget either, must we?"

"Forget what?"

"About the painting. Now why don't we go and have a sharpener in my room?"

Venetia said she wasn't meant to have alcohol with her new pills. "Last time I had a whisky in the lounge with old Maurice Dickinson I could feel myself coming out in quite a sweat."

"Hardly surprising under the circumstances, but what were you doing having a drink with him anyway?"

"I've absolutely no idea. I've a feeling I was once related to his wife."

"Well whisky's bound to disagree with one at this time of life, but a spot of sherry won't do you any harm, I'm sure. You've been taking communion on a Sunday, haven't you?"

"Communion's the only fun bit about Reverend Mulcaster's services. His sermons are diabolically long."

"Well, come on then."

It wasn't the same as having Hetty round, although the two did have their similarities. Within a short space of time Venetia had eaten all the crisps and an entire tin of olives Laura had opened.

The Brigadier rang as she was giving Venetia a top up. "Don't move, I'll only be a minute," she said, and took the phone into her bedroom.

"How did you get on with the chef?" he asked.

"Very interesting, but I can't talk now, Venetia's here and I've said I'll have dinner with her."

"I'll steer clear. Coffee tomorrow A.M?"

"Hair appointment. I told you."

"What time? I'll meet you in town."

Laura said she'd be finished at Dudley's at eleven-thirty.

When she returned, Venetia had found the Fortnum's tin that Laura kept for Parker's treats.

Chapter Twelve

"There you go my lovely!" Dudley stood back to admire his artistry.

Laura looked in the mirror. She raised one hand from under the protective gown and patted her hair – more curls she'd have to get rid of later.

"Very nice, thank you," she said as something caught her eye behind her own reflection. She could see the glass front door to the hairdresser's and on the other side of it was the Brigadier, his nose pressed to the pane. She swivelled round in her chair.

Dudley turned to follow her gaze. "Now who is this? Not your fancy man, Lady B?" He laughed.

"Certainly not," Laura said, as the door opened.

"Can I come in?" the Brigadier asked. "I thought I'd better remind you about the card."

"I hadn't forgotten."

"Aren't you going to introduce us?" The hairdresser held out his hand. "I'm Dudley. Dudley's Hair Designs, that's me."

"This is Brigadier Stanway," Laura said tersely.

"Brigadier… I don't think I've ever had a Brigadier in the salon. Can I interest you in a trim?"

The Brigadier stepped forward, his hand outstretched.

"That's a lovely bit of cloth," Dudley said, eyeing the Brigadier's suit. "Donegal if I'm not mistaken?"

Laura rose from her seat. "Help me out of this, Dudley," she said, tussling with the bow at the back of the gown.

"Has Mr. Dudley managed to locate the card?"

"He's not *Mr.* Dudley and I haven't asked him yet." Laura was becoming flustered as the only other customer in the salon, a woman under an old fashioned dryer, had lowered her magazine and was staring at them.

"Oh, I get it," Dudley said. "But honestly Brigadier, don't waste your money on hair restoring products. Not at your age. The ladies love a chrome dome." He squeezed the Brigadier's arm.

"It's not for me, you fool!" The Brigadier elbowed Dudley. "Can't you see I'm not bald?"

Laura pushed him to one side and turned to Dudley. "I'm sorry. He's confused. I should never have told him and now he'll get in a state. Nothing will pacify him until we find that card."

She turned back to the Brigadier. "Go and wait outside."

He sloped off, shutting the door behind him.

"Tut tut, Lady B. Quite a handful you've got there. But let me see. I put it out for when I came over to Wellworth Lawns but then that Mrs. Huxley cancelled – no cheering her up, I hear – and then I thought it could wait till you were next in. Half a mo, I'll go and find it."

He returned and handed Laura an envelope with her name on it. "You see I hadn't forgotten."

"Of course you hadn't, Dudley. You're a dear. Now how much do I owe you?"

"What's going on?" the woman under the dryer shouted. "I'm cooking under here."

"We wouldn't want that now, would we?" Dudley hurried over. "Pay me next time, Lady B," he called back to her.

Out on the street, Laura could see the Brigadier was trying to remain patient but agitation was getting the better of him. He was pacing back and forth outside Dudley's and when she got to the door, he was there first, opening it for her.

"Don't you know you should never disturb a woman when she's having her hair done? It's a cardinal sin." Laura marched off down the street.

"Just thought I was being helpful." He hurried after her.

"You thought I'd forgotten."

"I... Look out, Boxford." He grabbed her arm. "It's Fincham and Mellbury ahead of us." He pulled her into the doorway of the travel agency and began pointing at an advert for a cruise.

Laura stole a look down the street. "They've turned round. They're coming this way," she whispered.

"Needs must," the Brigadier said, as he embraced her.

They heard John Fincham's voice draw nearer. "... You must be aware of your position, Doctor."

"I'm fully aware of my position, thank you, John."

They were right beside Laura. The Brigadier bent further over her. She felt his rough tweed suit smothering her and was that his moustache touching the top of her head... On her freshly done hair?

The footsteps were passing them.

"You know I should say something..." she heard John Fincham say, and then the Doctor answered, "You bastard, don't you dare," as their footsteps faded.

Laura and the Brigadier disentangled themselves and saw that the travel agent was staring at them through the window. He came to the door and asked if he could help. "Saga have some great offers on this month," he said. "Their 'Autumn of Life Honeymoon Cruise' round the Hebrides is almost sold out."

"No, thank you," Laura said.

"Well move on then, you're cluttering up the pavement," the agent replied, ushering them off the premises.

"Well really! Come along, Boxford. Who needs the Paps of Jura when we can get a decent bevvie and a spot of lunch right around the corner." He strode off in the direction of the Huntsman's Horn Hotel.

"Don't keep calling me Boxford," she called out, as she hurried to catch him up.

"So what d'you think that was all about?" Laura said, putting down the menu.

"Bloody hell knows. Sounded like quite a stink brewing between those two. We'd better monitor that situation carefully. Now, what about the card?"

Laura opened the envelope and handed it to him.

"Barry Wong," he read. "Herbal Consultant for the Fiery Dragon Company. Did Dudley mention he was of oriental extraction?"

"Not that I remember."

"He must be a small cog in the whole nefarious business. 22 Butcher's Road, Cheltenham. I think he deserves a visit, don't you?" The Brigadier looked at his watch.

"I said I'd have tea with Sandra Abelson. She wants me to help with sponsorship for her next attempt on the channel."

"Tomorrow, first thing then. We'll have Creightmore banged to rights by lunchtime. Talking of which, we haven't ordered. I can recommend the pork pie."

The next morning, Laura went over to Strudel and Jervis' bungalow in the old kitchen garden and asked if they could print off directions to Butcher's Road.

"What is this?" Strudel asked, as Jervis brought up Google maps. "Not some secret trysting, I hope. You are knowing Ancient Eros will provide if you feel the need for companionship."

"Put a sock in it, Strudel," Jervis said. "It's none of our business what Laura gets up to."

"I was only trying…" Strudel let out a little sob. "…Helpful to be."

"Oh, my darling!" Jervis jumped up and embraced her.

Eventually Laura got away without further explanation. She walked back to the car park where she met the Brigadier who was bending down inspecting the tread on the tyres of her car with a coin.

"They're perfectly all right, I've had them checked," she said. "Now get in, let's go."

As the Brigadier adjusted his seatbelt, Laura looked in the mirror. She could see a disgruntled Parker curled up in a ball on the back seat, shaking spasmodically with indignation on his pink blanket.

Driving through the countryside, she began to worry. "I hope this isn't a mistake. What if we've got it wrong about Nurse Creightmore?" she said.

"Don't be silly, Boxford. Concentrate on the road. This could be exactly the break we've been looking for. The scrub hare never mistakes his brother's burrow."

Laura had a vision of the demented creature bounding around hither and thither in the dusty sand.

"Red light," the Brigadier barked as they reached the outskirts of Cheltenham. Laura slammed her foot on the brake.

The Brigadier consulted Jervis' map.

"I'm still convinced that Dr. Mellbury is somehow involved," Laura said. "It was when Alfredo and I talked of Nanny's death…"

"But who actually was Nanny? Next left…"

"Nanny was Nanny. She'd been with us forever and then, quite unexpectedly, last summer she died."

"It's as I said, the nurse and he may be in it together. Next right."

"Try and give me a bit more warning." Laura indicated and they turned down a pot-holed street, lined with pollarded lime trees, their roots uplifting the pavement slabs.

"Suspicious deaths. Creightmore, Mellbury, Barry Wong. Who knows? But I've a feeling we're about to find out. Stop here." The Brigadier indicated a house on the left hand side. There were few cars on the street and Laura drew up outside.

As the Brigadier opened his door to get out, Parker attempted to escape.

"No you don't," the Brigaider said, and hauled him back in by the collar. Laura was not sure if she or the dog were more incensed. As the Brigadier stood on the street, Laura patted Parker. "Don't you worry about the nasty man," she said. "I shan't be long."

A short path led to a shabby faded green front door. It was half glazed with a 1950s styled pattern of coloured glass in an oval above the letterbox. One small pane was missing. On either side, greying net curtains covered the downstairs windows. They walked up to the door, where a buzzer dangled from a wire at one side.

"Are you sure this is the right place? It says 'Pendleton'."

"Number 22. It's what it says on the card," Laura said. She pressed the bell and they heard a chiming from within. They waited but there was no response.

"Let's try round the side," the Brigadier said.

A rickety door in the same green paint connected the front of the house to the rear garden. The Brigadier tried the handle. He gave it a push but it remained shut.

"Credit card, Boxford? Old trick. Blade of a knife is more effective, but I've stopped carrying my Bowie with me; it was ruining the line of my suit trousers. Fine under combat kit, but tweed not so good. Warp and weft too loosely woven." He held out his hand. "Hurry up."

Laura delved into her bag and opened her purse. She handed him an old Harrods' card she hadn't used in years.

He slotted the credit card into the door latch.

"Where did you learn this 'trick'?" she asked.

"Time of the Mau Mau. Had a pretty narrow escape on more than one occasion. I recall a particular incident, them hot on my trail. Farm up in Sabukia. Hid in the grain store. Door just like this."

He turned the handle. "Got some of our men a bad name, that Mau Mau business. Not that I saw any shoddy behaviour myself. I'd have put a stop to that, I can tell you." He gave the door a shove with his shoulder and it creaked open. Ahead of them, beyond the dark narrow alley, the sun shone down on a mass of greenery. Laura followed him in, pushing the door half closed behind them.

"Good God," the Brigadier said, as they drew closer, "Buckwheat. Haven't seen this since Lesotho."

"That's not buckwheat, it's Japanese Knotweed."

"Whatever it is, you'd need a machete to get through it. Bloody rum in a suburban garden. This is more of an agricultural crop."

"That's exactly what it is. This man Barry Wong is using Japanese Knotweed as an ingredient in his hair-restorer remedy. Dudley told me. But what I'd like to know is why none of the neighbours has complained. It's a menace."

From behind them, Laura heard the back door scrape against the concrete path. She pushed the Brigadier into the undergrowth.

"What the...?" The Brigadier put his arms out to stop himself falling into a thicket of knotweed.

"Shh, didn't you hear? There's someone coming."

Chapter Thirteen

A small man of about sixty, with thin curly grey hair limped up the alley towards them.

"Oi, what do you think you're doing? This is private property. You're trespassing in my backyard," he said.

Laura began to apologise, as the Brigadier scrambled out of the herbage.

"Leave this to me," he said, removing a stalk from what remained of his hair. "My good man." He held up the Harrods' card. "The name's Stanford, Harold Stanford and this is Mrs. Boxtree. We are from the Environmental Agency. You do know the penalty for allowing this pervasive scourge to run riot, I presume?" The Brigadier grabbed a handful of leaves. "Japanese Knotweed." His shoulders went back, his chest puffed out as if he were back on the parade ground. "Number one on the Agency's list of illegal plant forms."

"You what?"

"You are Mr. Wong, are you not? Perpetrator most foul."

"Watch your language, mate! You won't catch me doing any perpetrating, I can assure you. For the life of me, I can't understand what you're on about. You've got it all wrong," he said.

"Not wrong, Wong," the Brigadier stepped forward returning the card to his breast pocket. "And I'm afraid you understand only too well."

He turned to Laura and gave her an exaggerated wink. "What was the fine imposed upon the Liverpool family... two thousand, was it?"

Laura nodded.

"Now listen here, matey, let me explain..." Barry Wong crossed his arms. "This house belongs to my old mother who has relocated to... New Zealand, leaving me with this overgrowth that I was totally unaware of until... well... I became aware of the problem only yesterday when I took charge of the property. Obviously I had no idea what the stuff was. What d'you say it is?"

"Japanese Knotweed," Laura said. "And I think you know exactly what it is." She delved into her bag and brought out Barry Wong's business card, handing it to him.

"Where d'you get this?" Beads of sweat appeared on his already shiny brow.

"From my hairdresser in Woldham; Dudley's Hair Designs, who I believe you supply with a product for hair re-growth that contains, among other things, Japanese Knotweed."

"And a very good product it is too."

"Ah ha. So you do know what it is, and I believe it to be utterly without curative merit," the Brigadier said. "But it is not only the hair-restorer that is of interest. We have reason to believe that you have been supplying hallucinogenic drugs."

"Hallucinogenic what? You must be joking. Oh no, you've got the wrong bloke there."

"I think not. You've been supplying a certain Nurse Creightmore of Wellworth Lawns, and judging by the state of your back garden, you could well be running an illicit laboratory to manufacture the stuff on these very premises. I think we had better look inside the house, if you don't mind, Mr. Wong." The Brigadier began to prod the little man on the shoulder.

"Hold on a minute." Barry Wong pushed the Brigadier away. "I sell a small line of highly sought-after alternative medicines." He remonstrated to no avail. Laura and the Brigadier, like a pair of well-trained sheepdogs, herded him back down the passage and round to the front door where they waited while he fumbled with the key.

"I imagine you have a valid licence to sell such things?" the Brigadier said. "And your accomplice, the nurse?"

"Accomplice? You're making me sound like a criminal." Barry Wong's hand was shaking as he opened the front door. "Celia, Nurse Creightmore," he said, standing on a pile of unopened mail on the floor of the hall. "Now, I admit I have furnished her with some of my remedies. No harm in that. She had the hair-restorer, the restorative tablets and the arthritis remedy for her oldies, that's all." Barry Wong wiped his brow with a grubby shirtsleeve.

"And what about your other remedies? The tea, for example," Laura said.

"Monkey glands. Explain that one away." The Brigadier snorted.

"That's for flatulence and, between you and me, it's got about as much to do with a monkey's glands as a burger's got to do with beef. One hundred per cent harmless plant extracts. Hay mostly. It's called Seaweed and Monkey Gland for, well to be honest, for marketing purposes. People think if it's got a fancy name, it's going to work. Like all that rhino horn rubbish. No more an aphrodisiac than eating oysters. Figment of the imagination. But please, let me explain. Come in. I'm sure we can sort this whole thing out over a nice cup of tea."

"One of your infusions?" Laura said. "No thanks."

"No no, I've got some Tetley's in."

Barry Wong ushered them into the front room. The walls were obscured by boxes piled high, all stamped with the dragon logo. In the middle of the room was a battered brown leather three-piece suite.

"I'll go and put the kettle on," he said.

The Brigadier followed him out as Laura perched on one of the chairs.

She heard clattering coming from the direction of the kitchen. They returned, Barry Wong carrying a tin tray with three steaming slopping mugs. The Brigadier took a mug and sat down on the sofa.

"I can see that you are both people of culture and class. Of a sophisticated nature, dare I suggest?" Barry Wong handed Laura a mug and sat down next to the Brigadier.

"Don't try flattery, young man." The Brigadier eased himself away from Barry. "It's the truth we're after, if such a thing exists in your criminal mind."

"Criminal? Now hold on a minute, you're at it again. I've done nothing wrong. I'm an honest salesman selling a small but elite range of products to a niche market. I've got the hair-restorer, my own personal remedy. Then there's the infusions and the tablets from my supplier. The restorative pills for lethargy and arthritis, as I've said before, Nurse Creightmore has been a recipient of these products. The insomnia treatment has never been sold to anyone at the home. Granted I gave a packet to Celia… Nurse Creightmore, but that was purely for her personal consumption. As I've tried to explain, they're harmless, that is of course unless they get into the wrong hands."

"But that's the point," Laura said. "You see, by selling or mis-selling them to Nurse Creightmore, they certainly ended up in the wrong hands. I myself can testify to that. I suffered greatly as a consequence of taking a remedy provided by her."

"What?" Barry Wong leaned forward spilling some tea on the carpet by his feet. "She must have made a mistake," he said.

"Whether or not Nurse Creightmore has made an error, you are still responsible for selling potentially lethal drugs," the Brigadier said.

"Lethal? What are you on about? The arthritis remedy has a tiny marijuana content, for sure…"

"Dope? I might have guessed." The Brigadier snorted. "Evil stuff. Had a young subaltern in Nakuru. Lost his head to it entirely. The brain of the addict is like a sodden soapy sponge in a matter of weeks. No good to anyone."

"I beg your pardon, but it's a well-known fact that marijuana can be highly beneficial in cases of age-related arthritis. But to be honest, the content is so minuscule, you couldn't get a mouse stoned if you tried."

"I'm no mouse and I can assure you, you can," Laura said. "I only took a couple of your pills and I was as high as a kite for hours. It was a terrifying experience and, what is far more serious, is that we have reason to believe that it may well have been instrumental in the death of a very good friend of mine at Wellworth Lawns: Mrs. Hetty Winterbottom."

"What? You're joking. But hold on a minute, a friend of yours at Wellworth Lawns? I thought you said you came from the Environmental Agency?"

"Let's not get off the point." The Brigadier wiped his moustache with his handkerchief.

"I think I've had about enough of this." Barry Wong rose from his seat. "You two barging in accusing me of God knows what. I think it's about time you slung your hooks. Come on, Granddad, shove it."

The Brigadier stood up. "Sit down, Wong, or I'll call the police," he commanded.

"It's Pendleton actually. Barry Pendleton."

"Wong, Pendleton, it matters little under what nom de guerre you travel." The Brigadier straightened his jacket. "The fact of the matter is that the pills you supplied to Nurse Creightmore may well have made you an accessory to murder."

Barry Pendleton looked at him and then at Laura. "But that's impossible. They're clearly marked. Look, you can see on the boxes here. They're colour coded. Yellow dragon; arthritis, minimum grass content. Red dragon; lethargy, a simple restorative, ninety nine per cent sugar."

"And what if it's a green dragon?" Laura asked.

"Green dragon? Insomnia. You've got a bit of skunk in there, granted, but Celia's never had any of the green ones for the oldies."

"Oh yes she has. The pills I took came from a box with a green dragon on it."

"But…" Barry Pendleton ran his hands through his hair. "No, she couldn't have… I made it quite clear to her… Oh God, she's made some kind of foul up." He looked up. "I'll have to go and see her."

"I think perhaps it would be a good idea if we all went to see Nurse Creightmore," the Brigadier said.

*

Laura let Parker out and he sniffed around the trunk of a tree while the Brigadier bundled Barry Pendleton into the back of the car.

The return journey from Cheltenham to Nurse Creightmore's digs in Woldham was tense. Parker spent the first five miles growling at Barry Pendleton. The effect was that an acrid stench emanated from the back seat of the car and it wasn't coming from Parker.

Laura stopped and the Brigadier changed places with Parker.

From then the trip improved. Parker and the Brigadier fell asleep and, as Laura monitored Barry Pendleton's expression of resigned dejection in her rear view mirror, she was sure he was not about to do a runner – difficult under the circumstances as the car only had two doors.

"I can't believe I could have done it," Celia Creightmore sobbed. She was sitting on the sofa in the bedsit that she rented above the gift shop in Woldham High Street. Barry Pendleton was next to her with his arm around her shoulder. Laura and the Brigadier were seated on two chairs they had found in the kitchenette. The only other contents in the room were an old TV, a dusty plastic plant and a box of tissues.

"But didn't you notice the green dragon when you gave them to this Mrs. Hobbs?" Barry Pendleton asked, passing her the box of tissues.

"I must have got confused, I don't know. I was that busy keeping up with orders and then all the other things I had to do. Enemas and more enemas and now I'm responsible for poisoning Lady Boxford and Mrs. Hobbs." The nurse renewed her wailing.

"Calm down, please," Laura said.

"But you'll report me to the police and I'll be taken to prison. Oh, I want to die!" She lurched sideways and hid her head in Barry Pendleton's crotch.

"Control yourself, Nurse Creightmore. There are other issues we need to clarify," the Brigadier said. "Now, did you or did you not give any of these pills to Mrs. Winterbottom?"

The nurse looked up. Her nose was running and she sniffed, "Hetty Winterbottom?"

"Yes," Laura said. "I know she had some with the red dragon."

"She was feeling enervated after she broke her ankle. She already took the tea infusion for her wind and when I told her about Barry's happy pills, as I call them, she said she'd like to try some. I never gave her anything else. I couldn't have."

"That's right," Barry said. "Because I only ever gave Celia the one box of tablets for insomnia." He turned to the nurse. "But why didn't you notice you hadn't got them? What happened about your not being able to sleep?"

Nurse Creightmore burst into tears again. "I thought I'd lost them, thrown them away by mistake, so I stole Mrs. Huxley's anti-depressants and left her with some lethargy tablets."

"Red dragon? Ninety per cent sugar. No wonder the poor dear hasn't been improving," Laura said.

"Yes… Oh, I am cruel. I deserve to be put away," she sobbed.

"And there is another matter," the Brigadier said.

"Oh no. What else could I have done? It can't be worse, can it?"

"Did you ever notice Mrs. Winterbottom's collection of paperweights?" The Brigadier leant forward and stared intently at Nurse Creightmore.

"Her paperweights? Why yes, she often talked about them to me. I used to sit with her while she was having her tea. Dear Mrs. W. I always had a soft spot for her. She was terrified her daughter might find out about the rare one; the one she kept for her emergency fund. It was sad she couldn't trust her own daughter."

"Why do you think she confided in you?" Laura asked.

"I don't know. I think she was lonely once she'd broken her ankle and you were always off playing bridge or walking the dog."

"And finally," the Brigadier said. "Did you remove the box of pills from Mrs. Winterbottom's room after she died?"

"I… I was mean. I thought I could sell them on. But what are you going to do now?" Nurse Creightmore's eyes glistened on the verge of another deluge.

"The Brigadier and I need to have a word in private," Laura said.

They walked down the stairs and into the alley that led out onto the High Street. It had begun to rain so they stood underneath the gift shop awning.

"What do you think we should do? She clearly didn't murder Hetty," Laura said.

"I agree, and it's in no one's interest to involve the police. I suggest we demand Barry Pendleton return his stock of pills to the supplier and, in the meantime, he and Nurse Creightmore will be indebted to us. She could be useful, after all she's well positioned to assist us in what now must be a hunt for evidence against the doctor."

"But what about her saying Hetty didn't trust her daughter? I'd say Gloria's looking highly suspicious."

"Yes, that too must not be overlooked, after all the galloping zebra attracts no flies."

"Wouldn't, 'leave no stone unturned' have been more apposite?"

"Possibly, Boxford, very possibly."

They went back upstairs. Nurse Creightmore and Barry Pendleton were still sitting on the sofa, but now they were holding hands.

"We have made our decision," the Brigadier said. "If the matter is to remain within these four walls, you must both desist from further intervention in the field of herbalism."

"Of course." Nurse Creightmore began to sob again. "I never want to see another dragon again."

"I'll hold my hands up, Brigadier," Barry said. "I'm out of Chinese imports and I'm going to get shot of that place in Cheltenham. Celia says they need a barman at the Rose and Crown."

"Here in Woldham?" Laura asked.

"Yes," Barry said, gazing at Nurse Creightmore. "You see I've asked Celia to marry me."

Chapter Fourteen

"Oh, Parker." Laura stroked the pug's ears. "I was so sure it was Nurse Creightmore, and now we're back to square one." She picked up the phone beside the bed and called the Brigadier.

"I've been making some notes here," he said. "The sun is breaking through and I predict a fine day. I suggest we traverse the policies for a de-brief?"

"Go for a walk and talk about it, you mean?"

They met in the hall an hour later.

"Let's go up to the pet cemetery," Laura said. "I've brought a rug to sit on. I think it will be warm enough."

"I admire your optimism." The Brigadier was carrying an umbrella.

They walked up the hill and put the rug down on the hollowed-out tree trunk. Parker began to whine, so Laura picked him up and he curled up between them. The Brigadier produced a scrap of paper.

"Now what have I written here?" He put on his glasses. "Charles Mellbury. The droppings of the sloth are multifarious. What do you suppose I meant by that?"

"I've also jotted down some notes." Laura had prepared a list that she handed to the Brigadier. "It's doubly complicated, as we still don't know if we're looking for a murderer, a thief or a murderous thief or anything else for that matter," she said.

The Brigadier took the sheet of paper. "How does this fit in?" he asked. "Things to do in February. Sow half hardy annuals?"

"Ignore that. I tore it out of an old gardening calendar. It starts with 'Suspects concerning Hetty's untimely demise'."

At the top of the list the Brigadier read:

"'Dr. Mellbury – Motive: Euthanasia/theft?' We're agreed there," he said. "So what's this? 'John Fincham – Motive; Hetty bed-blocking/theft. Only possible with the aid of above mentioned, Charles Mellbury'."

"Yes. Don't you remember when we were in Woldham and we saw them together? There was definitely something up between the two of them."

"But what's this bed blocking business?"

Laura zipped up her jacket as the sun went behind a cloud. She explained about Vince saving Chipping Wellworth and how she had acquired the room for Hetty. "But the more I think about it, John Fincham may have taken it as a personal affront to his authority. And now I've done the same for Venetia. I do hope that wasn't a mistake."

"Good God, but a favourable room rate is hardly cause for murder and, besides that, he'd never dare repeat himself. Not twice. It would be too obvious. No, I'm afraid I don't buy into that one, Boxford."

"But then there's what Jervis said about him needing money."

"What? Meaning John got Mellbury to dispatch Mrs. Winterbottom, then took the paperweight? It's getting mighty complicated. Who else have you got?" The Brigadier looked at the piece of paper. "What's this? 'Mimi? Bone and Bone, the undertakers? Alfredo… Alfredo?' Have you gone mad, Boxford?"

"Very possibly. It was getting late when I had that idea but I did think that perhaps someone could have forced him into poisoning her…"

"Alfredo poisoning Mrs Winterbottom? Great Scott, Boxford, I'm surprised my name's not on the list!"

Laura could feel herself redden. Luckily the Brigadier didn't seem to notice. "Don't be facetious," she said. "And anyway, it was you who encouraged me to look at all possibilities."

"But the cook? He's in the kitchen."

"He often took up Hetty's Eggs Benedict if they were short staffed. He knew how she liked the yolks, and he insisted they must be served immediately. Her last meal was three boiled eggs."

"Three? Still, point taken, but I think we're better off concentrating on our main suspect and that, to my mind, is Doctor Mellbury."

"But, don't you see?" Laura said. "That's what we thought last time with Nurse Creightmore. I think we should extend our lines of enquiry. You haven't got to the bit about Gloria Hemper."

"What, the daughter?"

"Yes. Let's just say Hetty died of natural causes and Gloria stole the paperweight. Actually she could have murdered her mother and stolen the paperweight. She was there the evening Hetty died."

"I thought you said she was with Mellbury, getting him to witness signatures? But now you're saying that Mrs. Hemper and the Doctor murdered Mrs. Winterbottom? I'm getting most confused."

"Maybe not the doctor. Maybe only Gloria. She's short of money. She didn't get on with her mother. Nurse Creightmore said Hetty didn't trust her. She could have returned later, after the Doctor had gone… Oh, it's so difficult not knowing if the two are connected, the murder and the missing paperweight."

"But you said maybe she wasn't murdered. That she could have died of natural causes, yet that's the thing you were so certain about, that she was murdered."

"Oh, I don't know what to think anymore. Last night I lay in bed almost overcome by the alarming amount of suspects and motives that seemed to be accumulating and, as you said about Nurse Creightmore…"

"What?"

"That you never know who might have knowledge about the value of the paperweight. That's why I put down Mimi and Alfredo. I'm trying to see it as a real detective would."

"We can count the police out," the Brigadier snorted. "Of course, there's a certain amount of cross-referencing that could be done. I can see that. Any one suspect could be associated with another for a multitude of reasons." The Brigadier studied the list again.

"I know," Laura said. "I mean, it could as easily be that dotty somnambulist on the second floor. I've seen him coming down the stairs with his arms outstretched. What is his name? He could easily be faking a trance."

"Not him, no. Fincham's taken to locking him in at night. Quite against fire regulations, but really Boxford, you must try not to enter the realms of fantasy."

"You're just like Mellbury. He thinks I'm mad and now so do you. Perhaps I am…" Laura stared out over the hills. A light mizzle was falling.

"Steady now." The Brigadier unfurled his umbrella and inched a little closer to her. Parker growled at him and jumped onto Laura's lap. "Of course I don't think you're mad. But I still think first thing's first. We'll concentrate on the doctor but keep an open mind to other possibilities, and we must try to get more detailed information on the Bacchus, so that we're in full possession of the facts when it comes to confronting the culprit."

"So that's our plan, is it?"

"The leopard creeps silently through the scrub."

"But is that really going to help? All that Masai nonsense," she said. "I mean, how on earth can two old things like us creep silently anywhere?"

The rain was heavier now, pattering on the umbrella and an air of despondency fell over them. They got up to leave. The Brigadier picked up the rug and shook it out, handing it to Laura. As they walked down the hill, he offered her his arm. "Something will turn up, mark my words. In the meantime, shall we go and see what's for lunch?"

Half way down the hill, they saw an apparition running through the rain towards them. Against the now blackening sky, with a turquoise feather boa flapping like a long wet rat's tail around her neck, was Strudel.

She reached them and grasped the Brigadier by the sleeve of his jacket. "I am needing you," she puffed, fluttering her rain-dropped eyelashes at him, "for a small discussion."

"What is it? You shouldn't be out in this weather. Is something wrong with Jervis?" he asked.

"No, nothing like that, but a small matter I should like to talk to you about. Why don't you and Laura come for some supper? We could play a hand or two of Bridge and I'll have time for my proposal to discuss with you."

"I'm intrigued."

Strudel turned to Laura. "Shall we say seven thirty?"

"That sounds a very jolly idea," Laura said. "Mind you, I'm not sure I'm feeling up to one of Jervis' Martini sessions."

"He has moved on to the Mojito, so there's no danger of that." Strudel flicked back a strand of hair that had fallen across her brow. "See you later."

As Laura and the Brigadier continued on their way, Laura hesitated.

"There is another thing…"

"Yes?"

"Would it matter if we told Strudel and Jervis?" she said.

"Do you think it necessary?"

"It's just I feel they might have an insight into the situation with Dr. Mellbury, and I thought perhaps with Jervis' computing skills we might get him to go on the internet for us, to find out about the paperweight. If we knew how many like Hetty's there are, for example, it might lead to something. But we can't really do that without involving them. It's a pity I'm so hopeless when it comes to modern technology."

"I quite agree, I'm no silver surfer either," the Brigadier said, as they walked around the corner and came in view of the main house. "But would you look at that?"

"What? Who?" Laura let go of his arm. "Should we go our separate ways?"

"No, I mean the sun's come out. So did Strudel and Jervis know Hetty?"

"Oh, yes. Hetty had quite a few dates through Ancient Eros before she broke her ankle. Actually, that's how she broke her ankle."

"What d'you mean?"

"She didn't care for whoever the man was that Ancient Eros had assigned her. They met for tea and it all became rather acrimonious as they were leaving. I think he questioned the number of crumpets she had ordered. She tried to hit him with her stick and lost her balance."

Strudel held the door open for Laura. She was wearing a tight emerald lace bodice cut low over the shoulders, and a black satin skirt. "Come in, come in," she cried excitedly. "Arthur's already here."

"Who's Arthur?" Laura asked. Despite her silver lamé slippers, she was feeling under-dressed wearing an ethnic kaftan she had once bought in a souk in Marrakesh.

"The Brigadier, of course. Don't tell me you didn't know his name. What have you two been up to? Don't think Jervis and I are not noticing." Strudel winked at Laura. "Come on, he's on his second Mint Julep... Well actually they're Irish Juleps – he's added crème de menthe."

"Mint Juleps?" A memory winged its way into Laura's head so vividly that she temporarily forgot her surprise at finding out the Brigadier's first name. "Heavens," she said, "I haven't had one of those since Tony and I were in Venice in the 1970s."

Whew, those sultry evenings on the Grand Canal. The boatman we hired at the Cipriani. The hanky-panky in the bottom of his boat... What was his name? Franco, that was it, such smooth hands for a gondolier!

"But I thought Jervis was making Mojitos?" she said.

"When I put this top on, he changed his mind." Strudel smoothed the fabric over her bosom. "Colour co-ordination is a thing of importance to his sensibilities."

They went into the sitting room where Jervis and the Brigadier were playing Racing Demon at a small card table covered in a dark, red velvet cloth, their Martini glasses half filled with the green concoction – a bunch of mint leaves floating on top.

"Stop that now, boys, Laura's here," Strudel said.

"Laura. Excellent." Jervis put down his cards. "Let me get you a drink." He jumped up and went over to the golden metal trolley on which stood bottles and all the paraphernalia for making cocktails.

He rattled the shaker. "Plenty left," he said, filling a glass.

"So," Strudel said, when they were all seated. "Spill the beans. I've seen you two coming and going. They are not calling me head of net-twitchings of Mulberry Close for nothing, you know."

Laura took a sip of the cocktail. "Delicious, Jervis," she said, removing a leaf that had got stuck to her top lip. "I hardly know where to start…"

"Shall I give them a resumé of events?" The Brigadier explained the circumstances of Hetty's death and the missing paperweight. "Boxford here had her suspicions from the start and I'm with her all the way. We're pretty sure of foul play. At first we thought it was something to do with Nurse Creightmore…"

"Hellfire!" Jervis took a swig from his glass.

"…But she's no longer in the frame," the Brigadier continued. "We've got a new suspect and, at the moment, we are in the process of investigation."

"This is terrible," Strudel said. "Jervis, top-ups. I hope that Jervis and myself are not in this picture."

"Goodness, no," Laura said, as Jervis held out the cocktail shaker. "But we thought you might help us."

"How's that?" Jervis filled Laura's glass.

"The internet. I thought that you might be able to research the paperweight. We've got a book, but it doesn't tell us much. We should know more about the glass manufacturer, Bacchus and Sons." Laura described the design. "It would be useful to find out how many weights with the silhouette there are in existence. Have they had any recent enquiries, that sort of thing. It could be that Hetty's daughter took it when she came to visit on the night of Hetty's death. But, either way, it would be helpful to know more about it."

"I'll get onto it right away," Jervis said. "We can email them. Bacchus and Sons, you say?"

"Not at this time, Jervis. We must first be having supper."

In the kitchen, Jervis poured the wine and, as they chatted away over Knickerbocker Glory glasses filled with prawn cocktail, Laura wondered if Strudel had forgotten the purpose of the evening. She had been so insistent that she needed the Brigadier for something, but now she was intent on gossip. She and Jervis had been to visit Bob Whale who was recovering back home with Dora, in one of the neighbouring bungalows. Dora was allowing him to eat far too much fatty food in Strudel's opinion. "She will kill him with chips and, as for Harriet Huxley who I am also visiting, I'm afraid she's quite past caring," she informed them.

"Harriet may feel an improvement soon, I hope." Laura explained about how Nurse Creightmore had intercepted Harriet's anti-depressants.

"This is good news indeed," Strudel said. "But I must tell you what else. This morning..." She waved her sundae spoon in front of her "... I am seeing Dr. Mellbury escorting a gentleman to Wellworth Lawns. And this, my friends, is his own father."

"His father? How d'you know it was his father?" Laura asked.

"I happened to be over there collecting a parcel and was thus bumping into them. I am asking who is this and he is introducing me. But it wouldn't take much to recognise the family likeness. There's a resemblance distinctly between the two of them, despite the father's beard. But too, he had a look that I almost knew; I can't work it out. As if from some other place I had seen him."

"Those awful blubbery lips I should think, but the old boy's come to live here, can you believe it?" Jervis said. "I call it downright cheeky. I'll put money on John Fincham bunging him a discount. Fincham and the doctor are hand in glove and up to no good, I'd say."

"Oh, Jervis, you are going too far now. Mind you, Ancient Eros will have a hard time fixing such a sight as him up with anybody who is decent by a half."

"Talking of the doctor..." Laura looked over to the Brigadier who nodded in assent.

"I knew it. What of him? Dish the dirt." Jervis said.

"Well, if you must know, he's our main suspect."

"You suspect Dr. Mellbury? What? Of Hetty's death?" Jervis rubbed his hands together.

"Yes. We think he likes to kill old people when he deems they're of no use anymore," Laura said.

"He is a man of little appeal of whom I have my doubts, to be sure." Strudel wrinkled her nose. "Ever since I had to see him about my poorly neck soon after Jervis moved in. He made a comment of Jervis the implication of which I was not amused."

"What did he say?" Laura asked.

"He said to me that... What did he say, Jervis, I cannot speak the words?"

"He told her that if I was into playing rough, she should tell me to knock it off."

"Rough sex? What a blaggard." The Brigadier thumped the table. "But then you two are comparatively young. He's never questioned your existence, has he? Both Boxford and I have been at the sharp end of his tongue. His suggestions that we might be better off dead are thinly veiled."

"He even suggested I have Parker put down."

"This cannot be true?"

"Yes, and we know for a fact that both Hetty and Nanny died unexpectedly. We were trying to remember if there were others."

Strudel's painted eyebrows rose. "I am remembering Nanny. I'll have to think back. Perhaps Dora will have some thoughts."

"The only thing is," Laura said. "We don't really want anybody else involved."

"No, no, I am quite understanding. I shall be most discrete."

Jervis refilled the glasses again. Laura was feeling distinctly tipsy now, but it was enjoyable to be amongst friends and Strudel's cooking was, if not on a par with Alfredo's, at least a change. She did think though, that Pork Stroganoff this late at night might not be such a good idea and noticed that Strudel had gone quite pink around the neck.

The colour was spreading, rising up, engulfing her face and then she thought that Strudel had two noses. She gave a little shudder and the second nose disappeared. Relieved, she took another sip of wine as Strudel regaled them with stories of the happy unions that Ancient Eros had recently affected.

"Oh, but Arthur," she exclaimed, "I had almost forgotten."

"What's that Strudel?" The Brigadier slurred.

"The little discussion with you of which I spoke. You must help me out."

"Are you sure about this, my love?" Jervis said.

"Do be quiet and fill up the glasses. Look at poor Arthur's here. He will be remembering his time in the desert."

Jervis unscrewed the cap from another bottle.

"As I was saying, Arthur," Strudel continued, "I have a little problem. One of my clients was to have had a liaison with Henry Gordon in number 14. You know he is living next door to Bob and Dora. Sadly he passed away the night before last. Quite un…"

"…Expectedly?" Laura sat up.

"Perhaps… But no, he had dehydrated himself playing golf with Sir Maurice, according to Dora."

"Maurice Dickinson and Henry Gordon? Silly old fools should have taken a buggy," the Brigadier said.

"I'm not so sure," Jervis said. "During the pensioner's Stableford Cup at Woldham Oaks, three chaps were hospitalised with water on the lungs. Their buggy hit a rock while traversing in the rough grass and they ended up in a pond." Jervis piled his fork with a lump of sauce covered meat and rice. "But Dora said Henry's first mistake was to stop for a bacon butty at the half way house."

"Don't be talking with your mouthful, Jervis."

Jervis finished chewing. "Of course he didn't help himself by going for a sauna at the Leisure Centre on the way home… And then the brandies at The Red Lion," Jervis continued. "Writing off his Yaris was not so clever either."

Strudel took up the story. "According to Dora, the farmer was in a temper and was saying, suing poor Henry he would be for the gate and the cow. Dora is hearing him fall into the wheelie bin and is going over then and calling Dr. Mellbury. He is putting Henry on a saline drip. He should have been all right after that. But sadly no."

Laura gasped and looked over to the Brigadier, but he had lost concentration and his head was swaying from side to side.

"I'm just going to look something up on my computer," Jervis said. His chair fell over backwards as he rose from the table. "Shan't be a tick."

"Pick it up, please. Most unusual now I think about it… But to get back to the story," Strudel continued. "Our client who was to be having the date with Henry, she'd been waiting weeks, and was looking forward with the greatest joy." Strudel leaned across the table and peered at the Brigadier. "Do you see where I am leading to?"

The Brigadier made an involuntary start and straightened himself on his chair. "What? Me?"

"Exactly, Arthur. I have a feeling in my bones that you will get on famously. Actually it's tomorrow. I'll waive your joining fee."

"I'm sure the Brig… Arthur doesn't want to be bothered with going on dates. He's quite busy enough as it is," Laura said.

"Oh, I don't know, it might be rather fun. Chance to get out my medals."

"That won't be necessary at teatime. The first date is always at teatime. I have found that the men prefer to pay, such a silly British thing, they find going Dutch embarrassing, and dinner is tending to be too expensive for the gamble that is involved. Jervis!" she shouted over her shoulder. "We are all sorted." She returned her attention to the Brigadier. "The tearoom in Woldham at four o'clock tomorrow. Jervis will be printing off the necessary details and delivering them to you in the morning."

They retired to the sitting room where Jervis was busy on his laptop at a desk in one corner.

"Jervis, stop that now," Strudel said. "We are needing nightcaps."

"Be right with you. Cognac or Grand Marnier? Or perhaps more crème de menthe would be in keeping. I think I've hacked into the doctor's surgery."

Strudel strode over to the computer and elbowed Jervis out of the way. She gazed at the screen. "Don't be idiotic, Jervis. This isn't the right Charles Mellbury. What are you typing in?"

"Woldham Medical Centre," Jervis said, handing round liqueurs.

"This man is of Woldham Military Centre. Turn it off immediately. And anyway what is this Woldham Military Centre?"

Jervis returned to the desk, his glass landing precariously as he put it down next to the computer.

"Never heard of it," the Brigadier said.

"Cripes, it's Woldham, Massachusetts." Jervis slammed down the lid of the laptop.

Strudel looked at the clock on the mantelpiece. "It is a trifle late for Bridge for now, but we could have a round or two of Vingt-et-Un. Jervis, more liqueurs. Schnapps for me!"

Chapter Fifteen

There seemed to be an out of tune brass band playing in Laura's head. She rolled over and shut her eyes again. Parker began licking her face.

"Not now," she groaned, as a cacophony of hand bells, tubas and bugles crescendoed under the pillow. She opened one eye and looked at her bedside clock. It was eight-thirty. Thankful for Parker's cast iron bladder, she grappled for the phone and rang down to the kitchen for a pot of tea and toast.

Some minutes later, she heard a knock on the door and Mimi came in with a tray. Parker jumped down from the bed, his tail wagging at the maid.

"Morning Ladysheep," Mimi said, putting down the tray on a table by the window. "I opening curtains now?"

As sunlight streamed into the room, Laura shielded her eyes with the bedclothes.

"Ladysheep not feeling good?" Mimi asked.

"Bit of a headache," Laura mumbled. She made an effort to sit up.

"I taking Parkie walk time for you, you not feeling well. I good for quick outside break in sunshine. Not see Mr Finch, mind you."

"Oh Mimi, that would be a help."

Mimi clapped her hands, "Come on, Parkie."

The pug snuffled keenly behind Mimi as she made for the door.

In their absence, Laura went to the bathroom and had a tentative look in the mirror. Her eyes were clear and bright – oh dear, she'd left her contact lenses in overnight... She took them out, put in a fresh pair and looked again. Her lips were red, but not, she noticed, courtesy of Elizabeth Arden but stained with claret. The wine they had consumed after the... before the...? Her eyelids fluttered. Clutching the wall, she made her way out and poured a cup of tea.

By the time Mimi returned, she was feeling marginally better. Well enough at least, to remember the maid's Parisian trip.

"Paris, oh la la!" Mimi held her hand to the back of her plait of hair. "Tom take me up the Awful Tower and we having meal in can-can restaurant." She twirled around. "Him buyed me nice necklace too!" She pulled down the neckline of her T-shirt in one hand and with the other lifted out a shiny golden chain with a little gold heart hanging from it. "Look, see," she said, her eyes sparkling in elation.

"Gracious, Mimi, is it real?"

"Is gold for sure. Tom I thinking very rich."

"Very generous of him. You are a lucky girl." Laura did not feel strong enough to pursue the conversation further but Mimi was keen to discuss the consistency of Parker's bowel movements.

"Him push, push, uh," she said by way of explanation.

Laura agreed to cut down the biscuit content of his meals.

By the time she had taken a bath, it was eleven o'clock. She rang Strudel to thank her for dinner.

Jervis answered.

"Morning, Laura, I trust you're well?"

"Recovering slowly."

"Recovering? You're not ill, I hope. Not Strudel's pork?"

"I think I may have had rather a lot to drink." Laura walked over to the bedside table and picked up the glass of water she had poured out the night before but then forgotten about.

"Really? Strudel gave me quite a flea in the ear this morning about being inattentive."

"Shall I have a word with her?" Laura gulped down the water.

"She's gone over to Dora Whale's to see what she can find out about 'you know what'."

"You know what?" The events of the evening were a blur in Laura's mind and a lone trumpeter had entered the fray.

"You know," Jervis said. "Sudden deaths. Henry Gordon in number 14. Oh, and by the way, I've discovered something about the paperweight. The silhouette could be of a young Queen Victoria. Either way they are extremely rare. The glass company doesn't exist anymore, but I've managed to track down an expert on them in Chicago."

"I don't think it was of Queen Victoria. Hetty's had a retroussé nose."

"Up-turned nose? I'll get back to you on that."

"Thank you, Jervis, and please ask Strudel to call me if she has anything to report from Dora."

Laura decided to call the Brigadier next. She couldn't remember what it was, but something about him stuck in her mind.

He answered the phone.

"Brigadier, is that you?" Laura said.

"Boxford, I thought we'd got over that last night."

"Over what?"

"My name of course."

His name? A tumbling avalanche of timpani vibrated in her temples. That's what she couldn't remember. What on earth was it? She brushed over the matter hastily and asked him if they should meet to discuss their next move.

"Bit tied up," he said. "Getting dolled up for my date and I seem to have mislaid my braces."

Another piece of the jigsaw of alcoholic amnesia slotted into place.

Somewhat irritated that he was not at her beck and call, she went to see Venetia instead, but she was out, so Laura returned and lay down on her bed. A few snippets of conversation wafted through her mind as Parker snored beside her. Dr. Mellbury was one of them, but everything was still too much of a blur to remember. What, if anything, of importance had transpired from the evening? Unable to make up her mind, she got up and went downstairs for lunch.

There was no sign of the Brigadier – what was his name... Horace? Geoffrey? Albert? Obviously he was too busy be-periwigging himself, so she joined Horticultural Society stalwart Gladys Freemantle who was sitting with Lance and Carol Paterson.

"You've just missed Dr. Mellbury's father," Gladys said.

Laura recalled another topic from the night before.

"Rum old cove."

Carol Paterson nodded her head in agreement with her husband.

"Eyes too close together," Gladys said. "He reminds me of a pelargonium grower I used to know from my days in Suffolk. I'm not overly fond of pelargoniums either."

Laura asked them which room Dr Mellbury's father was staying in, but no one seemed to know.

The Patersons didn't wait for pudding as they were off to an air show, so they left Laura and Gladys alone with their tarte au pommes.

"Charity plant sale nearly upon us again and then we've got the laburnum walk at Bodnant later next month." Gladys' large teeth protruded disconcertingly as she launched a spoonful of dessert into her mouth. Laura wondered why she'd never had them fixed.

"I'm never very good on long bus trips," Gladys continued, "though I'm better now I've got the nicotine patches." She patted her arm. "Even so, it's a worry not knowing when the next rest stop will be." She crossed her legs and gave a little tremble. "Do you remember when we went to that garden in... well I can't actually remember where it was... bloody miles anyway, and the bus got stuck in that bumpy old lane. Hours we were there."

Laura laughed. "We all had to go in a field, I remember."

"That was a relief. But then just as I was squatting, Maurice Dickinson came round the corner and Marjory Playfair had to shoo him away. He can be awfully thick skinned. And after all that, the garden wasn't up to much. Weeds everywhere. Not a gardener in sight. Where was it?"

"Herefordshire. I remember, all that hideous pampas grass and bindweed creeping up the dahlias."

"So invasive."

Laura was reminded of the knotweed. She made her excuses to Gladys and took Parker into the garden. *Bugger the Brigadier,* she thought. *I don't have to hang around for him. I'll go and see Creightmore, after all she owes me big time. I'll quiz her about Mellbury and any suspicious deaths.* Then she remembered Dr. Mellbury's father. Yes. The nurse might well know something about that too.

The sanatorium door was open and Laura walked straight in. Sitting at Nurse Creightmore's desk with his feet up, was a young man in a white coat scrolling down his mobile.

He noticed Laura and swung his legs down, narrowly avoiding knocking off a sheaf of papers. Dropping the phone, he grabbed them and pretended to read.

"Hello," Laura said.

"Bit of catching up to do," he said, putting the papers back on the desk. "Can I help you?"

"I was looking for Nurse Creightmore."

"She's gone on holiday I think. I'm standing-in."

"How long for?" Laura asked.

"Couldn't say. Is it something I can help with?"

"Thank you, but I'm perfectly all right."

Laura returned to the hall. "He must have thought I was mad," she said to Parker as they waited for the lift. "Going to see the nurse when there's nothing the matter. Still, if he stays here any length of time, he'll soon realise there's a lot of it about."

She got upstairs and tried Venetia's door again. Then she remembered that it was Saturday. Venetia always went to the 'Pub Outing' lunch on the first Saturday of the month.

Oh well, she thought, *it would be a kindness to see how Harriet Huxley is.* She certainly wouldn't be out.

*

Harriet was sitting in a chair wrapped in a knitted shawl. Her slate grey hair was parted down the middle and tied back, accentuating her long nose. She reminded Laura of Edith Sitwell on an extra melancholy day, perhaps having been told to think about something nice to say about her parents. She stared out of the window.

"I want to go to Switzerland," she said.

"Ah, the lakes! All that fresh air." Laura walked over to the window and looked at the car park below. It was a long way down. "But what you need is a better view." She watched as the laundry van reversed towards the back door, its safety mechanism beeping. "Why don't I go and see John Fincham for you? See if we can't have you moved to a different room. Something facing west on the floor below, that looks out over the hills. There's no snow at this time of year of course."

"That's not what I mean," Harriet said. "The Gravitas Clinic is what I had in mind."

"Oh dear, you're feeling no better?"

"No. Dr. Mellbury is a fascist bastard. I've asked him to put me out of my misery, but all he does is give me more pills. These are no more use than the last lot.' She swiped the plastic container feebly and it landed with a clatter on the floor. Laura remembered the nurse's confession; at least Harriet was taking her prescribed pills now. Perhaps, in time, her mental state would start to improve.

"Why don't we…" she was about to suggest a game of whist but Harriet had closed her eyes so Laura tiptoed from the room.

"It's too bad," she said to Parker. "Wellworth Lawns is meant to be a happy place. She felt suddenly nostalgic for the old days, the house full of young people and jolly maiden aunts. She returned to her room and got out an old photo album.

"Look Parker," she said, turning the page of one of the heavy leather volumes. "There's Tony and me on the day of the Church Fete. And who's that with us?" She peered at the picture. Two pugs stood at their feet. "Why it's Gibson and Gretel, your great grandparents. Or perhaps great, great… I can't remember. There have been so many of you." She turned the page to a photograph of the hunt meeting at

Chipping Wellworth. There they were, she and Tony, astride two immaculately turned out hunters, whose ears were pricked as they faced the camera. She picked up her magnifying glass to study the photograph more closely. She couldn't work out from what angle it had been taken. But then she realised that it was in the meadow that was now another car park for visitors to the bungalows.

She patted Parker at her side. "I don't know how far we can push John Fincham," she said, "but we must try for Harriet's sake. Come on let's go and find him."

The manager looked up from his computer, "You missed the Flexi Sole Sandal Company demonstration in the lounge," he said.

"What a pity, but I expect it was well attended." Laura picked up a brochure from the desk. "Interesting design."

"No, it wasn't well attended," John said. "Actually I'm quite upset. The chap had made a special journey all the way from Northampton with their new, post-bunion range. On a Saturday too. They're marvellous value. £19.95 a pair. Really, sometimes I think the residents here at Wellworth Lawns are most unappreciative of all the effort I put in."

"Everyone loves the Bingo nights and the race evenings are always a success."

"Yes I know, I should be grateful…" He sighed and looked down at his feet. "…But I had to buy a pair myself to please him. Terrible, aren't they?"

Laura had to agree. The shoes may have been the very latest in comfort, but as far as sartorial elegance went, they would not have looked out of place beside the Sea of Galilee circa 10 AD. They reminded her of a picture from *The Ladybird Bible Story Book*. John's red socks were no help either.

She steered the conversation round to Harriet Huxley. "I'm sure she would have loved to have come to the demonstration."

"Do you think so?"

"Definitely, and she would possibly have bought a pair, but you see, she's so unhappy. She's almost unbearably sensitive. What she really needs is a room with a view. Looking onto the car park from way up where she is, is doing her no good at all. I'm sure there must be some old codger who'll give up a west facing room on the first floor."

"It's not that easy, Lady B, and I've already done you that favour with Mrs. Hobbs. You must try to remember Wellworth Lawns, is a business now."

Laura thought this last comment unnecessary but continued anyway, "Venetia, I know. You were too kind. But this is important. Won't you check the register?"

John Fincham sighed and shuffled his computer mouse. "Oh, all right, let me see." He stared at the screen. "No... No... No... None of them will do. Hold on... He might – number 33. Now, which way does that face? I'll have to get the plans from Margaret." He rose from his desk. "I shan't be long," he said, as he disappeared into his secretary's office in the next-door room.

Laura sat and waited, then she thought she'd try and see who it was the manager had in mind; she might be able to exert more influence if she knew. She rounded the desk to look at the screen, but it had gone blank. She looked down at the mouse and began to fiddle with it. It slid off onto a piece of paper tucked beneath the mat. Laura recognised the bank logo and pulled it out an inch. It was a cheque. She pulled it out some more. It was written out to J. Fincham for two hundred pounds. Below the box with the figures, was a spidery signature, impossible to decipher but the name of the account holder was printed underneath, 'The Hon Venetia Hobbs'.

I'd no idea Venetia was an 'honorable', Laura thought and made a mental note to check Debrett's. *But more to the point, why is she writing cheques to John Fincham?*

She decided it was better not to confront him then and there, but to find out from Venetia – she must be back from the pub by now. It might be something quite harmless and she didn't want him to think she was snooping. She hid the cheque back under the mat and placed the mouse back where it had been.

He returned to say that room thirty-three did indeed have a view and he thought that Professor Wigg might be willing to do a swap with Harriet.

"He's a dear old thing," Laura said.

"Yes and his myopia is handy under the circumstances," John added.

Laura was startled by the latest home improvements in Venetia's room. She recognised her father's tiger skin that was now acting as a bedside rug. "Good Lord, what on earth's that thing doing here?" she said.

Venetia propped herself up on the bed. "Isn't it magnificent? I hope I don't stub my toe on its teeth though. John put it there. Rather sweet of him, don't you think?" she said.

"Except that…" Laura was reminded of the photograph of her father's hunting party in Mysore. Surrounded by guests and natives riding elephants, he stood with his solar topee perched on his head like a small Buddhist temple, gun in hand and his foot placed heroically on the dead beast. "…Oh never mind. Yes, it looks very handsome. But tell me, Venetia, you didn't pay for it did you?"

"Pay for it?"

"Write John a cheque for it."

"I don't think so…"

"Look in your cheque book."

"Why?" Venetia fumbled for her bag on the bedside table.

"Because I've just seen a cheque on his desk written by you for two hundred pounds."

"What?" Venetia pulled out a flannel from the bag and put it on the table beside her.

"That's your sponge bag, dear," Laura said. She took it to the bathroom and returned with Venetia's handbag that she found sitting in the basin. "You must remember what you wrote the cheque for." Laura fished into the bag and brought out Venetia's cheque book.

"I've no idea."

"Look on the stub. What have you written?" Laura handed it to her.

"I never fill in the stubs."

"Oh Venetia! Have you been taking more of Nurse Creightmore's pills?"

"I found one in the bottom of my bag as we were travelling back from lunch."

"What?"

"It's the last, I promise... Such enormous portions they give you at The Hare and Hounds, and I was feeling rather bilious on the bus." She rolled over on the bed and let out a long low moan. Laura looked at her as she began to snore, but then her eyes opened wide. "That's my panty-girdle, Doctor... hold me tighter." Then her eyes closed and her adenoids cranked back into action.

Laura returned to her room and poured herself a gin and tonic. She took a gulp. "Whew," she said, raising her glass to Parker who was sitting alert in his basket waiting for his dinner. "Hair of the dog, eh? But some ice perhaps."

She took the ice cubes from the small freezer compartment of her fridge and was getting Parker's bowl out ready for his dinner, when the phone rang. It was Strudel.

"Sadly I have nothing to report. According to Dora, it was a fact well known, that Henry Gordon had high blood pressure on top of the dehydration and the heavy drink. He was a dead man golfing."

"Too bad," Laura said, as she recalled the story from the night before.

"But I will keep my ears and eyes alert for more information that maybe on the radar coming."

Laura thanked her and put down the phone. She picked up the glass of gin. She could feel her strength returning; her mind clearing. Gin. Gordon's... Did Henry Gordon's high blood pressure really put the Doctor in the clear?

Parker whined beside her.

"Oh, my dear chap, I am sorry, you must be starving."

She fed him and then took him for a short walk. On her return she made herself another quick sharpener and sat down again. It had been a very long day.

Some hours later, she awoke. It was far too late for dinner so she took herself off to bed.

Chapter Sixteen

Another morning dawned with the sound of bells, but this time it was the telephone that was ringing. Laura squinted at the alarm clock and hurriedly picked up the receiver.

"It's Sally, Sally Beaumont. I haven't caught you in the middle of breakfast, have I? I know it's Sunday. "

"Gracious no." Laura winked at Parker who had crawled up from under the bedclothes and was gazing at her.

"Good. I thought I'd give you a call because I've discovered something from my cleaning lady."

"Really?"

"Yes, and I thought I'd take you up on your offer of lunch. Are you busy with anything today?"

Laura heaved herself up and pulled at a pillow as Parker scratched his ear with a hind leg. "Today?"

"It's rather short notice, but you remember I told you about Theresa, the cleaning lady I share with Gloria. Well, she told me something that I think you might find interesting about Hetty and her daughter."

Action stations. This is more like it. "Lunch? What a jolly idea."

Laura suggested they meet at Woldham Farmshop. "I hear it's been taken over by an ex-banker from London, he's brought in a new French chef."

"They're made from 100% re-cycled Chelsea and Westminster Council parking tickets," the waiter said, as he handed Laura and Sally a menu each. "So incredible for the planet," he continued, adjusting his hairband.

Laura and Sally both agreed to have the non-alcoholic cocktail of the day and the 'salad au crepitement de porc'.

"I've no idea what crepitement de porc are," Sally admitted.

"Neither have I, but I'm sure they'll be delicious," Laura said. "But do tell me what you've discovered from Theresa, I can't bear the wait."

Sally leaned forward in her chair.

"D'you want a cushion?" Laura asked.

"That might be a good idea. Normally I bring one with me."

"So, what's happened?" Laura said, once Sally had been bolstered up and their eye contact was more on a level.

"Well, Theresa knew exactly what the papers were that Gloria had taken for Hetty to sign on the night she died."

"But that's marvellous, tell me more." Laura found she was whispering.

"Gloria had left them on the kitchen table and, while Theresa was mopping the floor, she had a chance to read the title page. It was a document giving Gloria power of attorney."

"Why ever would Hetty have given Gloria power of attorney? She never entirely trusted her daughter. Did Theresa notice if the document was signed?" Laura asked.

"She didn't say. I can try and find out, if you like?" Sally took a sip of pomegranate and llama milk cocktail as the waiter put their plates of food down. "But if you don't mind my asking, is there a reason for your interest? Is there something I don't know? It might be helpful if I did."

"A touch of Cracked Andean?" The waiter pulled out a pepper grinder from under his arm. "The corns are harvested by indigenous Peruvian children to ensure the carbon footprint is minimalised."

Laura and Sally nodded in agreement and the waiter gave each of their plates a short sharp twist of the mill.

"You are right of course, I should have told you earlier," Laura said, as the waiter returned to the kitchen. "You see, I believe Hetty's life was... *cut short*."

"You don't... Do you mean you think she was murdered?"

"Yes."

Sally gasped.

Out of the corner of her eye, Laura glimpsed two women at the next- door table staring in Sally's direction, their heavy rimmed sunglasses incongruous in the dim lighting of the restaurant. "Shocking, I know," Laura said, putting one finger to her lips.

"But who... or why?" Sally whispered.

"I don't know but I'm determined to find out. And I don't know if it is connected to her death or not, but one of her paperweights is missing."

"A paperweight?"

"Yes, one from Stanley's collection. One of the rarest."

"Those things were nothing but a curse. Stolen, you think?"

"It's our best guess. I've got this old Brigadier on the case with me. We need all the help we can get."

Laura took a sip from her glass, then dabbed her mouth with a napkin. "Awfully thick, isn't it? Reminds me of something one puts on after sunburn. But as I was saying, we thought at first, it was the nurse at Wellworth Lawns who'd done for Hetty. Sadly, she's out of the frame. Utter waste of time." Laura eyed the salad. "Now our main suspect, is the doctor, Charles Mellbury." She picked up a piece of pork in her fingers and popped it in her mouth. "He was there on the night of Hetty's death to witness her signature."

"With Gloria, you mean?"

"Exactly. And this Power of Attorney could be the very document."

Sally let a nugget of pork fall from her fork back onto the bed of salad. "So you think he could have murdered Hetty after that?"

"It's possible. I went to the police but they didn't believe me." Laura looked at her plate. "I'd call these pork scratchings, wouldn't you? They give these things fancy names but, at the end of the day, it's a few old roasted sow's nipples on a bed of weeds." She picked up a leaf. "I mean, forgive me if I'm wrong, but I'd say this was dandelion." She put it in her mouth. "Still it's jolly good."

"It's all about the dressing. But why ever didn't the police believe you?"

"Ageism. And the doctor again; he told Inspector Sandfield at Woldham police station that I'm senile."

"That's outrageous."

Laura sensed the eyes behind the sunglasses trained on them.

"That's why I had to take matters into my own hands. I've got to find out what really happened to Hetty, and I'm convinced its all mixed up with Stanley's paperweight."

"The paperweights." Sally laughed. "I certainly missed a trick there. They weren't even mentioned in my divorce settlement. Still, I was just pleased to be shot of the old perv…"

The ears on which the sunglasses sat were straining to catch Sally's words.

"… And I'm not in the least bit bitter that Hetty inherited them. She was his sister, after all, and she needed the money more than me. I imagined she had sold them to pay for her care home fees."

The waiter came and took their plates.

"That's exactly what she did, except that she kept one back."

He returned as Laura was explaining about the Bacchus.

"Dessert ladies? The special today is Banane au crème Anglaise."

Laura and Sally both declined and asked for coffee.

"All the old nursery favourites seem to be back in fashion; banana custard, who'd have thought. But listen to me, I'm too spoiled at Wellworth Lawns."

"Get back to the story. You say it's the Bacchus that's missing?" Sally said.

"Yes, and what I don't know is if Gloria knew about it, and if she did, did she know what it was worth?" Laura watched as a waitress brought the card machine to the next-door table. "You see, if she did know it was valuable, and she was the one who took it, it might still be at her house." She turned to see one pair of sunglasses examining the machine, her nose almost touching it as she pressed in her pin number. Laura waited until they had got up to leave.

"The problem is," she continued, when they had gone. "There's no knowing if the motive for murdering Hetty was to do with the paperweight or not."

"I see. So it looks like Theresa has more work to do. She may have seen it." Sally bent down to retrieve her handbag from the floor beside her. She took out her diary. "Here we are, Theresa, Tuesday. Ten-thirty. That's my social life for the week," she said with a laugh.

"Are you happy in your cottage?" Laura asked.

"It's very tiny, so it suits me well."

"But I mean on your own."

"One gets used to it."

"You know you could always sell up and move to Wellworth Lawns."

"The trouble is I'm not old enough. I may last years yet. No, what I'd really like is a man in my life – silly isn't it, but someone to share the cottage with me. He'd have to be small, obviously."

Much against her better judgment, as they walked back to their respective cars, Laura delved into her bag and handed Sally one of Strudel's cards.

"Ancient Eros. A dating agency. I might just have to try it." Sally put the card in her pocket.

As Laura drew up in the car park of Wellworth Lawns, she saw John Fincham. He was carrying his battered old attaché case and heading for his Ford Mondeo that was parked under a horse chestnut tree, its leaves still half furled, poised ready to burst into great green high-fives. As she got out of her car and put Parker on his lead, she could hear the manager swearing. The tree was plainly the haunt of a sizeable bird that had taken the opportunity of effecting, what Laura thought looked like an abstract art installation on the roof of his car.

She strolled over to join him. "Hello, John, that's a nuisance. Looks like it could have been a buzzard."

"A buzzard you think, Lady B? Your talents are boundless. I would never have put you down as an expert on bird droppings. I wonder if we could incorporate it into a quiz night somehow?" He ran his hand over the roof of the car absently, as he thought through the concept. "Ornithological excreta identification. A photographic guessing game. Match the bird to the…" He looked at his hand before delving into his pocket for a handkerchief "…Mess."

"Bird's eggs might be easier. But it rather reminds me of a Jackson Pollock," Laura said

"A Jackson what?"

"You know, the American artist? He splattered oils to create his paintings."

John shook his head. "I've never understood modern art." He shoved his hand back in his pocket and pulled out the car keys.

The thought of oil paint gave Laura an idea. "Talking of art," she said, "I was in Mrs. Hobbs' room the other day."

John pressed the key in the direction of the car door. The lock popped up and he was about to open it when he stopped. "Oh yes?" he said.

"I must say, it looks very nice with all my old things in it."

"Waste not, want not. I found them in a store cupboard. I was sure you wouldn't mind; Mrs. Hobbs is your friend, after all."

"Not at all, John. No point things gathering dust. I can't think why they weren't already sold. Is there much more?"

"Only a set of chairs. No I tell a lie, I've put them in the staff room. Would you prefer me to have them sent to auction? The trouble is that Dimmock's gets such rotten prices."

"No no, much better they be used," Laura said.

"But a few old prints and a tiger skin are hardly what I would call art."

"No, I didn't mean that. I meant Mrs Hobbs' painting." It was a long shot, but Laura thought it worth a try. "I gather you are very kindly having it valued for her. Not at Dimmock's, I hope."

John gave a short laugh. "Very amusing, Lady B."

"But seriously, John, she's getting rather forgetful, you know. And there's another thing, she can't remember why she wrote you out a cheque."

John took a step forward and opened the car door. He tossed the attaché case onto the front seat before turning back to Laura.

"She should write things down. She's asked me to have it cleaned for her and the restorer wanted a deposit up front. Now, you mustn't concern yourself with these little matters." A blue vein appeared, like a river on the map of his mottled forehead. "You're not looking quite yourself," he said, his head at a slight angle as he scrutinised her. "A little unexpected slackness in the area of the lower mandible."

Laura was taken aback.

"Have you been eating plenty of greens?" John continued. "It's hard to get enough vitamin D at this time of the year, the weather's still so unpredictable. I'd recommend a trip to Dr. Mellbury for some supplements." He looked at his watch. "Well, I must get going, I've got a meeting in Woldham and I'm already running late."

"On a Sunday afternoon?"

"No rest for the wicked."

"Bad luck. Still, perhaps you could go to the supermarket carwash after your meeting? That's always open."

As he drove away, Laura thought about the encounter. It was a perfectly reasonable explanation about Venetia's painting but he was wrong to assume that Venetia would, or even could, take notes. She would never remember to write things down.

And then she thought about his comment on her physical appearance. It was not unusual for him to make these kind of personal observations, after all it had been his lifeblood for so long, but normally it was said in good spirit.

"You know what it is, Parker? It's tactlessness and we can't have a manager, however diligent at putting on entertainments, who is tactless." She pinched the skin around her jaw. *Slack? How dare he.*

"Anyway," she continued, as Parker, straining on his lead, headed for some bushes, "I will go and see Dr Mellbury. I can move my phantom depression on for one thing, and we can get back to the business of flushing him out."

Her arm was extended now as Parker's lead reached maximum.

And there was still that business about Harriet. Why had Mellbury not acted there? He had the perfect opportunity to get rid of her. Parker was tugging now: heading for the shrubbery. He, at least, was on the scent of something, that was for sure.

Chapter Seventeen

It was raining as Laura entered the surgery a few minutes early for her appointment. She sat down in the waiting room and flicked through a tattered copy of *Hello* magazine, water dripping from her hair onto a picture of the Queen. She was thinking that the Queen would never be caught out without a brolly when she heard the doctor call her name. Well, she'd had to wait until Tuesday for an appointment, but at least now he was running on time. She followed him into his consulting room.

He seemed distracted and morose as he slouched over his desk, but when she told him she was feeling suicidal, he perked up no end. He jumped up from his chair and rounded the desk, seizing Laura by the wrist.

"Nearing the end?" He checked her pulse and looked into her eyes with a torch. She could feel the hot breath emanating from his slack lips. "I think we should take some blood," he said, as he ticked boxes on a form with a flourish of his gold pen. "Make an appointment at reception to see a nurse." He handed her the form then stared at his computer screen. "I see you are already taking anti-depressants."

"You prescribed them," she said.

"Oh yes, so I did. When was that? Ah, here we are. So you haven't found them to have reduced these... symptoms?"

"No. I fear there is nothing left for me now. I am simply a burden on society. Worse than a badger."

"A badger? Interesting. Like a great furry balloon on the side of the road."

"I meant…"

"I know what you meant." The doctor typed using one fat finger and the printer whirred and spat out a piece of paper. He turned to her. "I don't suppose these will be any different." He handed her the prescription. "At your time of life, things can only appear grim; there's no two ways about it. However, I often find my patients recover simply because I've given them something. You've no idea how grateful people can be for a bottle of cod liver oil. Saccharine tablets, stock cubes, anything would do. I could save the NHS a fortune." He looked up and smiled the smile of a benign dictator; Mussolini came to mind. "Still," he continued, "count yourself lucky; at least you don't have TB."

Laura put the prescription in her bag and let herself out. She was cross with herself for allowing Mellbury to get the upper hand. She should have been more forthright, asked him his views on euthanasia. The badger analogy – how could she have been so stupid? And she had meant to ask him about his father. Why was he at Wellworth Lawns? She had discovered nothing and why had she agreed to have a blood test?

She took the papers to reception and was sent to wait in a queue for the nurse. On the positive side, she thought, leafing through a copy of *Farmer's Weekly*, she might glean some information from the nurse. But in the end, having whiled away the time reading an article on alpine tractors, the whole procedure did not take long and the nurse was not one that Laura knew.

She drove back to Wellworth Lawns and let herself into her apartment. There was a message on her answer phone from the Brigadier asking where she had been for the last couple of days. She ignored it. A short while in Coventry might teach the old bugger to pay her a bit more attention, instead of going off on Strudel's hair-brained dates.

She unpacked the peanuts and tin of olives she had bought in the supermarket and then poured the bottle of sherry into the cut glass decanter on her drinks tray. Parker stood beneath her, alternately licking his lips and snorting. As she listened to the glugging bottle she was reminded of her late husband. "You won't remember," she said to Parker, "Daddy often filled the Stolly bottle with cheap vodka when Uncle Johnnie was coming to stay. Johnnie was such a naughty boy."

Putting the empty bottle down, she clinked the glass stopper into place and gazed out of the window as the rain tapped on the panes. *Singing in the Rain*, she thought and hummed the tune.

Uncle Johnnie wasn't actually a relation of Tony's, but they pretended he was. It made life simpler when they joined him in his hotel suite on trips to New York. They'd have dinner with all the cast of Johnnie's latest Broadway show and then go back to the hotel for some games. Strip poker was such fun with Johnnie, and Tony was always so rejuvenated after their little 'capers'.

The ringing of the telephone disturbed her reverie. It was Sally.

"I couldn't wait to tell you," she said.

"What's happened?"

"Theresa rang me after she'd been to Gloria's, she knew I'd want to know."

"Know what?"

"She overheard Gloria in an awful temper. Something had gone missing. From what Theresa understood of it, Gloria thinks her son Charlie has stolen whatever it is."

"The paperweight?" Laura reached for the sherry decanter, but thought better of it.

"No way of knowing, but we've the perfect excuse to find out," Sally said.

"How's that?"

"Well, I didn't think that was much to call you about. Gloria and Charlie are always at loggerheads, but then Gloria rang me."

"She rang you?" Laura inched off the decanter stopper. "When?"

"Yesterday. I tried to call you last night, but you must have been out. Hetty has left something for you and I in her will."

"Oh, bless her. But what could it be?" Laura poured a splash of sherry into a glass.

"No idea. Shall I call Gloria and make a date for us to go over? She seemed to be keen to 'get the thing over and done with,' as she so pleasantly put it."

"The sooner the better," Laura said, downing the sherry.

Half an hour later, Sally called back. Gloria would see them the following day at four o'clock.

"Excellent," Laura said. "I'll come and collect you. We can go together."

As she put down the phone, Parker began to growl. "I'm coming," Laura said and took the rose motif Dolce and Gabbana waterproof poncho Vince had given her for her birthday from the peg on the back of the door. It was a striking piece that always drew comment. She was arranging it over her shoulders and apologising to Parker for being so slow to take him out, when the phone rang again. It was the Brigadier.

"Boxford?"

Still in some confusion about his first name, she was relieved when he continued.

"Arthur here. Where the hell have you been?"

Laura scribbled his name down on the pad of paper by the phone. "Here and there," she said. "Did you have a jolly time on your date?"

"Interesting. But how have you been getting on?"

"Quite a few developments, but right now I'm running late. Parker needs to do his business."

"What does that mean? Is it some sort of code?"

"No, it means it's that time of day. He needs to go out. I'll have to brave the rain, I can see it's not going let up."

"I'll meet you at the front door."

*

In the hall, Laura picked up one of the bright green corporate umbrellas kept in an old fashioned milk churn by the door. She hoped the combination of the pinks of the poncho and the umbrella was not too frightening. As she fought with the oversized contraption, emblazoned with the Wellworth Lawns logo, she thought of her granddaughter Victoria's husband. Dear Vince, he never did anything in half measures. "Maximise yer opportunities," he'd said. "Yer never know who might be looking down as they're passing overhead in a light aircraft during a shower and thinking, 'now where the chuff am I going to put my old dad'?"

The Brigadier was standing in the rain wearing a voluminous brown, waxed coat that almost reached the ground, a deerstalker on his head. He made no comment as to her fashion statement, but she noticed that his moustache had been shaped. It was altogether less protrusive above his lip… Really quite acceptable. His hair too, from what she could see, was neatly trimmed around his ears… and… She took a sidelong glance… *Even in them!*

They walked Parker up to the old pet cemetery. The rain pattered down off the trees onto the Brigadier's hat. Laura thought about inviting him to share her umbrella but there didn't seem much point as he was already soaked; the deerstalker sagging so that drips were going down the back of his cleanly shaven neck.

She told him about Sally and Gloria and Hetty's will.

"Good stuff," he said. "Might be getting closer to that elusive paperweight."

Then she told him about Venetia and the cheque. "John didn't seem to understand how forgetful she is, but either way, it's unclear what he's done with her painting."

"I'll pay young Fincham a call. See if I can't find out something. I've got a watercolour of the regimental goat. Needs reframing. Thunderbugs on the mount. You know the little blighters can even infiltrate a pacemaker."

"Have you got a pacemaker?" Laura asked.

"One of the first." He patted his shoulder. "There'll be no dispatching me in a hurry. You'd have to detonate it before my ticker gave out."

They walked back through the gardens, halting briefly when Parker refused to move as he inhaled some intoxicating aroma on a laurel leaf.

"There's something else," Laura said, reeling in the pug. "I went to see Harriet Huxley again. She said she'd asked Dr. Mellbury to help her end it all but he refused. So I went to see him."

"On behalf of Mrs. Huxley?"

"No. I knew he'd fob me off with patient confidentiality, so I pretended I was suicidal. I'm afraid his reaction was inconclusive. At first I thought I'd hit the jackpot he was so excited, but then he sent me for blood tests and prescribed more anti-depressants."

"Maybe he's playing a long game. You must tread carefully. The Gobi cactus flowers only when the rains come."

"For once I see what you mean."

"You could be in grave danger. Have you kept the prescriptions?"

"Yes."

"Good, they could prove to be vital evidence."

"I hadn't thought of that. That's cheered me up. Have you seen his father by the way?"

"Not yet."

"So that's still a mystery. Let's go in and have some tea and one of Alfredo's pastries. I'm starving and you must tell me all about your date."

They deposited their coats, his hat and the brolly in the hall and went into the lounge. There was no one about to take their order so Laura left the Brigadier in charge of Parker and went down to the kitchens.

"No faking staff out there? Madonna!" Alfredo said. "I'll getta the tea myself. Earl Grey?"

The Brigadier had allowed Parker the full length of his lead and the pug greeted her at the doorway as if she had been to Woldham for a week.

"You haven't been unkind to him, I hope?" she said, rejoining the Brigadier and taking the lead.

"Not much of a one with our canine friends, I'm afraid. Got badly bitten once. Pie dog in Mombasa. Still got the scar."

He bent down and pulled up one trouser leg.

"See these?" He pointed to a semi-circle of purple marks on his calf above another pair of spotted socks. "That's where the blighter sank his teeth in. Days of rabies injections."

"Parker would never bite," Laura said, as Alfredo appeared. "At least not intentionally. Only if a cake got in the way."

"You wanting cake? I thought you say pastry? Sweet Cistine ceiling, I'm losing the plot."

"No, no Alfredo, it's a misunderstanding. You're over-worked, that's all."

"I tell you..." Alfredo put down the tray. "Signor Fincham, he couldn't organise the staff rota for a singles party on a faking deserted desert island." He returned to the kitchen, his chef's hat swinging in one hand.

"Poor Alfredo, he doesn't care for John," Laura said, pouring the tea and helping herself to a Banbury cake. "But let's change the subject. How was your date?" She tried not to sound too inquisitive but there was no avoiding it and judging by his facial pampering he'd taken it pretty seriously. "Who was she?" she asked.

The Brigadier blew his nose and adjusted his hearing aid. Laura could see a drop of rainwater from his hair making its way down towards the device. She waited in anticipation but nothing happened. Perhaps the ear trimming had cured the problem? He cleared his throat.

"She went by the name of Tufty," he said, with the air of a schoolboy caught flicking a V sign behind the teacher's back.

"Brock Rockwell's widow?" Laura spluttered, struggling to keep control of the pastry in her mouth. She gulped some tea.

"Ah. That makes sense. I thought he was some sort of pet badger." The Brigadier put a slice of cherry pie on his plate.

"Don't say another word about badgers," Laura said.

"Something against badgers?" The Brigadier took a large mouthful of pie.

"Today, in particular, yes. But Tufty and Brock, they were notorious for car key parties back in the eighties." Now she could feel herself redden as she remembered the evening of the Hunt Ball when Tony chose to wear a kilt, the keys to the Land Rover attached to his sporran as a joke. "Not my sort of thing at all," she said. "Did she bring her hunting crop with her?"

"As a matter of fact, she did. She was using it as a lead. She had a most unruly foxhound attached to one end of it. The waitress wasn't best pleased but Tufty insisted it was a guide dog."

"Well, at least she couldn't use the whip for anything else," Laura said.

"Quite. But even so, by the end of tea, I was rather sorry I hadn't brought my father's cavalry sword. She was quite a handful." Parrying the imaginary weapon, the Brigadier caught the edge of his teacup with the flick of a wrist.

"But you saw her off, I hope?" Laura said, blotting the wet table with a napkin.

"It was touch and go." The Brigadier huffed and poured himself another cup.

"It doesn't say much for Ancient Eros's vetting procedure. You might have thought Strudel would do a bit of homework."

"How would she have known Tufty Rockwell was a dominatrix?"

"Fair enough. Still, I expect it's put you off the whole idea." Laura pulled off another piece of Banbury cake and popped it in her mouth.

"The vulture flies far afield for carrion. Strudel has persuaded me to try again."

Laura dropped the remains of the cake in astonishment. "What a disgusting analogy and really, another date?"

"I do beg your pardon, but yes; I'm going out on Friday afternoon with a retired midwife from Woldham. Strudel says she's highly respected in the nursing fraternity."

"Is Strudel an expert in midwifery now? But that reminds me; did you know Nurse Creightmore's gone on holiday? I wanted to interrogate her about Mellbury, but her stand-in didn't seem to know when she'd be back."

"I'll bring it up when I see Fincham." The Brigadier looked at his watch and wiped the dollop of red cherry filling that had landed on the sleeve of his jacket with another napkin. "I might see if he's in his office now. Will you be at dinner?"

"More food? Actually I'm having supper with some friends in the village."

She wasn't going out to dinner at all, but she was somewhat nettled by the Brigadier's newfound dating hobby.

"Tomorrow?" he asked.

"I'm sorry, but I'll be out with Sally Beaumont tomorrow. You see the leopard may have spots, but the zebra has a shorter tail, as you yourself might have said." She got up to leave.

"Hold on, Boxford. What d'you mean?"

"Other fish to fry. Come on Parker."

Chapter Eighteen

From what Laura could see of Gloria Hemper's house, Theresa, the cleaner, had her work cut out. She and Sally followed Gloria past a jumble of coats and shoes in the hall, to the sitting room. Piles of newspapers and magazines lay abandoned on the carpet next to the window ledge on which a selection of half-dead pot plants struggled to survive. The cushions on the faded sofa were in need of a good plumping, and a large marmalade cat lay sleeping in the middle of it. Laura sniffed the stale air. Perched on top of a table, a mass of discarded coffee mugs jostled with empty glasses and stub-filled ashtrays. *No wonder Hetty was always so disappointed in her daughter.*

"I haven't got long, so it'll have to be a quick cup of tea." Gloria pulled a loose strand of dark hair from the shoulder of her cream coloured jersey and dropped it on the floor. "I'll get the paperweights out so you can get on with choosing."

"The paperweights?" Laura caught Sally's eye.

"Yes. What did you think Mummy had left you? Money?" Gloria went to a desk in one corner and picked up an old shoebox from on top of another pile of papers. "Here," she said, handing it to Laura. "Mummy's instructions were that you had first choice and then Aunt Sally can choose one. Her will was quite specific about that. I can't think why. So if you'll excuse me, I'll go and get the tea."

Laura and Sally stared wide-eyed at one another.

"Quick, open the box," Sally said.

Laura pulled off the lid. Someone had wrapped the weights up in old bits of newspaper. One by one, she unwrapped them and laid them on the desk. There was no sign of the Bacchus.

The two women stared at them. They made a pitiful sight. Gloria had not even bothered to remove the gift, still in its box, that she had given her mother.

"Oh dear." Laura picked up 'The Diamond Cut', and lifted the lid. "Gloria gave it to her. Hetty was so grateful. She really thought Gloria had turned over a new leaf. Little did Hetty know how cheap it was. But we'll wait a minute before we choose, shall we?"

"See Gloria's reaction?" Sally's eyes narrowed. "I like it."

Gloria returned with three mugs on a dirty plastic tray. Seeing the paperweights displayed on the desk, she put the tray on the floor. "Help yourselves," she said taking her own mug.

Sally bent down and picked up the remaining mugs. She handed one to Laura. Gloria lit a cigarette and blew the smoke down her nose. "Have you chosen?" she said.

"Your dear mother was so fond of these." Laura picked up the modern Murano paperweight that she had given Hetty after a trip to Venice.

"Is that the one you want? Go ahead. Aunt Sally, what about you?"

"I can't quite make up my mind." Laura put down the weight and picked up 'The Diamond Cut'.

"I wouldn't bother with that," Gloria said. "It came from a charity shop."

Laura put it down and turned to Gloria. "I had a feeling there was one with a little silhouette in the middle of it. Hetty was very fond of it, I remember."

Gloria walked over. The ash from her cigarette dropped onto the floor near the tea tray. She scuffed at it with the toe of her pink furry slipper.

"This one, d'you mean?" She picked up one with the photo of an old woman in it.

Laura remembered Hetty had bought it in an antique shop near Chatsworth one year when they had been visiting the house. "It's Debo," Hetty had exclaimed. She loved the aristocracy and bought it there and then, even though Laura had told her it looked nothing like the late Dowager Duchess.

"Yes, that must be it," Laura said. "Funny how one's memory plays tricks. But I think perhaps I will take the Murano. Sally, what about you?"

"I'll have this one." Sally picked up the swirling pink Caithness glass.

Laura shuddered as Hetty's final expression flashed into her mind. "I remember Hetty got that for a very good price at the local auction," she said, as Sally polished it on her chest.

"Well, if you're all done…" Gloria began tapping her French polished fingernails on the table.

"I'll just finish my tea, if you don't mind?" Laura sat down on the sofa. The cat leapt out of the way as she patted the seat next to her.

"How are Abigail and Charlie, by the way?" Sally asked, as she sat down beside Laura.

Gloria frowned and lit another cigarette. "Abigail is fine, thank you. She at least has a job."

"And Charlie?"

Gloria's red lips puckered as if she'd smelt ammonia. "He's in London with his father. Jacked in his degree. Useless shits, the pair of them."

"So what's Ron up to these days?" Sally continued. "Still after the elusive deal?"

"God knows. He doesn't give me a penny, that's all I know." Gloria stubbed out her cigarette, twisting the butt into the already burgeoning ashtray.

"So Hetty's money hasn't saved the day?"

Laura felt a frisson of excitement at Sally's boldness.

"I beg your pardon?" Gloria's eyes widened and she raised her chin in defiance.

"And apart from dropping out of university, what's Charlie been up to now to get your goat so badly?" Sally had the bit between her teeth.

Laura was impressed by her strident, pocket-sized ally. "Pinching things for his drug habit, I suppose?"

Twist the knife. Laura studied Gloria's expression for a reaction.

"Who have you been talking to?" Gloria said, glaring down at her aunt.

"So it's true?" Sally leaned back on the sofa.

"I can't see that it's any of your business." Gloria walked away and lit another cigarette. "And now, if you don't mind, I have things to do."

"Shall we have a decent cup of tea at my house?" Sally said, as Laura drove them away.

"Oh yes, I'm shattered after that. I thought she might throttle you, when you asked her if she had money problems as we were leaving." Laura glanced at Sally. Parker had jumped into the passenger seat and was sitting on Sally's lap, puffing warm dog-breath into her face. "Push him into the back," she said.

Sally attempted to contend with the pug but he was adamant that his place was with her, so she gave up trying. "I saw no point in beating about the bush, and we weren't going to get another chance, were we?" she said. "I'm not sure it did a lot of good though. She wasn't giving anything away. I mean we've still no idea about the Bacchus. Did she know about it? Has she got it? Did Charlie steal it?"

"I've had a thought about Charlie," Laura said. "I think we should pay him a visit."

Sally found Ron Hemper's number in an old address book.

"I remember inviting them to Stanley's sixtieth. They were living in a grotty basement in Pimlico that Ron bought on the cheap. Rising damp, if I recall. I don't suppose he's moved. He couldn't afford to." She rang the number.

Ron Hemper answered.

"I'm with Hetty's old friend, Laura Boxford," Sally explained. "She's got something of Hetty's for Charlie. It's a sort of bequest. She and I are in London tomorrow, and we thought we could drop it in. Is he there?"

Laura listened as the conversation progressed.

"...Opposite the Halal butchers? Good, we'll see you there at midday." Sally put down the phone. "That's sorted, but what is it exactly, this bequest for Charlie?"

Laura took the Murano paperweight from her bag, "This," she said, "should flush young Charlie out."

On her way home, Laura dropped in on Strudel and Jervis.

Strudel was sitting on the sofa sewing sequins on a pale blue taffeta ball gown. "I am doing a little updating," she explained. "Also, I have to tell you more from Dora, who is talking with Harry Arnold, who is saying Dr. Mellbury is trying to kill him with the amount of pills he has to take."

"Really?" Laura said.

"But this is perhaps some gossip only. Harry Arnold is having very many complaints, and some would say the biggest of these is hypochondria."

Jervis looked up from his computer. "I've done all the booking for Ancient Eros," he called over. "Are we billing Arthur this time?"

"Perhaps we'll let him off after his encountering with, what was her name?"

"Tufty Rockwell." Laura said.

"You have heard?" Strudel said.

"You could have asked me about Tufty Rockwell and saved everyone a lot of bother."

"I'm not so sure, Laura," Jervis said. "Horses for courses and all that. Strudel's got the very man for her, in the equine field as it happens. Retired horse whisperer from Aston Magna. Not quite sure why he had to retire but there you go. Anyway, she'll have his jodhpurs off before he has time to think about a 'flying change', or what ever it is they get up to."

"Jervis, that's enough."

"Sorry, my love. Oh yes, and before I forget, Laura. Can you remember which way the silhouette in Hetty's Bacchus paperweight faced?"

"Is it important?"

"I'm afraid so. You see, because it came from America, my man in Chicago thinks it was probably made by a certain William T. Gillinder. He worked for George Bacchus in Birmingham in the 1860s. Then he emigrated to America. He set up his own glassworks and called it the Philadelphia Glass Flint Company. He copied some of the Bacchus designs."

"You mean it's a copy?"

"Not exactly. He faced his silhouette to the left, whereas the Bacchus ones always faced right. But it means it would be less valuable. Maybe six thousand dollars."

They looked at one another.

"To kill for that?" Laura said. "Life's cheap after eighty."

"But that's still not an inconsiderable amount. And you don't know for sure that it was the reason for Hetty's murder. I don't suppose there is a picture of it anywhere? For insurance, possibly?"

"I've been trying to think. It's not the sort of thing one takes a photo of, and Hetty would never have got round to having it insured."

"Do you know where she got it from? If we could prove its provenance, my man might be able to trace it, if it came up at auction. It's our best bet so far, I'd say."

"I'll ask Sally Beaumont, I'm seeing her tomorrow. Do you remember her? Hetty's sister-in-law. You met her at the funeral. The paperweight belonged to her late ex-husband." Laura gave them a brief outline of the circumstances in which Stanley had acquired the Bacchus.

"An addiction of feathers?" Strudel gave a whimper.

"What is it, my love?" Jervis jumped up from his computer.

"I have with my needle stabbed myself." She sucked her finger.

"Addiction, yes and that reminds me why I'm here. I wonder if you would be dears and look after Parker for me tomorrow? Sally and I are going to London to see Hetty's grandson. There is a distinct possibility he may be involved."

"The grandson?" Strudel looked up from her sewing.

"A most unpleasant young man, according to Sally. Penniless drug addled alcoholic. It could be that he stole the Bacchus from his mother."

Chapter Nineteen

"One of the benefits of being as old as I am, is that no one wants to sit next to you on a train," Laura said, squeezing herself into the seat opposite Sally. "They think it's catching. Varicose veins and walk-in baths."

"Exactly. The contagious nature of double chins." Sally shook her arms. "And batwingitis."

They roared with laughter so that the people sitting the other side of the aisle turned and stared.

Laura leaned forward across the table. "We're only confirming their worst suspicions," she said, as the train rumbled out of Woldham station.

The ticket collector punched their tickets and then the drinks trolley clanked to a halt beside them.

Best not, they agreed. They both had an aversion to train toilets and it was a reality that finding a loo in London in a hurry was impossible. They turned their attention to Charlie.

"You don't think he'll turn nasty?" Laura asked.

"You never know with drug addicts."

"My handbag's a pretty solid object carrying this paperweight. Oh yes, and before I forget," Laura continued, "Jervis says we should try and find out who Stanley won the Bacchus from. He's keen to get involved. He was busy Googling international art theft when I left Parker with them."

"The man from Las Vegas?"

"If he happened to still have any documentation about it, it would help with identification if it were to turn up at auction. Can you remember what the rehab place was called? Jervis said he could email them and see if they could go through their records."

"I'll have it written down somewhere. I'll go through my diaries. But what about patient confidentiality?"

"I'm sure that's not something that would put Jervis off his stride. Now, I think we've time for forty winks, don't you?"

"What number d'yer want?" the cabbie shouted as they crawled up the run-down Pimlico street.

"The Halal butchers," Sally said.

"Blimey, you've come a long way for a kosher sausage, ladies."

"Not the actual butchers; opposite. Look, there it is, number 48, basement flat." Sally pointed and the cab drew up.

"Basement flat in Pimlico? You wanna watch it at your age. Slavery's a big problem round here."

Laura handed him the money.

"Sure you don't want me to wait?" he called out.

"We can look after ourselves," Laura said, and thanked him as, clutching the handrail, they descended the steps to Ron Hemper's flat.

They rang the bell and waited in the dank concrete area. A minute passed and then Charlie answered the door wearing tracksuit bottoms and a crumpled grey T-shirt with a skull printed across the chest.

"Hello, Charlie," Sally said. "This is Lady Boxford."

Laura smiled at him. "We met at your grandmother's funeral."

Charlie grunted, ignored Laura's outstretched hand and let them in.

The flat had all the characteristic hallmarks of the Hemper family: it was a tip. Charlie had obviously seen no need to spruce the place up for the benefit of his guests. His offer of a cup of coffee came as a surprise.

"Thank you," Sally said.

"Just a glass of water for me," Laura looked round for somewhere to sit. The sofa bed – still in bed mode – was the only available option.

The kitchen formed part of the living area, so Charlie did not have far to go to make the coffee. The pipework clanked as he filled the kettle and steam filled the room.

"We're out of milk," Charlie said. He handed a mug to Sally and backed away to lean on the edge of the sink, his arms folded over the skull on his chest, Laura's glass of water forgotten. Sally took the mug and sat next to Laura.

"I expect you're keen to see what I've brought you as a memento of your late grandmother." Laura said, delving into her handbag. She had wrapped the Murano paperweight in some pink tissue paper. She held it out to Charlie.

He opened it. "What the fuck's this for?"

"Don't you know?" Sally said.

"How'm I meant to know what a crazy coloured lump of glass is for?"

"It's a paperweight. You're very lucky. It could be one of the valuable ones, couldn't it Laura?"

They looked up at Charlie's bemused expression. "Valuable?"

"Some of them are worth thousands," Sally said.

"You're joking." Charlie inspected it with casual eagerness.

"Didn't you ever see your grandmother's collection?" Laura asked.

"No. Why would I?"

"They were in your mother's house, that's why." Sally put her mug down on a makeshift bedside table.

"So?"

"So I know what you've been up to." Sally stood up and took a step towards her nephew. She was close to him now. "Stealing things to feed your habit." She reached up and prodded him in the chest. "We could easily go to the police, you know."

"What are you on, Aunt Sal?" Charlie pushed his diminutive aunt gently to one side. "Is that what my dear Mother's been saying about me? That I'm a junkie? She really takes the biscuit." Charlie ran one hand through his hair and scratched the side of his head. "Look, I've never seen a collection of paperweights. Sure, I took the pearls. It was in Gran's will; they were for Abigail and I knew Mum'd flog 'em if I didn't get them out of there. I'm not a total loser, you know."

"You stole your sister's pearls. Where are they?" Sally held her ground.

"I didn't steal them. I've got them for her, for safe keeping." Charlie opened a kitchen drawer and took out an oblong leather case that Laura recognised as Hetty's.

"I'll give them to her when I see her next."

Sally took the case and opened it. She handed it to Laura.

The single strand with its little paste clasp, yes, it was Hetty's. Dear Hetty, it always was a trifle tight around her neck. Laura nodded, closed the lid and handed it back to Sally.

"You promise to give it to your sister?" Sally said to Charlie. "What about your debts?"

"I'm not in debt. Okay, Dad's bailed me out, but I've got a job. I'm starting next week. Jesus, this is like the fucking Spanish inquisition."

"Well, I shall be informing your sister of the situation, all the same."

"Go ahead. She already knows. She agreed with me. You've no idea what Mum's like. She's probably got through the cash on Sauvignon Blanc already, if I know anything about her."

"How much money did Glor… your mother inherit?" Sally asked.

"About six grand," he said.

"Six thousand?" Laura was taken aback. Hadn't Jervis said the Bacchus was worth six thousand… dollars. How precarious Hetty's situation had been. Even with her discount, she would have had to sell the Bacchus fairly imminently if she had wished to stay at Wellworth Lawns… And then what? It didn't bear thinking about. She stood up. "You don't know anything about the paperweights, do you Charlie?" she said.

"I've told you."

"So shall I take this one back?" Laura said.

"You mean you were kidding me? It's not worth anything?" Charlie rolled it about from hand to hand like a cricket ball.

"No."

"What an effing waste of time." He gave it back to Laura.

"It was a very good act if he was putting it on."

"I think he was being genuine," Sally said. "I felt rather sorry for him, poor boy."

"With a mother like that." Laura tapped her fingers on the carriage window as they clattered back to Woldham. "She's probably so desperate for a drink, she'd have sold the Bacchus to any old passing antique dealer."

Sally leaned her elbows on the table that divided them and put her head in her hands. "So we're back to Gloria."

"Unless she did know its true value... And knew how near Hetty was to having to sell it herself?"

"You could send your Brigadier round," Sally said. "Get him to pose as a valuation expert."

Laura drove Sally home from the station and then collected Parker.

"So Strudel gave you a small lamb bone to occupy you during the Old Time Dancing, did she?" Laura said as she opened the door to her apartment.

Parker staggered into his basket and lay there panting, his belly distended haggis-like. *Trouble later,* Laura thought and picked up the phone to call the Brigadier.

"I'm done in. This dating lark certainly takes it out of one," he said. "Just got back from tea with my retired midwife."

"*Your?* So, I'm to understand it was more successful than the last encounter?"

"I should say," the Brigadier effused. "I'm accompanying her to the CD fair at Cheltenham Town Hall tomorrow afternoon."

"Are you interested in CDs?"

"Music? Oh yes." He began humming *The Dam Busters'* theme.

There seemed little point in telling him about Gloria and Charlie. Laura hung up the phone and called Venetia, even though she was only in the room next-door.

"Being alive is exhausting. I've just watered the plastic geranium by mistake," Venetia said.

"Shall we go down to supper?"

"I think I've already had supper. Hold on, what's this…"

Laura heard banging as Venetia put the receiver down on a hard surface. Then she picked it up again. "Yes I'm fairly sure I have. It looks like some sort of pie."

They arranged to have lunch the next day.

At least that's something to do tomorrow. But still Laura had a feeling of being on pause. Once again, she had pinned her hopes on the wrong person and now she was directionless. What else could she do to find out if Gloria had the paperweight? It was too annoying that the Brigadier was so easily distracted.

She picked up the copy of *Good Housekeeping* magazine she had swapped with Sally on the train, and flicked through the pages. She came to the horoscopes and scanned the page for her sign. 'Remember when you first learned to ride a bike…' *What am I doing reading this rubbish?* But in her mind she was back in the India of her childhood. She was running down to the stables, the little bike bashing into her ankles. "Prem?" she called out to her father's syce. "Please can I have another lesson?"

She felt the stabilising hand on her back as he guided her down the dirt track and over the bridge. Past water buffalo cooling themselves amongst lush water lilies in the lake. Then the dizzy feeling as she wobbled on and Prem's voice as he encouraged her: "You can be doing it." Then, further away as he shouted, "Pedal memsahib… You are on your own being now."

Laura put down the magazine. *I can. I can do this on my own*, she thought, as a malodorous stench wafted up from Parker's basket. I'll dump the Brigadier, philandering old sod… Yes, I'm perfectly capable of getting to the bottom of Hetty's death without his help.

*

As she walked Parker the next morning – his bowels were indeed in disarray – she began to formulate a plan. Sally's idea was a good one, but Dudley was the way forward. She would get him to pose as the valuation expert. He didn't have the gravitas of the Brigadier, but his theatrical nature could prove an asset. She would give him a crash course in the arts and Gloria would be seduced into revealing her hand. But she couldn't bother Dudley on a Friday or a Saturday – they were his busiest days. Sunday would be rude, so she'd have to wait until Monday. Sally had said she would call her if she found the address of the rehab place but, until then, there was nothing for it but to wait. She went to collect Venetia.

"I'm growing sunflowers for the charity plant sale," Venetia said. "The windowsill is perfect for it. So light and sunny. My old room would have been quite hopeless. Oh Laura, I'm so lucky."

"I don't think the Horticultural Committee will be expecting you to provide the plants. Gladys Freemantle generally has a team in Woldham who do the growing and the local garden centres are always very generous."

"I like to do something though. I had quite green fingers once upon a time. Oh, I do miss baking too. They have a cake stall don't they? I used to dabble in watercolours too, but that's not much use is it?"

Laura looked around the room. "Is your painting still at the restorer's?" she asked.

"What painting? I can't remember, and I've a feeling there's something very exciting happening this afternoon and I can't remember what that is either."

"I'd hardly call the demonstration of personal alarms in the lounge exciting."

"Was that it? I suppose it must have been."

"There's a charity fashion show this evening."

"Yes, that's it. Oh, I'm looking forward to that."

*

"Aren't the dresses pretty!" Venetia said.

"Not my cup of tea." Gladys Freemantle frowned. "Thoroughly unsuitable for the fuller figure."

Laura yawned as a lot of overweight middle-aged models with high-heels and thick ankles showed off a collection of skin-tight jersey dresses. She remembered the pink silk Balenciaga sheath dress Tony had bought for her in Paris. She had worn it out to dinner and afterwards they had gone to a bar on Rue Mouffetard and played on the pinball machine. Later, Tony and Didier had gone to drink Champagne cocktails in the hotel bar overlooking The Quai D'Orsay, but Laura had preferred to stay in bed.

Now she longed for sleep. Anything to get through until Monday.

Chapter Twenty

Sitting in church on Sunday, Laura prayed for a breakthrough. 'Lead us, Heavenly Father, Lead us,' she sang with gusto, as she thought about the Bacchus.

She listened to Reverend Mulcaster as he delivered the sermon on forgiveness that he was so fond of. Laura knew it well and was anticipating its end when the Reverend got waylaid and started mixing it up with his one on miracles. He was half way through the raising of Lazarus when he realised his mistake. "Oh yes, the healing powers of our Lord!" he concluded abruptly. And now we will all stand for hymn number one hundred and eight, 'Glory be to Jesus'."

Glory? Gloria. Laura opened her hymn book. Healing? She stood as the organist began to play. Could there be a connection between Gloria and Dr. Mellbury? She sang the first verse. They had been together in Hetty's room the night she died. Had they between them given her a helping hand into the next life?

She went up for communion and found herself kneeling next to Maurice Dickinson, his greasy ginger hair smoothed onto his scalp like a thick layer of caramel sauce. As Reverend Mulcaster placed the wafer in her upturned hands, she had the glimmer of an idea; perhaps Jervis could help? Out of the corner of her eye, she watched as Reverend Mulcaster handed Maurice Dickinson the wine. He took the chalice in both hands, raised it to his lips and drank the goblet dry. Then he got up, handed it back to the vicar with a curt burp and staggered out of sight back down the aisle.

By the time Reverend Mulcaster had consecrated more wine, Laura's knees had all but seized up, but her mind was clear. She needed Hetty's death certificate details but she didn't want questions asked if she were seen to be making enquiries. She would get Jervis to try hacking the surgery files again, or even perhaps those of the undertakers, Bone and Bone.

Perks of the trade, she thought as Reverend Mulcaster handed her the now brimming chalice. She took a sip of the heady sacramental fermentation. It was enough to revive her. She might even send Jervis under cover to sniff out Gloria. He'd have to disguise himself. Perhaps Francesca Northbridge had a wig? Well, he would think of something, it was simpler than having to train up Dudley in the art of valuations.

She strode dizzily back to her pew. *Why didn't I think of that before?*

But the Brigadier's absence still rankled. She leant forward to pray, clenching her hands together. She thought she heard a voice. 'Don't hang around waiting for him.' The words wafted in her ear. 'Enrol... 'And then again, 'Enrol...' The voice was fading. Laura clenched her hands harder and now her buttocks too. The voice returned. Quite clear in her head. '...Before its too late...' Yes, there *was* something else she could be getting on with.

There was no answer when Laura knocked on Strudel's door, so she walked round to the back of the bungalow and peered in the kitchen window. Strudel and Jervis were practicing a samba to the music of a steel band coming from a CD player by the sink. She waved and Strudel came round to the front door and let her in.

"How are you, my little friend?" she said, bending down to pat Parker.

His tail wagged in gleeful recognition as he trotted past her into the sitting room and they watched through the open door as he leapt onto the sofa.

"So Laura, how can we be helping you today?" Strudel said, smiling as Parker scratched around to make himself comfortable.

"I've decided to join up."

"Join up?" Jervis had appeared at Strudel's side. "Are you suggesting armed combat, Laura? Bit risky at your age I'd have thought."

"I mean join Ancient Eros. I'd like to go on a date."

"At last. But this is marvellous news. I have been feeling your romantic inclinations were in need of rejuvenation for some time. I will get the registration form this very minute." Strudel hurried out to the kitchen.

"And I've got news for you," Jervis said. "I've been back in touch with my Bacchus expert. He's sent me some pictures. The trouble is, the ones with a silhouette are so rare; there are very few images available. Hang on while I print them off. They might jog your memory."

"I'm waiting for a call from Sally," Laura said. "She's going through her old diaries to find the name of the rehab place in Las Vegas, where Stanley won it."

Strudel reappeared carrying a sheaf of papers. "Did I hear you mentioning Sally? Such a nice person and I think I have the very gentleman for her."

"Sally?"

"Yes, Intelligent and with culture. He may be a little on the infirm side – I forgot to ask what she is feeling about wheelchairs. Motorised of course, but it will be a good start and I am hoping that in his seated position, he will be of approximately the same height as her."

"Sally?" In an instant Laura remembered the card she had given her.

"Yes. It is something of a gamble, but we can't hope for Valhalla on a first liaison."

"I think you mean Nirvana, my love." Jervis said over the sound of the printer buzzing back and forth.

"Nirvana. Possibly. This is something for you also to bear in mind, Laura. Sit here; this won't take long." She handed Laura a pen and the registration form.

"Is Sally a member?"

"Yes. She telephoned. I asked her round… Only yesterday, wasn't it Jervis?"

"What was that, my love?"

"We got her signed up over tea."

"Here we are," Jervis handed the pictures to Laura. "Do you recognise any of them?"

"Hold on, let me think." Laura was feeling over-wrought at having to answer all the questions on the Ancient Eros registration form. "Did Sally fill in all of this?" she asked.

"Oh yes. But you can skip the questions about your income." Strudel looked over Laura's shoulder. "And I don't think we need you to fill in the section on replacement joints and pacemakers. You would be telling us if you were planning a foreign trip, would you not?"

When Laura had finally completed the form and written out a cheque for fifty pounds to Ancient Eros, she and Jervis studied the photographs of the different silhouettes. The more Laura deliberated, the more confused she became.

"You see, this is a Gillinder. The head is facing left," Jervis said.

Laura stared at the picture. "Now I think about it, I'm sure Hetty's faced the other way…"

"So it could still be a real Bacchus and Sons. That's good news."

Jervis said he'd fetch a magnifying glass, while Strudel went to make a pot of tea. As Laura sat and waited, she wondered if Strudel had a secret sliding scale of membership fees, because she couldn't for the life of her believe that dear Hetty would have forked out that amount and she couldn't imagine the Brigadier being profligate with money, or Sally for that matter. Perhaps they took the whole thing much more seriously than she realised?

Still, she felt better that she was now part of this elite group, and she could always make excuses if she didn't fancy going out on one of Strudel's somewhat ill-conceived pairings.

She returned to the prints of the paperweights. Even with a reviving cup of tea and the aid of the magnifying glass, she could not be sure which was most like Hetty's.

"This is exhausting," she said.

"Take them with you. You can look at them again later when you're feeling fresher."

"Thank you, Jervis. I might show Sally; see if she remembers." Laura put the pictures in her bag. "Come along now, Parker. We've taken up much too much of Strudel and Jervis's time."

"If Sally's remembered the place in Vegas," Jervis said, as they walked to the door, "I can email them and ask if they remember Stanley's card playing friend. If not, I can always try a little hacking."

"I've told you before, Jervis, this will end in trouble." Strudel turned to Laura. "Jervis had a most strange communication from the Pentagon, asking if he was needing more bullet proof golfing shirts for the Woldham Military Centre."

"Oh dear, but Jervis, that reminds me, I've been concentrating so hard on filling in forms and looking at these pictures I'd completely forgotten the most important thing."

"What's that?"

"Dr. Mellbury. Do you think you could hack into Bone and Bone the undertaker's records? I thought we could find the death certificates of Hetty and Nanny and possibly Henry Gordon. They might give us a clue."

"I would do happily, but I believe they're a matter of public record." Jervis gave a sigh of dejection. "I'll look them up anyway, it's no trouble."

As she walked back down the drive, a white van flashed past her. With a spray of gravel, it parked by the steps to the main entrance. Mimi jumped out and slammed the door behind her.

"Hello, Ladysheep," she called out.

The driver's window wound down. "Evening, Lady Boxford," Tom said.

"This is very smart." Laura pointed to the side of the van. There was a cartoon picture of a man in a cap with a large toolkit in one hand. Beside him, a sign read, 'Tom's Plumbing and Electrical Services,' followed by a series of phone numbers.

"Is Tom's." Mimi beamed with pride. "She a hundred and serty-fix horses how you say?"

"Honestly Meems, how often have I told you? A hundred and thirty-six horse power." Tom flicked his floppy blond fringe back from his face and patted the steering wheel.

"Aww Tom, you so silly, that's what I say."

"I'm impressed. You must be doing well, Tom," Laura said.

"Not bad, not bad at all. We've got another on order for the new division I'm setting up on the other side of Woldham." He started the engine. "I'd better get going; burst pipe in Nether Swell. See you later Meems." He wound up the window and drove off, scattering more gravel as he went.

Mimi and Laura walked into the hall.

"I get going too. My shift I thinking late already." She trotted off in the direction of the kitchens.

"Where do you suppose Tom found the money to go buying fleets of vans just like that?" Laura said to Parker, once they were safely in the lift. "I suppose he could have taken out a loan."

She continued the conversation as the lift doors opened. "But Tom…What about Tom?" They walked down the corridor. "Of course, it couldn't possibly involve Mimi. But what about Tom and the doctor?" She opened the door to her apartment. "I'm afraid there is only one thing for it. Much as it displeases me, we are going to have to ring the Brigadier."

She was about to pick up the phone in the sitting room when she noticed the messages light flashing. She pressed the button and listened. 'You have three messages. Message one… "Boxford, are you there?" Message two… "Where are you Boxford?" Message three… "Boxford, where the bloody hell are you? I have news of the most important nature."'

She dialled his number. He said he was coming round.

A few minutes later, she heard a rapping on the door and let him in.

"Boxford."

"Brig…"

"You go…"

"No you…"

"Ladies first, I insist."

"Oh, all right," Laura said. "I think Tom Scott Hopkinson is mixed up in it."

"Have you gone mad? The old Etonian handyman?"

"Yes. I don't know why I didn't think about it before. With his education, he'd more than likely know all about paperweights. He'd be bound to know what a Bacchus is worth. Have you seen his new van?"

"I'm sorry to disappoint you…"

"What if he was in it with Dr. Mellbury?"

"… I'm afraid it's all up."

"What d'you mean?"

"It's all up. That's why I've been trying to get hold of you since last night, but you never answer your telephone. Creightmore's been arrested."

Chapter Twenty-one

"What d'you mean 'arrested'?" Laura slumped onto the sofa.

"I was at the CD fair." The Brigadier collapsed down beside her. "With the retired midwife. She was interested in pomp rock. Pomp and Circumstance; military marches. That sort of thing."

"But what's this got to do with Nurse Creightmore?"

"I'm getting to that. I mentioned the Band of the Blues and Royals as we were talking to a stall-holder who she knew from the hospital. Retired porter. He specialised in the Electrical Light Orchestra, not an ensemble I was personally familiar with and I told them so. For some reason, this caused considerable mirth between the two of them and they exchanged telephone numbers."

"That must have been very annoying, but what has it got to do with Nurse Creightmore?"

"She began texting him when we went for a cup of tea – I was getting most impatient. I could hardly bring myself to eat my sausage roll – but then he texted back the news. He'd heard it from a friend at the hospital who knew someone who cleaned at the police station."

Laura's own patience was running thin. "What, for goodness sake?"

"Telling her that Nurse Creightmore was in custody. Well, the minute I got back, and that was not a minute too soon, I went to find Fincham."

Laura sat up. "I can't believe it. Glass of sherry?"

"Yes please."

Laura jumped up and hurried to the drinks tray. "Did John know about it?"

"Of course he pretended not to, but I got it out of him in the end. Threatened to go down to the police station myself. He told me in the strictest confidence, mind you it will probably be all over the papers by tomorrow."

"So, what did he say?" Laura handed the Brigadier a generously filled schooner.

"They're going to charge her..."

"With what? Do get on with it." Laura put out a bowl of nuts.

"The suspected murder of Hetty Winterbottom and Henry Gordon."

Laura gasped. "Why?"

"That remains to be seen. They're doing an autopsy on Henry Gordon. Obviously it's too late for Hetty."

"But it can't be Creightmore. We must go and see Barry Pendleton and find out what's happened. She must be innocent. I told you, it's Tom and the Doctor. Tom will have keys to everywhere. I feel so sorry for poor Mimi. It's likely he's been letting Dr. Mellbury in, and together they've been killing people then looting their possessions."

"I'm sorry, but I think you're wrong and we can't go blundering in trying to find Barry Pendleton. He'll probably be being questioned anyway."

The Brigadier tossed a handful of nuts into his mouth. "There will be some perfectly good reason for Tom having a new van. He's most likely made it up with his mother. Strudel told me about his being disinherited by her, but it's my opinion that the maternal instinct is too strong for that sort of threat to last long. The warthog waits for the drought to pass."

"If I have to continue the investigation alone, I will."

"Steady there, Boxford. I'm not saying I won't support you; it's just that in the face of this latest development, it seems to me that the case is closed. You should be pleased."

"But look how silly we will look when she's found innocent, which I am sure she will be. The scent will be even colder."

"So what are you intending to do?"

"Speak to John about Tom. See if he knows how he's come into this money all of a sudden."

"Are you sure about that?"

"You're the one always talking about leaving no stone unturned. And I must call Sally. She's finding out who Stanley won the paperweight from. Then Jervis can hopefully find out precisely how much it's worth. In all of this there's been no mention of the paperweight by the police as far as we know."

At dinner, the news had got out and the dining room was a-buzz with gossip.

"I suspected there was something not quite right about her." Gladys Freemantle loaded her spoon with a profiterole. "Ever since I started taking her herbal tea, I have found my memory worse, not better as she promised. D'you know I stared at a mound of Alchemilla vulgaris in the border this morning and I simply couldn't remember what it was called."

Carol Paterson's dimpled cheeks flushed, "Is that a downstairs problem?" she asked her husband Lance. The once great pilot shrugged his shoulders and carried on eating.

"But you've remembered now," Laura pointed out to Gladys.

Carrying a plate of cheese from the sideboard, Maurice Dickinson bumped into Laura's chair as he passed their table. "Couldn't help overhearing," he butted in, putting one arm on the back of Laura's chair and breathing warm rancid breath down the back of her neck. "She had a look about her that I never trusted, fiendish eyes," he said; then carried on back to the table where he was sitting alone.

"What does that idiot know?" Laura huffed. "Fiendish eyes, I ask you."

"Man's a fool," Gladys said.

Laura looked over her shoulder as Gladys' deep voice reverberated around the room, but Sir Maurice appeared not to have heard.

"I've always rather liked Nurse Creightmore." Venetia picked up the last profiterole on her plate and popped it in her handbag.

"Is that a good idea?" Laura asked.

"I may feel hungry later."

"But it's all sticky and…"

"No, I should say we've all had a lucky escape," Gladys continued, dabbing her mouth with her napkin.

"We really shouldn't judge.' Laura could see her words fall on run down hearing aids as Carol Paterson accused the nurse of killing her first husband.

Laura saw little point in contradicting her. Everybody, including Lance, knew that Carol's first husband had fallen off the ferry to Dover after a tiring wine tasting trip to Calais, many years earlier.

The following day, Phil Sandfield and his sidekick Lizzie came to interview Laura. The young policewoman was a good deal more respectful than on their previous encounter.

"It's really down to you that we got our first lead," she admitted.

"Of course, we did have our suspicions," Phil said, in cheerful defence. "And I imagine we will be uncovering a good deal more. Did you happen to use any of her products, Lady Boxford?"

"No," Laura lied, "but what possible motive can she have had, I mean has she mentioned the paperweight?"

"The paperweight?" Lizzie looked at Phil.

"Such matters are part of the on-going investigation. Strictly confidential at the present time, but she'll get her day in court, her and her accomplice."

"Barry Pendleton? Have you arrested him?"

"How d'you know about him?" Lizzie asked.

"Barry? Oh it's nothing. Nurse Creightmore told me about her boyfriend some time ago."

"Right then," Phil said. "I think that's all we need to know for the present. I'm sure we needn't disturb you any longer. I've put one of our men on the front drive to keep those nosey reporters out. If there's anything else you think of, I've left instructions with Mr. Fincham of where I can be contacted."

"I don't suppose that Dr. Mellbury could have been in it with her?" Laura said, as the inspector and Lizzie reached the door.

They looked at one another. "It's been an emotional time for you, Lady Boxford," Phil said. "Have you thought about a holiday?"

John Fincham's office door was slightly ajar and Laura could hear a female voice.

"Really, Mr. Fincham, I can't understand your filing system at all and how you expect me to do the accounts, I do not know. This is not the way I'm used to working."

It wasn't the voice of his old secretary, Margaret. Laura knocked briefly and walked in.

John was sitting at his desk staring at his computer screen. He looked up at Laura. "Ah Lady B, good choice, most becoming if I may say so. It's an old maxim of mine; if you can't afford surgery, wear a decent necklace. Diverts the eye and gives the illusion of softening the lines."

Laura felt the jade around her neck and saw that the young woman standing at the filing cabinet had turned round and was looking at her. She was wearing a short black skirt and appeared to have lost her shoes.

"You haven't met my new secretary have you? Mandy, this is Lady Boxford. Wellworth Lawns used to be her home, so there's not a lot she doesn't know about the place."

The girl said hello and continued searching through the filing cabinet.

"Is Margaret ill?" Laura asked.

"Had to let her go," he said, lowering his gaze and shuffling the computer mouse about as if he were polishing the mat. "Work was getting on top of her. She was coming up to retirement."

"I'd have thought she might have said goodbye. I would have liked to thank her for all her work," Laura said. "Does Vince know?"

John turned to the secretary. "Leave that now, Mandy. Take the rest of the afternoon off. You can have another go at it in the morning."

The girl slammed the drawer shut and went over to her desk. She picked up her bag and then bent down and put on a pair of black high heels. "Have another go at it yourself. I can't deal with this."

"Thank you, Mandy, that will be all."

"I'm going to call the agency," she said, shutting the door behind her.

"Dear me," John said. "She's rather officious. Still, I'll soon get her into my way of thinking."

"Perhaps you should see if Vince could send his accountant down for a day or two to show her the ropes. I was going to ring Victoria later, I could ask her for you," Laura suggested.

"That will not be necessary, Lady Boxford. Now if you don't mind…"

"No no, but actually it was Tom Scott Hopkinson I wanted to talk to you about. Have you seen him with Dr. Mellbury recently?"

"What?"

"I suppose you've seen his new van?"

"Yes, very practical. He works hard."

"Are we paying him an awful lot? I mean, how much is he earning?"

"What's all this about, Lady Boxford? I really don't think you should concern yourself with such matters. I am the manager here and Mr. Outhwaite, Vince, has given me a free hand to run things as I see fit. Now, if there's nothing else, as you can well imagine, I've quite a lot on my plate at the moment, what with the police and all those reporters asking Alfredo leading questions."

"Have you told Vince about Nurse Creightmore?"

"Of course I have. He's fully apprised of the situation. I'm talking to his crisis management team later to formulate a damage limitation plan. Now if that's all?"

The three-ten at Wetherby was a dismal affair. "I'm glad I didn't put a bet on that," Laura said to Parker, as she turned down the volume to answer the phone.

It was Sally. "I tried to call you, but you were out," she said.

"Don't worry." Laura told her about Nurse Creightmore's arrest. "I'm sure the police have got it all wrong."

"I believe in female intuition," Sally said. "You must follow your instincts. Have you any other ideas?"

Laura told her of her suspicions about Tom's involvement. "I'm speculating, I know, but I can't very well go up to him and ask him where he got the money from, can I?"

"It's hard to know what's for the best," Sally said. "All you can do is keep an eye on him. But perhaps this might be of help, I found the name of the rehab clinic. As I thought, it was in an old diary of mine. I told Jervis, I hope you don't mind? We've emailed them."

"Stanley was only ever at the one place, wasn't he? You're happy about the date?"

"Not exactly, I said to Strudel I wasn't wheelchair averse as long as he didn't need lifting and I certainly didn't want to have to deal with any personal hygiene procedures…"

Laura wondered how easily people got distracted when it came to Ancient Eros.

"… Strudel's opted to postpone the rendezvous until she's made a more in depth survey of his condition."

"Not that date, I mean about the rehab place. He only went there once, didn't he?"

"Oh sorry. Yes, just the once. So, after a series of emails during which Jervis pretended to be Stanley's partner and said he wanted to have a surprise reunion for Stanley and all his fellow inmates to celebrate a decade of being clean, the clinic sent a list of all those who had been on the programme with him. All Jervis's idea."

"He's a wasted talent."

"He's going through the names one by one. He said he thought it would be quite simple to hack into a few personal details to find a multi-millionaire, ex-gambling addict, but the records don't show who was in for what addiction. The other problem is that, apart from Stanley, it appears they were all multi-millionaires. So it's going to take a little time, but Jervis is confident we'll find our man."

Feeling more positive about the situation, Laura turned up the volume on the TV. Parker jumped onto her lap and they watched a handicap hurdle. It was what Tony used to call an untidy race; the jockey's elbows flapping like ducks on takeoff as their sweat flecked mounts raced for the line.

"Oh Parker..." she sighed. She stroked the top of his soft head as she remembered the racehorse Tony had bought from Paddy Mulligan in Ireland. They'd named the mare Theresa Crowd. It was a private joke that only they and Paddy fully appreciated.

As she picked up the paper to study the form for the next race, she heard a knock. "Who can this be?" she said, walking over to open the door.

Inspector Sandfield greeted her.

"Hello again Phil," she said. *He's seen the light. Finally he might ask me some sensible questions.* "This is an unexpected surprise, twice in one day. Come in."

Phil Sandfield stepped into the room. He was followed by Lizzie. Behind them, lurking in the corridor, Laura could see a woman wearing a white coat. She was talking to Dr. Mellbury.

Chapter Twenty-two

D r. Mellbury closed the door behind them. Then he took a few steps into the room. The woman in the white coat followed him and now stood beside the mantlepiece. Her hair was tied back so severely that it accentuated not only her cheekbones but the very shape of her scull. It looked painful. She put on a pair of heavy black framed glasses and inspected a photograph of Laura and Tony taken in Capri. Laura's gaze jumped from person to person. Lizzie, stood against the door, her feet planted firmly apart. Inspector Sandfield swayed too and fro like an inexperienced sea captain caught in inclement conditions, his hands behind his back. His face was shiny and pale and he looked as if he may also have been suffering from sea-sickness.

"Are you ill?" Laura asked him.

"There's nothing wrong with the Inspector," Dr. Mellbury said. "It's you that's not well, Lady Boxford."

"Whatever can you mean?" Laura said. "I'm feeling as right as rain."

"Ah, that's what you think, but I'm afraid it is an incorrect assumption, unless of course you are referring to acid rain or some other sort of irregular precipitative occurrence. No, I am afraid it's a figment of your imagination that you are in good health. All part of the picture of clinical depression; suicidal tendencies; stark ravingness, believing you are a badger – call it what you will – that was revealed by the pathologist's report on your blood sample. Lady Boxford it is my duty to inform you that you are a danger to yourself and possibly others, and that is why Inspector Sandfield is here today to section you."

"Section me? Whatever are you talking about?" Laura turned to the inspector. "Phil, what's going on? Has the doctor lost his senses?"

"I'm afraid not. We have indeed come here to detain you."

"Detain me? What do you mean?"

"Under section two of the Mental Health Act. I do apologise."

Dr. Mellbury rounded on the inspector. "Don't apologise, man." He turned back to Laura. "You can come with us without restraint to the ambulance…"

His expression reminded Laura of a toad grown fat on slugs.

"… Or the WPC can go and fetch the strait jacket. It's up to you?"

"I… I simply don't understand what is going on here. And who, might I ask, is she?" Laura pointed to the woman in the white coat, who was still peering at the photograph. She looked round.

"Sorry, I should have introduced myself. I'm Cheryl Dixon. I'll be your psychiatrist."

"This is absurd."

"Look, she's not going to do a runner, is she?" Lizzie said, relinquishing her post by the door. "Why don't you sit down, Lady Boxford, and I'll explain the procedure."

Reluctantly, Laura sat back down on the sofa next to Parker. Lizzie took a chair beside her, as the others remained standing. She explained to Laura that she was being taken to the secure unit at Woldham hospital for an initial period of observation and possibly medication, because of her blood test results and her recent medical history. Lizzie said that there was no point refusing, because it was the law. She would be able to appoint a 'nearest relative' once the paperwork had been completed and she was safely installed in the unit.

"You'll probably only be there a day or two…"

"Depending on my report," Cheryl, the psychiatrist, piped up.

"Well, I'm sure it won't be long," Lizzie continued. "So you'll need an overnight bag, nightdress and a change of clothing. Oh and don't forget to pop in some slippers." She leaned forward smiling and patted Laura on the knee.

"Slippers?" Laura was in a state of shock. Everything around her had suddenly become blurred. She looked at Parker beside her and tried to focus. He licked her hand as she put it out to stroke him.

"Don't you worry yourself about the dog, Lady Boxford," Lizzie said.

"Parker?"

"Write that down could you, Inspector Sandfield? That's Parker with a 'P' is it, Lady Boxford? I've arranged for him to go to kennels the other side of Woldham."

"But he's never been to kennels before. He'll never cope. He must come with me."

"No dogs in the hospital, unless they're guide dogs," Cheryl said.

Dr. Mellbury looked at his watch. "Let's get this show on the road. I'm meant to be at the theatre this evening."

"Cool it, Doctor," Lizzie said. "Now, why don't you lot wait outside with the ambulance while I get Lady Boxford organised."

Lizzie helped Laura pack her case and they gathered Parker's food and bowl and put them in a bag with his blue furry lined bed. Laura became anxious about the bed as she knew he didn't really like it. In fact it was almost unused, since he was invariably on the sofa or in her bed. Lizzie suggested she put an item of her own clothing with it so that the dog could smell her. Laura chose an old cashmere jumper. She was about to put it in the bag when she had another thought. She opened up her case, took out the bottle of Chanel No5 and gave the cardigan a quick spray.

"That's a good idea, Lady Boxford," Lizzie said. "So now, if you're ready, shall we go down?"

Lizzie picked up the suitcase and Parker's possessions. She said that the dog was accompanying them in the ambulance as far as the hospital and then she would personally take him on to the kennels and make sure he was settled in.

By this time, Laura was beginning to look on the young PC as her only ally in the developing nightmare and she thanked her with the gratitude of one on the way to the gallows.

She put on her grey wool coat. Then she put Parker on his lead and they stepped out. Laura locked the door behind her and put the key into her handbag. As she looked up, she saw Venetia coming up the passage.

"Laura," she said, "I think my sunflowers are about to come through. I'm sure I saw the earth move. Will you come and see them?"

Squeezing her friend's arm, she said, "Later, I'm a bit tied up right now," and walked on towards the lift.

As luck would have it, there was nobody around in the hall to see the ignominious procession.

"That doesn't look much like an ambulance." Laura observed the black van parked outside in the driveway.

"It's a 'secure ambulance'," Lizzie explained, as Inspector Sandfield opened up the back and escorted Laura and Parker into the caged area she was to sit in.

"I'll come with you," Lizzie said and climbed in with the bags. "Honestly, all this must seem rather unnecessary but we have to follow the guidelines."

"Right, I'll meet you at the hospital," Dr. Mellbury said, as the inspector slammed the doors shut.

Chapter Twenty-three

Leaving Parker was a heart wrenching experience. Laura couldn't remember anything so bad. Far worse than when Tony ran off with the Thai masseuse – she'd known it wouldn't last – but now, as she sat in the reception area of Woldham hospital's secure unit, she realised that she had no idea when she would see the pug again.

Dr. Mellbury and the psychiatrist Cheryl, had disappeared and all she could do was wait while her 'responsible clinician', a round faced young woman who had introduced herself as Molly, gathered the paperwork.

"There we go," Molly said, putting the papers in a neat pile on the desk. "I've got your 'patient pathway' sorted out. It looks pretty straightforward. Dr. Mellbury has prescribed some medication for you while you are under observation and the psychiatrist will be formally assessing you tomorrow."

She got up and, taking a key from her pocket, opened the medicine trolley and began rattling pills into a small container. "Here we are," she said, picking up a jug of water and filling the plastic beaker on the desk. "You'll feel much calmer after you've taken these. They will settle you down." She handed Laura the pills and watched her as she dutifully swallowed them.

"Now, if you'd like to follow me, I'll show you where you'll be staying and then you can have a nice rest." Molly picked up the suitcase and

Laura followed her down a corridor, Molly's rubber soled shoes squeaking on the shiny surface of the floor. They rounded a corner into a ward with six bays. Walking past two sets of closed curtains on either side, they reached the end bay. Opposite, with her curtains open, sat a woman in a pair of man's blue striped pyjamas that reminded Laura briefly of the Brigadier. She had on her head a faded pink cloche hat that was pressed firmly down, hiding her features.

"Here you go," Molly said, putting down the case. She patted the pillow and smoothed the already pristine sheets.

Laura picked up her case and put it on the bed while Molly drew the curtains round her. Then she sat Laura down on the chair beside the bed and took her blood pressure.

As Laura rolled the sleeve of her cardigan back down, Molly said she would go and get some water while Laura made herself at home. "You can get into your nightwear if it makes you feel more comfortable," she said, closing the curtains behind her.

Laura looked at her watch. It was seven-thirty – far too early to go to bed. She unpacked as best she could, placing her nightie under the pillow and putting the rest of her things in the small cabinet on the other side of the bed. There was nowhere to hang her coat, so she left it on the back of the chair.

Molly reappeared with a jug of water and a plastic beaker. Laura was about to ask if there wasn't something stronger but she suddenly felt very tired.

"I've sent down for a sandwich as you've missed dinner this evening, I'm afraid," Molly said. "You can order your meals for tomorrow though. I've brought the menus for you to fill in. We can decide who you'd like to choose as your 'nearest relative' in the morning."

Laura concentrated on Molly's comforting blue eyes.

"That person can then do what extra shopping you need. Chocolate biscuits are what most people want."

"My 'nearest relative'?" Laura said, struggling with the arm of her cardigan – it was getting very warm.

"That's it." Molly's tender smile radiated affection. "You're allowed to communicate with one relative or friend. You can ring them in the morning and tell them all about it."

Laura thought that Molly was the loveliest person she had ever met. "How wonderful," she said, as she lay down on the bed and fell into a deep sleep.

The next thing she remembered was being woken up and given some more pills. Someone walked her to the washroom and a little later breakfast arrived. The tea was delicious, and the scrambled egg brought back wonderful memories of post-war rationing. She took a bite of toast. How unusual to have white bread so lightly browned, and margarine. *I haven't had margarine since heaven knows when. What a treat it all is.* "Isn't this heavenly!" she said to no one in particular.

"They've got you on the right medication then," came a deep voice from nearby. Once Laura had focused her eyes, she recognised the woman in the pyjamas and pink cloche hat in the opposite bay.

"Mind you, you have to be careful or the nurses turn into herons and try to eat you."

"Really?" Laura said.

"Yes. It's one of the down sides to being an old trout. Have you seen the mayfly this year? I'll be fat as anything if they continue swarming like this." She swatted the air with one hand and made gulping movements with her mouth.

While Laura took in this spectacle, she heard muttering to her left. At first it was indecipherable, but gradually the words became clearer and formed a sort of jaunty rhythm: "Flat cap black cap, mutton roasting."

It was rather like listening to the caller at a hoedown.

"Woolly back wig. Shearing high. Court gown gone, going down."

"Ey up, the judge is awake," the cloche hatted woman said.

Laura looked round to see from where this stream of consciousness had come. The curtains of the bay beside her had been opened. The 'judge' in the bed had plainly exhausted herself with her verbal dance and was lying with her head on the pillow, her eyes closed, a mass of frizzy dark grey hair spraying out from her face like a gigantic wire wool pan scourer.

Once upon a time this apparition might have startled me, Laura thought, *but now all I see is a serene and lovely angel floating down from heaven.* She wondered briefly if the woman had met Tony on her intergalactic travels before she fell asleep again.

Sometime later Molly arrived. "Morning," she called cheerily to Laura. "Shall we think about your, 'nearest relative' now. Then I can go and get the phone."

"I don't think I need bother anyone," Laura said. "I'm perfectly all right. I've got everything I need."

"But you have to have someone. Shall I look in your bag and see if I can find a name or something? Have you an address book?"

"I'm not sure. You can look if you like." Laura waved her hand about in the vague direction of where she thought her handbag might be.

Molly went through the bag but said she could find nothing.

"You could ring my home, I suppose," Laura said.

"That's a good idea. You're Wellworth Lawns aren't you? We had Mrs. Huxley here not so long ago."

"Dearest Harriet." Laura knew it wasn't quite right but she could feel a smile enveloping her face.

"So I'll do that," Molly said. "I'm sure someone there will be able to help. Oh look, here comes Professor Dixon. She'll be wanting to see how you are."

"Good morning," Cheryl said. "You can leave us to it, thank you Molly."

Cheryl Dixon sat on the chair beside the bed and took out a sheaf of papers and a pen from her briefcase. She did not look nearly so stern as Laura had remembered. Her features were softer, less cadaverous.

Cheryl put on her glasses and looked at her notes. "So you believe you are a badger?" She stared at Laura. "Are you afraid of dying?"

"Oh no," Laura said. "Most definitely not, although it's so nice here, I should be sad to leave. Do you think I am dying?"

"Well obviously we are all dying." Cheryl made a tick on the top piece of paper and then turned it over. "It's a question of when. So you haven't had any suicidal feelings this morning?"

"Gracious me, no."

Cheryl made another tick and turned to the next sheet of paper. "And if you did, what do you think your preferred method would be?"

Laura gazed at the psychiatrist. There was something almost familiar about the dark scraped back hair and black framed glasses. She'd had the same fleeting thought the day before as Cheryl had held the photograph of Tony and herself. What was it?

Cheryl coughed and pushed the glasses further up her nose.

That's it, the glasses, Laura thought. The Egyptian Prince. Granted, his were darkened and he wore a headdress, but the similarity was there. They had met him in the hotel in Chantilly that year. She and Tony had gone over to France to look at a racehorse Tony was thinking of buying. The Prince had taken them out to dinner in his chauffeur driven car. He'd ordered quantities of champagne and oysters and later, my, what a time the three of them had had! Laura could feel another grin spreading across her face.

"Shall I put it another way?" Cheryl asked.

"Sorry, I've forgotten what the question was."

"Your preferred method of suicide."

"Ah. I think gluttony would suit me. Yes, over-eating. Can we put that down?"

"It's not on the form. I think for the purposes of this initial appraisal, we should stick to the approved list. Would you like me to read it out? We've got overdose, slit wrists, suffocation, shot-gun, jumping from heights…"

"I'll take that." Laura lay back on her pillows as the memory of the Prince wafted around in her head.

"Bridge? Into water? Brick or other heavy object attached? Suitcase of small change is popular…"

"Mmmm?"

Cheryl sighed. "High rise building?"

Suddenly Laura was in Cairo. It was evening in the Prince's palace and a hot dry breeze skimmed over her as she and Tony lay on the roof terrace. They turned simultaneously and smiled as they heard the click of the door. "Ohh," she sighed.

"Let's try a different tack. What about getting yourself somehow run over? Or culled? Or injected with TB? That could be another possibility."

"I'm not sure I'm keeping up with this," Laura mumbled as the Prince unwrapped the kufiya around his head, tossed it onto the floor and began to undo the buttons of his flowing robes.

"I think we'll call it a day for now," Cheryl said. "I'll be back to see you on Thursday."

Laura had no idea what day it was but it didn't seem to be of the slightest importance and she closed her eyes.

Sometime after the psychiatrist had gone, Molly returned and helped Laura get dressed – Laura looked down at her nightie and wondered how she had got into it – and then she sat in her chair until the most delicious lunch of brown stuff and potato arrived with some more pills. The curtains next to her had been closed again. She heard a male voice. "Open up, your honour, come on now." Laura supposed that, for the sake of propriety, the judge was being fed behind them. After a while, during which time some grunting had taken place, the nurse drew back the curtains. The judge was fast asleep and the ward was quiet. It was all too comforting and Laura dozed off again and dreamed of being a bubbling wavelet on a desert island, gently swooshing back and forth in time with the tide as it lapped onto the sandy beach.

All too soon, Molly was back. She invited Laura to join in with the afternoon's activity group.

"It's called a 'care spell'," she explained. "I think you're going to weave a waste paper bin."

"How thrilling." Laura had a faint feeling that her words had not come out as she had intended. It reminded her of an old record on the gramophone that had been put on at the wrong speed... Too slowly? But Molly smiled sweetly at her and took her arm as she got up from her chair. Then Laura followed the jaunty rounded derriere undulating beneath the uniform as the nurse walked down the corridor.

There were five other patients in the activity room. Mrs. Cloche Hat was there.

"You've met Francine, haven't you?" Molly said to Laura. The two women smiled at one another and nodded. Sitting next to Francine was a young woman with long, jet black hair who Laura had seen briefly coming out of the washroom. Molly introduced her as Celestia.

There were three other patients, all male, who Molly explained had been asked to join in from the men's ward. They were sitting quietly watching as the teacher demonstrated what she wanted them to do with the pile of rushes and sticks at her feet.

"Are they dry?" One of the men said, looking agitated.

The teacher looked over to the assistant – another bright young girl in her hospital uniform – who was in charge of the men.

"Yes they're quite dry," the assistant said and turned to the teacher. "Len was late for his medication. He'll be fine presently."

Laura looked at Molly.

"He's got a thing about water," she whispered. "He can't come in contact with it in case it washes away his DNA and he doesn't know who he is."

"Oh dear, poor soul," Laura said. "Shall we go and comfort him?"

"No. It's a common phobia. He'll be fine, but please don't ask for anything to drink."

The teacher handed out the sticks. Then she gave them all a circle of plywood with holes punched around the edge. They were to push the sticks into the holes to form the base of the waste paper basket.

When they had accomplished this, the teacher demonstrated how to weave the rushes.

"In and out you see," she said. "Keep the tension nice and even."

"Jaw, jaw jaw." It was a young man. *I wonder if he has tooth ache?* Laura thought.

"That's enough James," the teacher said.

"But I've already made six."

"Should've kept taking the tablets," said the man with aquaphobia.

"Shut it, you nutter," James said.

"Who are you calling a nutter, you schizoid?"

"D'you want a bath?" James said.

"Noooo." The man jumped up from his chair and rushed for the door, hotly pursued by the assistant.

"Now look what you've done, James," the teacher waggled a finger at him.

"I'd love a bath," Francine said. "I can feel my gills constricting and my fins are going all scaley and these rushes are reminding me of the river bank..." She began to gurgle. "Do you mind if I go and take a shower? I can feel a spate coming on."

She too left the room while the rest of them sat quietly weaving.

Laura had managed to get a third of the way up her basket when the teacher said it was time to stop. She took out a marker pen and wrote their names on the bases of the baskets before collecting them up and throwing them into a corner of the room.

"Come on Celestia and Laura," Molly said. "Let's go and get a nice cup of tea."

They followed her back to the ward.

"D'you think you could weave a noose?" Celestia asked.

Molly looked at her watch. "Like clockwork you are," she said. "I'll get your medication right away. Laura, I think we'd better top you up as well. Professor Dixon said she found some of your answers to her questions disturbing and we want to knock that on the head, don't we?"

"D'you want to end it all too?" Celestia's impenetrable expression seemed to brighten.

"No," Laura said. "I'm looking forward to finishing my basket. I need a new one. I always seem to have such a lot of waste paper to throw away."

"Waste. A waste of space, that's what I am. " Celestia had arrived at her bed; it was on the other side of the ward to Laura's, opposite the judge. "A waste product of society." She sat down and stared at the curtain.

Laura sat with her while they had their tea and medication. The curtains round the judge had been opened again but she was still fast asleep.

Feeling drowsy herself, Laura went and lay on the empty bed next to Celestia and from there they chatted. As they drifted in and out of consciousness, Celestia told her story. It was clear Celestia was feeling the full effect of her medication's calming influence. Laura too, was as high as a kite on a cocktail of valium and a new product hot out of a drug company lab that Cheryl, despite Molly's questioning look, was keen to try out.

Waking and sleeping fitfully, they resumed the conversation as the afternoon wore on. The girl had had a series of unhappy love affairs that had led to her finding herself in her present slough of despond.

"My mum ran away with a man she met on holiday in Cornwall when I was twelve," she said.

Celestia had travelled back alone with her father, who had confessed as they drove up the M5 that he was gay and would Celestia mind calling the next door neighbour, Morris, Mum from now on.

"I didn't mind that so much but Morris, I mean Mum, started wearing all my real Mum's clothes. It was when I found him in the kitchen cooking steak and kidney pudding in her wedding dress that I had my first suicidal feelings."

"How old were you then?" Laura asked.

"Thirteen."

Laura got off the bed and clasped Celestia. "You poor darling," she said. "You must come and stay with me."

Tears of joy poured down Celestia's face. "I've never had a proper Gran," she said.

"You haven't got a pond you could take me home to?" Francine said from where she had been listening in the next bed.

"How do you get along with carp?" Laura asked.

As suppertime drew near, Laura began to feel a little more energised. She suggested to the others that they play a game. She was reminded of being in the sick room at boarding school when there had been a minor measles epidemic and she and a few other girls were kept in the darkened room for days on end, their hands bandaged so they couldn't scratch their faces. They had resorted to long sessions of I Spy.

Francine was rather slow to grasp the concept and Laura reminded her more than once when she and Celestia drew a blank after much fruitless guessing, that the object had to actually exist in the room.

"You see," she said, "there aren't any kingfishers in the ward."

"Yes there are," Francine replied, pointing to a nurse who had arrived to take the judge's pulse. As the nurse took her wrist, the woman sat up, her frizzy hair rampant about her head.

"Sheep shed doors of life and burning hillside. Twenty years. Foot rot gumboots sliding. Lamb... Bananas... Liquid... Cosh." She fell backwards onto her pillows.

"It's all right, your honour," the nurse said. "I'll give you your injection in a jiffy."

It was hard to know if the judge had taken this in, as she appeared to be asleep again.

"What's wrong with her?" Laura asked.

"She either thinks she's a Welsh hill farmer or she's in a coma. Occasionally she thinks she's delivered the death sentence." Francine eased the cloche hat from her forehead. "Your go, Celestia."

Celestia looked around. "I spy with my little eye... something beginning with..." Celestia looked down at her wrist. "W. And I want a knife."

"Oh dear," Laura said. "I thought you were feeling better?"

Celestia began to cry.

"Hold on," the nurse said. "I've got your pills. Let me just finish with the judge here."

Laura returned to her own bed and they were all peaceful by the time the supper arrived. She lifted the plastic lid from her plate and found a piece of white fish swimming in a thin yellow sauce. The fish was marbled brown and a dollop of grey mashed potato and a carrot sat next to it.

"Mmm, cod in cheese sauce. My favourite."

"You sure know how to hurt a person's feelings," Francine said. "You could have chosen macaroni cheese if you'd had any sensitivity about you."

"What's that Francine?" Laura said.

"Fish. It could have been a relative of mine."

"I'm so sorry," Laura said, guiltily bolting down the last mouthful.

Molly came in to see how they were after supper. She told Laura she had contacted Wellworth Lawns and John Fincham had finally returned her call, suggesting that Laura might care to choose her granddaughter as her 'nearest relative'. He had given Molly Victoria's number.

"Shall we ring her?" Molly asked.

Chapter Twenty-four

Victoria arrived the next morning. She appeared to have had no trouble getting in and marched through the ward with the confidence of one married to a very rich man.

"Granny," she said, hugging Laura who was still in her nightie at eleven o'clock. "We're going to get you out of here. I've got a meeting with the psychiatrist in ten minutes. You get dressed and I'll come and collect you when I'm done. I shouldn't be long. Vince has got his lawyers primed in any case. They say Dr. Mellbury hasn't got a leg to stand on and they've issued a notice of malpractice to the Medical Board. I left Vince in Leeds drafting a letter to The Lancet."

"But darling, I'm quite happy here and I haven't finished my waste paper basket." Laura felt a drip of saliva seep out of the corner of her mouth and run down her chin. She reached for the tissues on the bedside cabinet but somehow missed and ended up knocking over the jug of water.

"What have they got you on?" Victoria looked horrified and shouted for someone to come and dry the floor.

A man appeared with a mop and bucket and, when he had finished, Victoria said she had to go or she would miss the psychiatrist.

"Now don't forget, Granny, start to get dressed so you're ready to go when I get back."

"You can't leave us," Celestia said, when Victoria had gone.

Francine's trout lips sagged. "I thought you were taking me to that carp pond of yours."

"Sleeping lemmings. Shooting sheep, probation, custody. Gabriel Oak... Life term."

"She seems a bit better," Francine said.

"Perhaps she will have to come too?" Laura looked at the judge, but she was asleep again. "Oh dear. I will talk to my granddaughter and see what she can fix up."

"We'll wait," Celestia said.

"We haven't any option." Francine sighed and gobbled an imaginary mayfly.

"Shall we have a little nap?" Laura suggested.

She was chatting to the wavelets beside her as they eddied back and forth. One wavelet was called Spume and he was telling her about a sometimes bumptious cousin of his called Spindrift who liked nothing more than acting the white horse in rough weather.

"Personally I'm a laid back sort of a wavelet. I don't see the point of crashing about spraying salt everywhere. Fancy a spot of nude sunbathing?" he said.

"Mmm. Lovely..."

"Granny?"

"Mmm..."

"Granny!"

Laura was not sure where Victoria had come from and asked her if she had been washed up too.

"Washed up? What are you talking about? Get a grip, Granny."

Laura felt her neck lazily with one hand and opened her eyes. Victoria was still talking.

"I've spoken to the psychiatrist," she said. "What a woman. She was under the impression you were on the verge of suicide. How she got that idea, I do not know. Luckily your carer, Molly, was there, otherwise I think you might have been in here, drugged up to the eyeballs, for heaven knows how long. Anyway, Molly didn't think there was much wrong with you and, providing you can walk unaided, they agreed I can take you home. They've printed out a care plan but I don't think there'll be any need for that. A few decent meals and you'll be quite yourself again."

"But the food is so good here. The most delicious Cod Mornay."

"We'll get Alfredo to make you a bowl of his zuppa di pesce. You know how much you like that."

"Oh no, I remember, I couldn't possibly eat fish. It would upset my friend Francine. She's a trout, you know."

"Granny, stop being silly."

"But I'm happy here with all my new friends."

"I'm sure they're very nice but they're here for a reason. Now come on, you'll soon forget all about this unfortunate episode."

"And my waste paper basket... I'm making it you know."

"I'm sure we can get Molly to have it sent on."

"But..."

"I've rung the kennels. We've got to collect Parker by one-thirty, or they close."

"Parker?" Laura felt a sense of urgency fight its way through the haze.

"You wouldn't want him in there for any longer than necessary, would you?"

"Parker?" Laura raised herself up from the bed. Her limbs felt heavy and her brain like porridge. "You'll have to help me," she said.

Victoria called for a nurse and, between them, they managed to get Laura dressed and packed.

The others were still sleeping as they tottered out of the ward, Laura clinging onto Victoria, the nurse following with Laura's coat and case.

"Oh dear, I do feel bad not saying goodbye. I'll have to see how I can get hold of them..."

"Plenty of time for that once we've got you home," Victoria said, as they got to the door and waited for the nurse to unlock it.

Laura started to fumble in her bag.

"Granny what are you doing," Victoria asked.

"My purse. I must leave a tip."

"It's not a hotel."

"Oh." Laura felt a gust on her face as fresh air whooshed up the corridor. It had the effect of waking her from her semi-trance like state. "Where are we?" she asked.

"Woldham Hospital, Granny. Christ, they've managed to institutionalise you in less than forty-eight hours. I don't know what Vince is going to say about this."

Victoria left Laura sitting on a bench and went to get her car. When she returned, Laura was feeling a little stronger and, with Victoria's help, she managed to get in and they drove to the kennels.

Parker rushed yelping to the car, his lead fully extended; Victoria some yards behind. She caught up and lifted him onto Laura's lap. He couldn't decide whether to whine or yap or lick her face, so he did all three standing with his front feet on Laura's chest, his curly tail wagging furiously so that he almost unbalanced himself.

"Parker." Laura stroked his head. Her wet face felt like it had been crawled over by a snail, but the tightening, like a drying face pack, had the effect of focusing her mind further. "I feel as if I'm coming round from an operation," she said. "Did I have one?"

"No, but they may as well have given you an anaesthetic, the amount of drugs they'd got you on. Honestly, Granny, how did you let them, and anyway what on earth gave Dr. Mellbury the idea that you wanted to take your own life in the first place?"

Laura felt too exhausted to explain and she, like Parker, dosed off with a sense of relief that both had escaped a fate depriving them of their liberty.

Victoria woke her as they drove up the beech-lined avenue to Swinley Court, the hotel in the next-door village to Wellworth Lawns. Victoria had booked her usual suite and another interconnecting room for Laura.

"Just for a few days," she explained. "So that you can fully recuperate and we can get to the bottom of this."

The manager welcomed them in and showed Laura to her room.

"I think my grandmother would like to rest now," Victoria said. The manager backed out silently over the thick pile carpet.

Laura lay down on the bed with Parker by her side.

"I'll get his stuff out of the car," Victoria said. "And then I'll pop over to Wellworth and collect some things for you."

"You are a dear," Laura said. "I know I've been such a nuisance. Old people are a liability, I'm afraid."

"Don't be silly, Granny. It's not your fault. I've called Vince. He's arriving in time for dinner. He's going to see John Fincham in the morning and have it out with him about Mellbury. They may have to change the practice that looks after the Wellworth residents."

Laura gulped and felt her mouth go dry.

It was not until lunchtime the next day that they all got together in the dining room.

The head waiter was flustering around Vince, offering him the wine list and flapping a huge white linen napkin over Vince's knees as Laura and Victoria joined him.

"We'll have the Chablis," Vince said. He looked up. "Oi, oi, oi, who've we got here then, flower?" He rose and welcomed Laura, kissing her on both cheeks.

The waiter pulled back a chair for Laura, tucked her in and then went to fetch the wine.

"So this is a right pickle you've got yerself in." Vince laughed. "I've spent all morning getting that Fincham to take heed of what I'm saying and I'm still not sure he's got the picture."

"What picture is that, Vince dearest?" Laura asked feeling herself redden.

"Oh, Granny," Victoria said, "John seems to be reluctant to fire Dr. Mellbury. For some odd reason, he thinks you were genuinely ill."

The waiter arrived with the wine. He poured a little into Vince's glass and took a small step back to await approval. Vince nodded and the waiter filled their glasses.

"I mean, the very idea our Laura here could have gone soft in the head is absolutely daft. Doesn't know his arse from his elbow that man Fincham." Vince took a hefty slug of Chablis. "For the life of me I can't understand why I employed him."

Laura felt herself redden again and took a sip of wine. "I'm afraid I have a confession to make," she said.

It took most of lunch for Laura to explain how she had managed to get herself sectioned under the Mental Health Act.

"So let me get this straight…" Vince wiped his mouth with the napkin. "You told the doctor you were feeling suicidal, made him believe you were out of your mind, because you thought he'd murdered your old chum Hetty, even though this nurse has been arrested for it."

"That's it in a nutshell, but it's because I don't believe Nurse Creightmore did it."

"So you don't go along with Inspector Sandfield, with all his years of expertise behind him?"

"Vince dearest, don't be beastly to Granny."

"I am not being 'beastly' to yer gran, but I've come down in t'helicopter to sort this out and now's I've got here, it seems yer gran's brought it on herself and I'm the one with the ruddy great dollop of ketchup on me face."

"'Egg' dearest, you're getting upset, and 'my'."

"Flippin 'eck Victoria, when I say ketchup I mean ketchup and I don't need an elocution lesson now."

"You know it only goes to pot if you get in a state." Victoria jumped up from the table and nuzzled Vince's neck.

His face lit up. "Oh what the 'eck. You're absolutely right as usual."

"So you can go back this afternoon and straighten things out. John hasn't spoken to the doctor yet, has he?" Victoria asked

"No. I'll tell 'im…"

"Tell him I did lose my marbles, temporarily, but I'm all right now." Laura felt it was the least she could do.

"Perfect." Victoria clapped her hands together. "Say she's made a complete recovery, marbles all back in place and she promises not to get into any more trouble."

"And you'll knock this detectivising on the head?"

"Oh Vince, you're doing it again. Poor Granny, she's only recently lost her oldest friend and there you are like a bull in a china shop making the most inappropriate analogies."

"I only said she should… Oh I give up. Humble apologies, flower."

"No no, Vince. It is I who should apologise for causing so much work for everybody. I promise I shan't get into any more scrapes."

They ordered coffee and Victoria made some suggestions as to how she and Laura might spend the rest of the afternoon.

"We could take Parker to the arboretum; he'd like that, wouldn't he?"

"That's a lovely idea. He needs a treat after the terrible time he's had." Laura bent down to pat him.

"That's right, you two ladies go and amuse yourselves while I…"

"Don't start again Vince dearest."

"No, it wasn't that pet. It's the fact that Fincham's got himself in a muddle with the VAT. The last lot of figures he sent were all over the shop. I was going to read the riot act at 'im but now…"

Laura blushed again.

"Oh Vince! You've done it again. Upset Granny for no reason. How could you?"

"I give up," he said. "Anyone for a brandy?"

Chapter Twenty-five

As Victoria drove down the windy lanes to Wellworth Lawns, Laura assured her that she would drop her role as investigator and leave the matter of Hetty's death to the police. Victoria suggested she tell her friends that she had been away on a short break with her and Vince all the time.

"Try to be pleasant if you come across the doctor. I've had a word with him and he said he's happy to draw a line under the episode," Victoria said. "And, after all, he was only acting in your best interest."

Laura declined to question Victoria on this. It seemed ungrateful to disagree. She waved from the steps outside the front door as Victoria drove away, then turned to Parker. "Smacked wrists, eh? I suppose I was rather a naughty girl pretending to be ill, and he did say I had something wrong with my blood." Laura thought about this a moment longer. Dr Mellbury had never said exactly what it was that the tests had shown.

"But I feel bad about my nice new friends from hospital. You would have liked them." She patted Parker as they waited for the lift. How they would have fitted in at Wellworth Lawns, she wasn't sure. "Perhaps I'd be better off writing a letter to someone or other about them," she said, as Parker stared up at her, his head to one side.

*

Mimi brought Laura up a cup of tea as she was watching the racing from Haydock.

"You having nice holiday?" she asked. "Me, Tom going London time this weekend. Him taking me Hyde Park Hotel for earwaxing."

"Earwaxing?"

"Yes, you knowing. Take it easy time."

"You mean *re*laxing."

"Yes, earwaxing."

"But how…" Laura bit her lip. She was desperate to probe further but it had only been a couple of hours since she'd promised Victoria that she would stay out of trouble… still it didn't seem right. "How can Tom afford it?" she asked.

"Tom making many money. New business in old people home Chippington way. Him employing many staffs."

"Shouldn't he be saving his money?"

"I saying that, but Tom mother very rich lady. She want him go Oxford after Etoncoll. Tom say he want be plumber, no lawyer, so they no speak many time. But now she nice again and giving Tom plenty money." Mimi giggled and touched Laura's forearm. "Minding you, Tom no tell her he going out with Bulgarian girl. We thinking get married but not want her change mind." Mimi sucked in her lips and pretended to fan her face.

"How lovely, but you know what they say: the course of true love never runs smooth."

Mimi looked puzzled and asked if there was anything else she needed.

Laura felt stupid. "Wrong again, Parker. How could I have ever suspected Tom? I think Dr. Mellbury might have been right all along. I'm two sandwiches short of a picnic and probably a slice of quiche as well." She finished her tea and, after a while, felt strong enough to check her phone messages.

One was from the Brigadier asking where she was. There was another from Sally and another from Strudel asking if she was going to the raffle in aid of the Air Ambulance and the Horticultural Society that evening. Much as Laura loathed the idea of it, the raffle would keep her busy and, more importantly, out of trouble. Laura rang her.

"But where have you been? I had such a nice gentleman all lined up for you. Unfortunately, he became too impatient and now he is going out with someone else," Strudel said.

Laura did as Victoria had suggested and told Strudel she had been with her granddaughter at Swinley Court. They agreed to meet at the raffle. She put down the phone and decided to walk next door and see if Venetia was going.

Venetia's chair was stuck in dentist mode again and she was gazing at the ceiling.

"Thank heavens you're here, Laura. It won't come down. Where have you been?"

Laura hurried over and pressed the button on the side. The chair lurched itself into an upright position.

"How long have you been like that?" she asked.

"I'm not sure." Venetia felt her mouth. "But I would never have kept my teeth in overnight. No, now I remember, I went to look at my sunflower pots and then I came here for a sit down, but I can't remember when that was. Have you seen them? They're sprouting!"

Laura looked over at the window ledge. The sun was shining in and Laura was reminded of Hetty's paperweights. Now the space was taken up by cardboard pots of a size suitable for a radish. The nascent sunflower seedlings looked as if they might boomerang out at any moment scattering the small amount of drying compost that surrounded them. "You may need to pot them on," she suggested.

"Do you think they will be ready in time for the plant sale?"

Laura thought it doubtful and changed the subject. "There's a raffle in aid of the air ambulance this evening. Are you going?"

"Oh yes. I knew there was something I was looking forward to."

*

The recreation room was alive with the merry chatter of elderly folk clanking around on Zimmer frames and walking sticks.

Laura and Venetia bought raffle tickets and made their way past a table laden with tinned cans, other sundry items and half a dozen crocheted ballerina dolls dressed in pastel shades of lace.

"Gladys Freemantle has been busy with her loo roll holders," Laura remarked, picking up one of the dolls. Venetia was too busy eyeing a jar of home made chutney to take heed. Laura looked round and saw John Fincham talking to Dr. Mellbury behind a makeshift bar festooned with plastic flowers and helicopter pictures.

"Hello there, Lady Boxford. You're looking better." The doctor, swaying slightly, raised his glass.

Laura nearly walked away but Venetia was pulling at her arm. "Have you been ill?" she said.

"No," Laura whispered, "I've no idea what he's talking about." And to the doctor, ignoring his comment, "Evening, Doctor. Not here in your official capacity, I hope?"

"Purely social, I'm reading out the winning tickets."

"I wouldn't bank on that," John said. "Look, isn't that Marjory Playfair?" They turned in the direction of John's gaze. A couple of women were heaving a body off the floor.

"They seem to have the situation under control," the doctor said. "What's yours, Lady Boxford? Mrs. Hobbs?"

"No, please, let me buy you two a drink. It's all in a good cause." Laura got out her purse.

"Very generous, Lady B." John swilled his quarter-filled pint glass around. "I'll have a half. As you say, it's in a good cause. The air ambulance was so efficient when Dolly Burridge got trapped in the manhole."

"I'll have another glass of red, if you insist." Doctor Mellbury clutched the bar with one hand.

As John poured the drinks and handed them out, a strange looking man with a beard came up to the bar and ordered a whisky.

"Take it easy, Dad," Dr. Mellbury said.

"Pot calling kettle?" the man said.

Laura was about to ask for an introduction when they were interrupted. It was Gladys Freemantle. "I'm sorry, Doctor," she said. "But you'll have to come. Marjory is definitely dead."

Dead? Marjory Playfair had been renowned for her skills at the annual Wellworth tug-of-war. Laura checked the Doctor's expression.

He was unfazed.

Could he be employing new tactics? Some sort of delayed action drug so that he was distanced from suspicion. Laura recalled the calamitous efficacy of the hospital medication.

"That's rather bad timing," the doctor said. "Still, I told her to take it easy after the bypass surgery. She would insist on having her hips done at the same time. Not a clever idea when you're ninety three."

Laura watched as he followed Gladys unsteadily across the room. *I must call a halt to these silly fantasies now, before I really do go round the bend.*

"Never a dull moment," John said. Turning to Laura, he wiped a fleck of froth from the side of his mouth with a handkerchief. "Most becoming jumper you've got there, Lady B. The polo neck will hide a multitude of sins. Bane of my life for thyroid work, mind you." He turned back to serve another customer.

Venetia was asking if there was time to go to the ladies before the raffle, when Gladys Freemantle's voice boomed out:

"Ladies and Gentlemen, your attention please. Sadly, Marjory Playfair has just passed away, but I know she would not have wanted to spoil our evening and she will be with us, at least in spirit till the ambulance gets here. So, Doctor Mellbury has agreed to go ahead with the draw."

Laura stayed by the bar as Venetia joined the clamour round the table. She could see Jervis and Strudel standing with Bob and Dora Whale on the other side of the room near the door and then she saw the Brigadier walk up and join them.

The doctor stuffed his hand into the bucket Gladys Freemantle was holding and drew out a scrumple of paper. Opening it out, he couldn't resist reverting to his Bingo techniques. "Knocked knees…"

There was a hushed silence.

"…Double threes. And the prize is…" He picked up one of the loo roll dolls. "This." He inspected it, lifting up the lacy skirt.

"Don't be cheeky, Doctor," Gladys wheezed smacking him on the wrist. "I made that."

"Whoa, Gladys, and very charming it is too." He handed it to the winner and took another number from the bucket. "Pressure sore, number four."

'Oohs' and 'aahs' greeted the lucky recipients. Laura found herself the owner of a pair of gardening gloves and even Venetia won a plastic bird nut feeder. Then, from behind the table, Doctor Mellbury called out, "Barely alive… One hundred and five." He picked up a can of frankfurters in tomato sauce. "I say, that's me," he announced.

The grand finale was a large box of Milk Tray.

"Mine I think," called John from behind the bar. He hurried up to the table with such indecent haste that a couple of people were inadvertently thrown together. It could have ended as a stack of dominos but disaster was averted by Bob Whale's bulky frame, so that the effect was more one of a Mexican wave.

"Thank you, thank you," John said, holding up the box of chocolates. Everybody cheered.

"No, really," he said. "This has been a marvellous evening and, yet again, a wonderful effort by all concerned."

More cheering and then a hush as John beckoned for quiet.

"And now," he said, "I have an announcement to make."

All eyes were on him.

"It is my sad duty to have to tell you that soon I shall no longer be with you."

A collective gasp.

"Don't worry, I'm not ill."

Relieved laughter.

"No, the truth of the matter is, that for some time now, I have felt the need to be nearer my dear mother in Brazil, and so it is with great sadness that I will be bidding you all farewell as I go to take up the new post that I have been offered, running a care facility in Rio."

"Do they get to be old in Rio?" Bob Whale called out.

"Actually it is an orphanage."

"Good on you!" Bob Whale put his hands together and the room filled with clapping and cheering.

"We'll miss you," Gladys Freemantle cried out and this was followed by "hear, hear," from all around her.

John thanked them all for their support. "But don't worry, I haven't gone yet. I'll be with you for a while longer."

Laura felt a tap on her shoulder. "There you are," Strudel said. "You are becoming most elusive. But I am envious of your stay at Swinley Court."

"Swinley Court? Swanky Court I'd say." It was Jervis. "Shall we go and have some supper. Bob and Dora are saving us a table and Arthur's joining us."

"Arthur?"

"The Brigadier, silly." Strudel nudged her and laughed. "Had you again forgotten?"

"Of course I hadn't, it was just that… I wasn't sure that there'd be room, I'm with Venetia you see." Laura looked round and saw Venetia chatting to the life sized cut-out photo of a member of the air ambulance crew.

"Of course there'll be room," Jervis said. "Venetia doesn't take up much space, does she?"

"No but Bob Whale does."

"Well, we'll have to squeeze up. Cosy. Mmmm."

"Jervis please."

"I'll go and get her," Laura said.

By the time she returned with Venetia, the rest of the table were seated. The Brigadier was at the far end sitting next to Strudel.

The conversation at dinner centred round John's announcement. Everyone agreed he had done a good job and that his enthusiastic approach to in-house entertainment would be missed.

Then Strudel said she had breaking news from Ancient Eros. There was to be a wedding. An octogenarian gentleman from Woking who had signed up through the website had become engaged to a cousin of Strudel's in Bavaria.

"How ever did they meet?" Dora Whale asked.

"Helga is going to stay with a friend she has in London and from there the train she took." Strudel was puffed up with pride.

"Silly moo fell off the platform and was in Woking General for six weeks with a broken pelvis, ankles, wrists… You name it, Helga broke it." Jervis laughed.

"That's as maybe, my love, but the accident had the effect desired and the two of them are to be wed in the registry office of Woking on this coming Saturday. Jervis and I are to be present."

"That is a result, I must say," the Brigadier piped up.

"Oh, don't you worry, Arthur. I have not given up on you. We will be mating you up any day now with a new partner."

Laura sat quietly. So, the Brigadier was still at it. *And what a lot of idiotic banter, and how soon people forget.* "Fading mem'ree, eighty three," as the odious doctor had said.

Chapter Twenty-six

"Wanting croissant, Ladysheep?" Mimi whispered, placing a basket of pastries in front of Laura. There was a hushed air in the dining room, broken only by the occasional hum of a passing mobility scooter. Laura asked Mimi what was going on.

"Oooh Ladysheep, you not hearing? Mrs. Huckle dead last night time."

"Mrs. Huxley?" Laura felt an unnerving sense of exhilaration. Harriet, dead… Had the Doctor struck again – twice in one night?

"What happened?" she asked.

"She falling out her window." Mimi shook her head and sighed. "Her landing in the car park. Coffee?"

Laura gasped. "She threw herself?"

"Not throwing. She jumping. Shhh. People very upset morning time. Professor Wigg, he all ready for swapping rooms and all." Mimi pushed down the knob on the cafetière.

"Of course," Laura whispered. "Was Dr. Mellbury there?"

"No, my Tom he find her six o'clock time. She landing right by him van. Tom, he very upset. Bad mess. He call amb'lance. Then Doctor Mell arriving. Him no shaved nor nothing."

Laura finished her breakfast and went to find Venetia. She was still in bed, used tissues scattered around her.

"It's too awful. Mimi told me when she brought up my tea." Venetia took another tissue from the box beside her and blew her nose. "Poor Marjory."

"It's not Marjory. Well it was Marjory but now it's Harriet Huxley. She always said would take her own life, but nobody believed her."

"Her too? I can't keep up with all this death. Where am I? Is it time for some of my pills? I'm feeling thoroughly unwell. D'you think I'm dying too?"

"Of course not. You stay right where you are and I'll go and find that new nurse."

"This is too frustrating," Laura said, as Parker bowled along the corridor to the sanatorium. Harriet's death proved nothing. It was a tragedy, plain and simple. Dr. Mellbury could have helped her – he had had every opportunity – but in the case of the only person who really wanted him to assist them, he had singularly failed. She sighed as Parker continued to pull on his lead. "Perhaps Victoria's right. I should leave matters well alone."

Dudley picked up on Laura's downcast air with his usual nonchalant perspicacity. "I dunno what it is, but it's affecting your curls. D'you fancy a go with the straight'ners Lady B? Bit of a change might perk you up." He caught her eye in the mirror and gave her a wink. "Only joking, I can tell you've brushed 'em out."

"Oh Dudley, I could do with being cheered up. You heard about Mrs. Huxley's defenestration?"

"What ever next." Dudley shook his head. "These women's problems."

"She threw herself out of the window."

"Oh, my Lord."

"Horrible, I know, but she wanted to die. Not like Hetty."

"Mrs.W still on your mind? That's what's getting to you, isn't it?"

"It's with me all the time."

"Bound to be; you and her went back a long way. I can remember the first time you brought her in here. Blimey, who ever'd have thought of giving a woman her size a mullet."

Laura smiled as she recalled the style. Hetty had been cutting her own hair for some years, and was reluctant to take advice. Eventually, Laura had persuaded her that there came a time when professional help was required.

"Oh, but she could be a pest, could Mrs. W," Dudley continued, as he waited for the curling tongs to heat up. "Blue rinse, eh? Those were the days. But seriously Lady B, what's up?"

"Oh Dudley, I don't know, it's this Nurse Creightmore business…"

"Shocking, I must say. I had this matron from Woldham in the other day, wanted a perm, but that's another story. She used to work with the Creightmore woman before she went into the private sector. Said she was one of the nicest people you could hope to meet. Really caring, she said, and that's rare in a nurse these days. Mind you, you can't believe what you read in the papers… But then again, you never can tell, can you? Doing anything nice for the weekend?"

"What, like being taken out to the theatre, followed by a candlelit supper and a spot of dancing? Don't be absurd, Dudley; nothing ever happens when you're my age. It's a waiting game without a referee, that's all it is."

"I think we'll have some spray, all the same. You never know, a handsome man might ring you up out of the blue and ask you out. What's happened to that old General you had in tow? He seemed keen." Dudley got out the can of hair spray.

"He's a Brigadier and he's far too busy going on inappropriate dates with other women to bother with me. That's if I wanted him to, which I don't."

"Woah. Touchy. But seriously, you shouldn't sit and mope." Dudley pressed the nozzle and soon the air in the salon was thick with an indefinable smell.

"Poof, is that new?" Laura asked.

"Bit strong, d'you think?" Dudley read the label on the can. "'Honey and avocado, with a hint of chilli'. Blimey, I should try it on my salad."

"I'm so glad you rang," Sally said. "We were worried about you."

"Who's 'we'?" Laura asked.

They were sitting having lunch in Woldham's first ever noodle bar. Laura had managed to load up her chopsticks with a mound of steaming Pad Thai that now slipped back into the bowl.

"Strudel and Jervis. The Brigadier. He was the one that found out where you were."

"What? You mean…"

"In Woldham Hospital, yes. Don't worry, it's only us four that know. Strudel rang me, so I went over and that's when I met Arthur."

"Arthur?"

"Yes, the Brigadier. He was keen to 'spring you,' as he put it, but we thought it best not, so we kept him busy with Gloria. He cycled over and pretended he was from Dimmock's and he'd heard she had a rare paperweight."

"What happened?"

"She sent him away with a black eye. Still, nothing ventured and all that. Meanwhile, Jervis has identified the man who Stanley won the paperweight from. Did he tell you?"

"I saw him the other evening but he and Strudel were too busy congratulating themselves about their first Ancient Eros wedding."

Sally held her chop sticks in mid-air. "I know, amazing isn't it?"

"Really?"

"Maybe it's different for you, Laura. You're so self-sufficient, perhaps you don't need male companionship."

"I suppose after Tony died I couldn't ever see myself with someone else," she said. "And then the effort of the whole thing and the idea of having to… Well you know, one would have to think about all those ghastly things like having ones legs done, I mean keeping one's moustache under control is bad enough but imagine having to worry about all those unseen bits and bobs. Depilation is a form of torture. But can you really see yourself with another man?"

"Actually…" Sally smiled.

Laura's put her chop-sticks down on the paper table cloth beside her bowl and stared at her friend.

"I haven't gone as far as needing my legs waxed," Sally continued, taking up her napkin to wipe her mouth. "But I have met someone. He's called David."

"David what?"

"Marshall. He's sort of small, which is useful, and fat, which is kind of comforting, and he used to be a wine merchant, which is handy. He's got the most marvellous cellar." Sally took another mouthful and looked at Laura. "Do eat up or it'll get cold. It's delicious, don't you think?"

Laura took up the chopsticks again. She was feeling dizzy with all this information and perhaps it was this palpitation combined with eating Pad Thai that brought back the memory with such clarity. She hadn't eaten Pad Thai in years, not since she and Tony had been in Singapore. Tony had left her alone in the hotel one afternoon while he went to see a man about a packaging contract. She had gone to sit by the pool. It was a glorious day, not humid, just a gentle breeze rustling through the bamboos and the occasional squawk as a parakeet hopped about nearby. She was lying on a sun lounger, her eyes closed, when a shadow passed over her. She had looked up and found herself staring into the eyes of Umar Mamat.

Later that afternoon, Tony had reappeared and joined them. My, that had been fun.

She felt a glow of heat rising up her neck and pincered a prawn. "Perhaps I should consider finding a man," she said. "Where did you meet this David chap?"

"Ancient Eros, of course; Strudel is a saint. That's how I found out about this place. David makes a point of keeping up with all the latest happenings. We came to the opening."

There were so many questions Laura wanted to ask, she hardly knew where to start. "How did David get invited to the opening?"

"He knows everybody. Shall we have a bowl of lychees?"

Laura heard a whole load more about Sally's new beau over the pudding and it was not until they were sipping little bowls of green tea that she remembered the Bacchus. She reminded Sally that she had not finished the story about the man from whom Stanley had won the paperweight.

"Well, Jervis emailed him. He left him my name and number and explained that I wasn't on the Internet and blow me if Chester McKinley the Third didn't ring me at six o'clock the very next morning."

"The Third?"

"I know, and he was charming. Remembered Stanley and all the pranks they'd got up to in the clinic – we didn't get into too much detail. He'd gone in for his gambling addiction, so it obviously didn't work for him."

"How do you know?"

"Because he's invited David and me to his casino in Las Vegas."

"Gracious, I can't keep up. You're not going, are you?"

Laura sat in disbelief as Sally bridled like a debutante.

"You only live once," she said, and tittered. "Anyway, the Bacchus wasn't one of the ones made in Philadelphia by the man Gillinder, who moved from England to set up on his own. Chester was quite miffed we could have even thought he would have some cheap American counterfeit, as he put it, in his collection. He told me its current value is probably in the region of twenty thousand dollars. Shall we get the bill. My treat."

"This is all too incredible," Laura said, as Sally got out a credit card.

They walked out onto the street. It was a bright sunny afternoon but still a chilly spring breeze gusted down the High Street. Sally asked Laura if there was somewhere she could buy a sunhat in Woldham.

"It'll cloud over any second, mark my words and anyway it would blow away in this."

"Not for England, silly, for Las Vegas."

Laura felt a moment of pique. She was definitely being left behind.

"You must meet him, David I mean," Sally chattered on. "Yes, that is a good idea. I think I'll have a little dinner party. Invite Strudel and Jervis and maybe the Brigadier. Have you seen him, by the way? Oh look, talk of the devil." Sally pointed across the street to where the Brigadier was emerging from the florists, carrying a small bunch of carnations. She waved and called out, "Arthur, over here."

The Brigadier launched himself into the road, narrowly avoiding being mown down by a passing motorbike.

"Steady there," Sally called.

He stepped up onto the pavement. "Afternoon, ladies," he said, and then to Laura, "Boxford, have you been avoiding me?"

"Whatever makes you think that? Mind you, it looks as if you're fully occupied yourself, even if I were."

"Yes," Sally said. "Who's the lucky lady?"

"Elderly poetess from Evesham. I've had to buy a copy of her book. Whole thing's costing me a fortune but then Strudel suggested I do my homework after the last escapade. The mongoose prepares himself before he takes the cobra... Well, perhaps not the cobra..." The Brigadier stepped sideways as a couple passed them.

"What happened?" Sally asked.

"Strudel said she informed me, but I can't have been paying attention..."

Laura noticed a bright spot of red high on each of his papery cheekbones.

"...Can't think what came over me. I haven't told that story in years. It must have been something to do with the wallpaper in The Market Café."

"All those black and white stripes? I've never been fond of it," Sally said. "Very good hot chocolate but the décor can make one feel quite giddy."

Have these people nothing better to do than hang about in teashops all day long?
"What story was that?" Laura asked.

"Tanzania. Up country. Short of rations. Not an impala to be seen. Had to resort to zebra. Bloody tough meat at the best of times but the men were ravenous."

"She must have understood that," Laura said.

"Trouble was I went into some pretty graphic detail... Machete sharpening... Gralloching technique... She was from the RSPCA."

"Ah, that's bad. So that was the end of her. Still, better luck this time and if all goes well you must bring the poetess to dinner." Sally put one hand on the Brigadier's arm. "I was telling Laura I'm going to have a little party to introduce you all to my new friend David. I thought I'd invite Strudel and Jervis as they were the ones who got us together."

"David? Splendid, they told me that was going strong."

Laura thought she might be sick. Listening to these two rabbiting on about their love lives was enough to make any sane person retch and she could feel the Pad Thai rising. "I must be going," she said. "Parker's been alone for hours."

She returned to where she had left the car in the shade of the library building. Looking in the window as she unlocked the door, she saw Parker curled up in a little ball sleeping on the driver's seat. He woke up and stared blearily at her. "You are my faithful little man, Parker," she said, as she picked him up and put him on the other seat. "Lets go for a nice long walk."

By the time they got to the pet cemetery the sun had gone in and there was a dampness in the air. Wrapping her coat around her, she crossed her arms and looked down the hill to her old family home. The house imposed itself on the landscape, gloomy in the fading light and the bungalows looked like a straggle of parcels, as if Santa Claus had just tipped them out of his sack. Cars were coming and going in what had once been the peaceful environs of the estate. For a moment, her heart beat faster as she saw Tom's van race down the drive… She put the thought from her mind. How could she get things so wrong? Everybody was in agreement that the right person was in custody. *Blast,* she thought and then, *I'm sorry, Hetty, but it's time I moved on. I haven't given up on finding the paperweight but, bugger it, I'm being left behind and I must speak to Strudel.*

Chapter Twenty-seven

"**H**e will be perfect for you."

"But Strudel, he's the one you had lined up for Hetty. You told me so. Unless Ancient Eros has got two antique dealers from Burford on its books?" Laura repositioned the phone so that it was lodged between her shoulder and her ear while she picked up Parker and put him on the sofa beside her.

"No no, it's the same one. But why is this a problem?"

Laura didn't like to speak ill of the dead but she could not see how Strudel could imagine she and Hetty could possibly have the same taste in men. Hetty'd had a photo of her late husband Algie on their wedding day and, even in his youth, he was no oil painting. His morning coat was straining and the trousers barely covered his shoelaces, which was surprising considering he was a good two inches shorter than Hetty and she could hardly be described as Amazonian.

"I just thought the kind of man that would go for Hetty, might not be the same as the type that might go for me, that's all." She turned to the photograph on the table taken on her wedding day. Tony, tall and elegant, the tailoring of his suit a million miles from that of Algie's. His strong jaw and aquiline nose, as he looked lovingly at her in her cream satin and lace. She picked up the picture, listening to Strudel at the same time. But was Tony looking at her? His eyes seemed to be directed to the very top of her head. Through all these years, she'd never paid much attention to Tony's best man Bill Vane-Williams standing the other side of her in the photo. But perhaps Tony was admiring her tiara…

"I don't think you should look at it like that," Strudel was saying.

"No?" Laura eyed the photograph more closely.

"They may not have got on anyway…"

Oh yes they did! Was Bill actually winking? Had it started before they were married? "Sorry, Strudel, what were you saying?"

"You should not be worrying at this stage. You must tango first before seeing if it will take two. Do you not agree?"

"You're quite right, Strudel. Set it up."

Laura put down the phone and looked at Parker. "Bill Vane-Williams… What a naughty man he was." She patted the dog absently as she stared out of the window.

Laura knew that Basil Miller wasn't for her. She didn't mind the fact that he had facial hair like Colonel Sanders – Tony had been inordinately fond of popcorn chicken – or that he poured the milk in first, which was a habit she had not been brought up with, but he would keep calling her 'your ladyship' and the very idea that she might actually have to touch him made the hairs on the back of her neck stand up.

It had been his idea that they meet at Swinley Court. He had asked her if she knew it. Laura explained that she had only recently stayed there for a short break with her granddaughter.

"Most auspicious," Basil said.

Laura didn't see why it was, but agreed to meet him in the drawing room at four-fifteen on Sunday afternoon.

She arrived early and found herself a seat overlooking the gardens. The waiter asked her if he could get her some tea but she said she would wait until her companion arrived. She smoothed her skirt. It was a striking combination of red and black that somehow made any old jumper look good. The orange plastic necklace may have been a mistake but its size alone was a talking point. She glanced around for a magazine. There was a selection fanned out on a table by the door so she got up to choose one. As she neared the table, a good looking grey haired man in a dark suit put his head round the door and looked about. *That'll do me*, Laura thought, but a group sitting by the fireplace caught the man's attention. He waved and went to join them.

Laura chose a magazine and sat back down. She flicked idly through the pages looking at the houses for sale. South Devon... *Don't want that.* Surrey – historic priory? *Too dark, low ceilings...* She looked up as a couple entered. Battersea Park Road – *surely some mistake?* Thatched cottage in Hampshire... *too many spiders.* Northumberland? *Far too cold.* She looked up again as another very presentable old chap limped past her and settled down on his own.

She began to read an article on Whippets. It said they were the perfect companion and she tutted. She was becoming indignant as the article listed all the members of the aristocracy who favoured the breed. "Ridiculous," she said and heard a cough beside her.

"Lady Boxford?"

She looked up. What could this enfeebled shaking person want? He was probably a whippet owner.

"Basil Miller." He held out his hand. "Ancient Eros?"

Skip the Eros. "Hello, do call me Laura," she said.

"Most kind, your ladyship."

He sat down and they ordered tea and chatted amicably about this and that while Laura wondered how soon she could politely get away.

"I expect you are wondering how soon you can politely get away," Basil said, as he finished the sandwich on his plate.

"I... Was it that obvious?"

"Would you like me to be honest?"

At this they both began to laugh. Basil explained that he was no more inclined to go on a date than he presumed she was.

"My housekeeper signed me up," he said. "I only agreed to meet Mrs. Winterbottom from Wellworth Lawns in order to keep her quiet. It was something of a relief when I was informed that she had died." Basil lifted his teacup shakily to his lips.

"Hetty was a very dear friend of mine."

"Oh my goodness, your ladyship, I'm so sorry."

"It's not your fault. Please, do call me Laura."

"If you're quite sure?"

"Of course I'm sure."

"But I do feel bad. She died quite suddenly, didn't she?"

"As a matter of fact she did, but still it got you off the hook."

"Ah, but Strudel Black doesn't give up that easily. I managed to get out of meeting various others on the grounds that it was the Antiques Fair at Grosvenor House and then there were other exhibitions I was attending. All lies of course, but Mrs. Black kept pestering me and my housekeeper kept pestering me and... well here I am."

"Thanks a lot." Laura crossed her arms.

"Oh, I do beg your pardon. How very tactless of me."

"Think nothing of it," Laura said, as Basil squirmed. "Shall we have another round of sandwiches?"

Having broken the ice and, fortified with a fresh pot of tea and more sandwiches, Laura found that she was actually rather enjoying herself. Basil Miller was most knowledgeable and had many amusing stories about discovering antiques in unlikely places. His main field of expertise was silver and he recalled the time he had been transporting a canteen of Georgian cutlery that belonged to... (Laura's eye's widened as he told her the woman's name) to London when he had been taken short in Tewkesbury.

"I only left the car for five minutes but it was long enough for it to be stolen. Of course the silver was uninsured."

"What did you do?"

"As luck would have it, she had not told her husband. She intended to use the proceeds keeping a young gentleman of her acquaintance in a rented flat. All this came out sometime later when the young man in question began to blackmail her."

"How on earth do you know this?"

"She told me. It was after the car had been discovered abandoned at Leamington Spa station. The thieves hadn't bothered to check the boot."

"So you got the cutlery back?"

"Yes, and sold it for a very decent price. She said her husband was quite unaware of the existence of the canteen and so would be none the wiser."

"That was a lucky break."

"It's surprising what you find out in my line of business. Selling the family silver can be a delicate matter." Basil tapped the side of his nose and then, "Oh God," he said. "I've put my foot in it now."

Laura laughed. "Don't worry, I imagined Strudel had put you in the picture and, you might say, we went one better in selling the family home. Anyway, I'm more than happy with the way it turned out. The present situation suits me well."

Basil wiped an imaginary bead of sweat from his brow and they both laughed.

"You've got Sir Maurice Dickinson there at Wellworth Lawns, haven't you? I used to do a bit of business with him when he was at the Ashmolean, before he got his knighthood. And then of course they had to sack him. A lot of red faces on the board."

"He was sacked from the Ashmolean as well?"

Basil nodded. "Rather ignominious it has to be said."

"He's certainly not my favourite person, I'm afraid."

Basil leaned forward. "I'm inclined to agree."

"Why? Dish the dirt." Laura found Basil's indiscretion quite charming.

"Another family silver story. He wanted help selling off some stuff. Some very desirable objects, between you and me." Basil began to whisper. "It was soon after that his wife died in rather curious circumstances."

"Really? How?" Laura leaned forward.

Basil looked at his watch. "D'you think the sun is over the yardarm?"

It was not an expression Laura was fond of, but on this occasion she agreed whole heartedly and asked for a gin and tonic.

By the time they'd finished their second drink, there was not much Laura didn't know about Sir Maurice Dickinson and his late wife and a whole host of other people Laura knew, or had heard of. It was riveting stuff and she felt as if her own situation was par for the course when it came to the incompetence of the ruling classes in looking after their goods and chattels for the next generation.

"One more for the road?" Basil suggested.

Laura said she really had to go as she had left Parker in the car and had promised to take him for a walk. "But shall we meet again?"

"You mean I haven't bored you with my stories?" he said.

"Not a bit, I haven't heard such good gossip in years."

Basil tried to pay the bill, but Laura insisted they go Dutch. They tottered out into the evening light; felt momentarily guilty at the prospect of driving when near the limit; dismissed it and agreed to telephone over the next few days.

"By the way," he said, winding down the window of his car, "that's a very nice piece if I may say so. Original 1930's bakelite is very rare these days."

Laura's hand went automatically to the necklace. "Yes," she said, her confidence in him increasing tenfold.

As he drove away, Laura and Parker set off around the grounds of Swinley Court.

"So, Basil told me," she said untangling his lead from a lavender bush. "Sir Maurice Dickinson sold a rare and extensive collection of glass..."

There was no sign of the Brigadier at dinner but Laura saw Venetia sitting on her own and went to join her.

"What have you been up to, Laura? I never seem to see you these days." Venetia buttered her napkin. "I even resorted to having lunch with Dr. Mellbury's father the other day."

"I'm sorry. I haven't meant to desert you, anyway I'm here now. What did you make of him?"

"A sort of older, dirtier version of Dr. Mellbury."

"That's what I thought."

"Most disreputable looking altogether and I'm sure that beard is false." Venetia's eyes widened. "I kept imagining him on Crimewatch."

"Really dear, your imagination will get the better of you one of these days."

They laughed but then Venetia became serious again.

"And he was rude as well. He kept looking around as if he might see someone more important. Why he should think that I don't know, but there's another thing I've been meaning to tell you. I think I've seen Mr Fincham's replacement. In fact he's standing over there." Venetia pointed to one of the regular evening staff.

"That's Sidney, dear. He's a waiter."

"He must have been promoted." Venetia raised the triangle of paper to her lips before Laura had time to stop her.

"Here, have mine." Laura handed her the clean napkin and Venetia wiped the layer of butter from her face.

"How are the sunflowers doing?" Laura asked, changing the subject.

"I spent the whole afternoon watering. You must come and see them."

"What a good idea. We'll have our coffee sent up to your room, and there's something I want to talk to you about."

The sunflower seedlings were bent double. Their dehydrated stems had collapsed like cooked spaghetti.

"I thought you said you'd watered them?" Laura went to fetch the plastic jug from Venetia's bathroom.

"It must have been a figment of my imagination. Dr. Mellbury said it's quite normal. He's given me some new pills. The funny thing is I can remember exactly who did what, when and where, as long as it's thirty years ago.'

"But that's such a useful attribute. Then you'll remember saying you were related to Maurice Dickinson's wife?"

"Hilary? Yes, I believe I was. We used to go to tennis parties with them. I remember one afternoon in the summer of 1983. I'd a brand new pair of shorts from Peter Jones. I remember they cost very nearly twenty pounds but I'd got Osbert's credit card in my bag. It was a very nice one, brown leather with a gold buckle. I'd bought it in a shop on The King's Road. It was…"

"Venetia, I'm sorry to stop you, but could we get back to the story?"

"Oh yes, where was I?"

"At the Dickinson's tennis party. Tell me, what was Hilary like?"

"That's right. Osbert and I were playing doubles against Hilary and Maurice. It was a scorching afternoon but we were winning comfortably. Then Maurice started playing a most ungentlemanly game."

"What happened?"

"He began to return my serve with a ferocity he really shouldn't have. Osbert got quite cross with him, so I whispered to Osbert to do the same to Hilary but he was far too well mannered to stoop so low. They beat us six four in the final set. We rather stopped seeing them after that. A pity really, it was such a lovely house."

"Wasn't it her's?"

"She inherited it from a maiden aunt. Priceless things inside. Of course Maurice started flogging them when he lost his money at Lloyd's, or was it her money? Anyway he got the sack from somewhere for something or other and that seemed to start the ball rolling. Did I say Wimbledon? I mean Cheltenham, well anyway all his directorships went tumbling out of the members' box window." Venetia turned to the curtains, drawn against the cold night air. "How could I have said that?" she said.

"I'm sure Harriet wouldn't hold it against you. Do carry on."

"Well, Hilary became a complete recluse by the end, and she wasn't old. And then she just upped and died. Poor dear can only have been in her early seventies."

Laura felt for the comfort of her Navajo bracelet; so Basil Miller wasn't making it up. "More coffee?" she asked.

"Oh no I never drink coffee. Dr. Mellbury says it's bad for... something or other."

"Why didn't you tell me?"

"What?"

"That you're not meant to drink coffee."

"Why?"

"You've just had a cup, that's why."

231

Chapter Twenty-eight

Laura threw back the bedclothes, exposing Parker whose nose had been pressed uncomfortably close to her right thigh. A surge of suspicion rose in her mind like a jumbo jet on takeoff. Maurice Dickinson, short of funds, sells his wife's glass collection. Hardened by the social stigmatisation of his failure, he murders her.

Laura leapt out of bed, rushed through her morning ablutions and began to get dressed. "But that's just the start of it, Parker. He drinks his way through a fortune. Becomes embittered against the world and ends up here…" As she buttoned her white shirt she was reminded of the evening after Hetty's death, when she'd seen him in the hall. "Finally, I think we may be onto something," she said, pulling on the Cameron Hunting tartan shift she always thought of as battle gear. "But we're going to need the help of the Brigadier."

She crossed the dining room to where he was sitting alone reading the paper, a half pint glass of grapefruit juice in front of him.

"That doesn't look like much of a breakfast," she said.

"I'm on a new regime. Liquids only." He took a sip and winced. "As long as you don't order a cooked breakfast, you're welcome to join me. My resolve would fail at the smell of a rasher."

"You're not dieting, are you?"

"What?" The Brigadier huffed and adjusted his hearing aid. It let out its ubiquitous piercing whine. "That fucker Mellbury said he'd got it fixed," he said, and pushed it in again.

"So are you watching your figure, or not?"

"It was brought to my attention by a certain poetess that I was in danger of becoming obese."

"Ah. The poetess. So you're getting yourself in shape for her?"

"The very opposite. I have no intention of seeing the wretched word-smith ever again."

"Not a success?"

"The wildebeest is no match for the lioness when scrub is sparse."

"That makes sense. Nowhere to hide?"

"A predatress."

"Another?"

"The trouble is they're none of them old enough. I don't want some nubile young thing hanging off my elbow."

"How old was she?"

"Late sixties. Still, she was right, too much of Alfredo's cooking has ruined my physique." He took a slurp of black coffee and eyed the croissants that had appeared in front of Laura.

She put the plate on a nearby empty table. "You're quite right. It's wholly unnecessary to eat so much. But listen, I've important news." She told him what she had learned about Sir Maurice Dickinson.

"Boxford, you should let well alone. Your imagination is getting the better of you. The police are in charge of the case now and, until such time as Nurse Creightmore is proved innocent, we must believe that they have the right man, or woman in her case."

"But I've said it before, the trail will be stone cold by that time."

"But at least you won't be accused of being a busy body."

Laura put down her coffee cup with a start. "I never thought to hear you say such a thing. I remember once, not so long ago, you said you wouldn't give up. And now here you are accusing me of being nothing but an interfering trouble-maker."

"Come, come, Boxford. Don't take it badly…"

"I am. I'm taking it very badly."

"Oh, all right, I suppose a little light-hearted prying will do no harm. I've never liked the man. Not since he told me he thought Sandra Abelson was... No, perhaps I'd better not repeat what he said, the slanderous cad. What did you have in mind?"

"A dinner party at Strudel's. We can invite Sally to make up the numbers. She'll have to wait to introduce us to her man, whatever his name is."

Whether or not Sally and Strudel were of the same opinion as the Brigadier, that the police had the right culprit and Laura should leave well alone, they agreed to the conspiracy.

"We will some fun be having with that old snob," Strudel said, as the three women wandered round the charity shop looking for potential prizes that Glady Freemantle could use for the tombola at the Horticultural Society plant sale.

"And how are you getting on with Basil Miller?" Strudel asked, picking up a small china owl.

"I liked him. He's the one that told me about Maurice's glass collection."

"And on the scale of amour?"

Laura followed Strudel to the till as she went to pay for the ornament. "Friends," she said.

"This is a pity, yet I am not disheartened. A man who's working life was spent in the field of farm machinery has recently joined Ancient Eros. A modest profession but he has a very nice black Labrador?"

Laura politely refused.

Sally joined them. "Look." She held out a small wooden rhinoceros. "Remind you of someone? Maurice Dickinson, I'd say by your description Laura." They laughed but decided that it would not do for the tombola.

As they left the shop, Sally asked about Maurice Dickinson's glass collection. "Do you know what it entailed?"

"Not exactly. Basil Miller said that Maurice asked him to value it shortly after his wife died. Basil said he didn't know enough about glass and told him to take it to an expert. It means we've got to find out what was in the collection from Maurice himself. We might also try and find out why he hates women."

"How do you know he hates women?"

"It's a feeling that's all. Something the Brigadier said."

"Not much to go on."

"We'll see."

From Maurice Dickinson's reaction to her invitation, Laura guessed he thought she fancied him.

They were gathered in Strudel's sitting room, Jervis pouring Blue Curacao and rum into a jug of fruit juice with slices of orange and lemon floating on the top.

"It's called a Blue Zombie," he announced. "To go with Strudel's necklace." He handed round the drinks.

Strudel was wearing a low cut, black satin dress. Its lack of flamboyance enhanced Strudel's liberal display of décolletage. Around her neck, a string of lapis lazuli beads dangled above her rugged cleavage. She was bending down to stroke Parker and now she stood and fingered the beads, "Aren't they lovely?" She showed them to the Brigadier who was standing by the cocktail trolley next to Jervis. "Jervis is a present giving," she said.

"Most becoming," the Brigadier remarked.

"I used to have a pair of urns made out of lapis at the bottom of the staircase. Magnificent they were." Sir Maurice Dickinson gestured with his arms from the sofa where he was sitting, legs apart, brass blazer buttons straining. On either side of him Laura and Sally held onto their cocktail glasses as they were squashed further into the sides.

"Careful Maurice," Laura said. "You nearly knocked Sally's drink out of her hand."

Maurice turned to Sally. "I beg your pardon. I'm still getting used to confined spaces. Not a problem you would have encountered, I imagine."

Jervis looked at him with a bemused expression. "But surely you should be used to it by now. You yourself lived in one of the bungalows before you moved over to the main house, only last week wasn't it?"

"Ah yes, but that's the point. I never did get accustomed to it. It's like putting one's gun dog in a Fiat Panda."

"I'm surprised you know about the interior of a Fiat Panda," Laura said.

"There's not a lot I don't know about, but as I was saying, one of the reasons for getting rid of that ghastly little box of a place was so that I could have a decent sized room."

Strudel's jaw dropped. She turned to Maurice. He seemed unaware of the impact he was creating and leaned heavily over Sally to put his drink down on the occasional table at her side.

Laura smiled at him. Now was the time to strike. "So that's why you wanted Mrs. Winterbottom's room?"

At that moment, Parker, who was lying near his feet, let out a yelp and ran off in the direction of Strudel.

Sally reiterated Laura's line of attack. "And have you got a decent room?" she asked.

"One of the best." He pulled his shirt cuff down from under the sleeve of his blazer – Laura did not recognise the buttons – and snorted. "I haven't seen you around," he said to Sally.

"Sally doesn't live at Wellworth Lawns," Laura said.

"Bad luck." He gave Sally a pat on the knee. "Over at that place the other side of Woldham, are you? I had a poor relation there once."

Sally looked at him and then at her fingernails. She clenched and unclenched her fist once and then again.

"Sally has her own delightful cottage," Laura said.

"I've heard the new manager comes from Glasgow." The Brigadier tried steering the conversation into calmer waters. "But there's so much gossip about, I'm sure it's quite untrue. Someone even said his name is John French. Now that would be a coincidence."

"Some silly misunderstanding, no doubt," Jervis said.

"Sally, Laura," Strudel said. "Could you help me in the kitchen for one minute."

With Parker, they followed Strudel out and closed the door behind them.

"How are we to get through this evening?" Strudel asked.

"He is the rudest man I've ever met," Sally said.

"As ignorant as a pig."

"That's as maybe but we are making excellent progress," Laura said. "He's already admitted he wanted a bigger room and I know for a fact that he's not in one of the best rooms."

"So that's what that was about, I could tell it was important," Sally said.

"He wanted Hetty's. I didn't put two and two together at the time. You see, he was going to have it until I complained that I didn't want a man next door to me. That's why Venetia got the room."

"I see." Strudel nodded as she opened a can of gherkins. "But what I was not understanding was how Venetia was to pay for it." She opened the fridge and took out the plates of pickled herrings, placing them round the table.

Laura explained about the rent.

"But Maurice would have had to pay the full amount?" Sally said.

"Yes."

"How?" Strudel garnished the fish with the gherkins.

"Exactly." Laura wondered if she'd remembered to restock her bag with Rennies. "He's going through his money fast. According to the Brigadier, his bungalow was mortgaged. He'd have had every reason to need the Bacchus. We've must find out about his glass collection."

"Is he having children to bail him out, perhaps?" Strudel popped a gherkin in her mouth and threw the can away.

They heard Jervis calling from the sitting room. Strudel looked up at the cuckoo clock above the fridge and gasped. "Oh dear, we have been taking very long in here." She opened the door and called the men in to dinner.

Maurice laughed when he saw the dainty fish knives and forks that Strudel had laid out for the starter. "Haven't used these since the sixties," he said, picking one up. "Mind you we had a bloody nice set ourselves. Silver, obviously."

Jervis tried to change the subject. "D'you care for old time dancing, Maurice? Strudel and I give lessons if you're interested."

"Not my bag." Maurice crammed the entire starter onto his fork and launched it into his mouth. He picked up the empty wine glass by his plate and flicked it with his fingernail. The glass pinged. He tutted and put it down.

"Jervis, the wine, how could you be forgetting? Sir Maurice must be supposing we are coming from the Sahara."

"Ah, the desert." The Brigadier's eyes glazed over as Jervis filled their glasses, "Now I remember having one helluva thirst in the Kalahari once."

It was one of the few occasions when Laura was heartily relieved to sit back and listen as the Brigadier set off on one of his African jaunts. But he hadn't got far into the mirage tale before Maurice stopped him short.

"Is this Hock?" he asked, sniffing his glass.

"Been out of fashion for a while," Jervis said. "But Strudel's partial to it, aren't you my love? She says it reminds her of her homeland. Anyhow, my wine chappie in Woldham say's it's making something of a comeback."

"Always liked a glass of Hock of an evening in the club in Mombasa," The Brigadier said. "Not too strong in the heat. Glass of today's Chardonnay would have knocked a man sideways. As I was saying, we were three days out, not a drop of water…"

"You don't use the wine merchant in Woldham, do you?" Maurice butted in.

"Yes, why?"

"Shocking storage facility. Selling stuff that's been up and down the Fahrenheit scale like a prostitute's thong." Maurice sniffed the glass again. "Just as I thought." He put the glass down in disgust.

"My late husband always used them and we never had any cause for complaint." Laura picked up her glass and took a sip. "Delicious, and made all the more so for drinking out of Strudel's exquisite Bohemian cut glass." Laura had no idea if the glasses had come from

Bohemia or a Tesco Clubcard offer. She glanced at Strudel who remained silent and then turned back to Maurice. "I imagine you had some pretty fine glass yourself in the good old days?"

"Oh yes, some of the finest decanters in the country. Museum pieces." He took a gulp of the 'undrinkable' Hock.

"Just decanters?" Sally said.

"Christ no! We had scent bottles that had belonged to the last Tzarina..." He took another gulp. "...Vases. Lalique and Tiffany. Balusters of the late Qing dynasty. Eighteenth century goblets from Newcastle..."

"How marvellous. Candelabra?" Laura asked.

"Air twisted, hobnail cut, ormolu based, funnel bowled. Scroll and strap cartouches. Medieval, Georgian, Regency... You name it."

"Paperweights?"

"Clichy, Baccarat..."

"Bacchus?"

"Hundreds." Maurice put his empty glass down and let out a long self-satisfied burp.

Laura looked around the table at the array of raised eyebrows.

Sally tried to cover up the indiscretion. "You must have been sorry to see it all go," she said, but Maurice wasn't listening. He had already begun to list the porcelain that had been in his wife's collection.

As Strudel took away the plates, he started on the paintings.

He finally let up after the goulash. His shirt was splattered red with paprika sauce that had fountained from his mouth as he ranted on about Constables, Gainsboroughs and Canalettos.

"Nothing modern?" Laura said. The red daubs on his shirt reminiscent of a Miro.

Another floodgate of pompous boasting was opened, but it reminded Laura of Venetia's little painting that John Fincham had taken to be cleaned. It would certainly pay for a couple of weeks' rent. Did Maurice know about it? How close was Venetia to being his next victim?

*

Sally was the first to leave, as she was driving home and had had to endure the evening on one small cocktail and a glass of wine. The Brigadier was next to make his excuses.

"Oh yes, Arthur," Strudel said. "You must have your beauty sleep. You are having another big day tomorrow. And don't forget, no talk of blood thirsting matters."

Laura felt far too guilty leaving Strudel and Jervis alone with Maurice, so eventually, after a third glass of port, she suggested to him that they walk back together. She clapped her hands and Parker jumped down from where he had taken up residence on Strudel's lap.

"Come along then, Maurice, I think its time we let Strudel and Jervis get to bed."

As Jervis closed the door behind them, Maurice let rip a mighty audible gust from his rear. "That Strudel woman's not a bad cook for a Kraut," he said.

Laura had, in her most private moments, thought that her position at Wellworth Lawns stood for something that engendered a certain respect, but this was manifestly not true in the case of Sir Maurice. They made their way back in silence and it was not until they were getting out of the lift that Maurice continued. "All in all," he said, "that wasn't such a bad evening. Better than I'd been expecting. Shall I come to your room for one last snifter?"

"It's far too late, Maurice," Laura said, thinking about the Munnings that hung in her sitting room. The horse in the painting looked a bit like Theresa Crowd, and Tony had bought it after the mare had won at York and my, what a celebration that had been. Tony, Paddy Mulligan and she had gone on one helluva bender at that nightclub in Harrogate.

Chapter Twenty-nine

Sally was the first to call in the morning; then Strudel; then the Brigadier. The opinion was unanimous. Sir Maurice Dickinson was the rudest bore they had ever come across and, chances were, a thieving murderer to boot.

"You never told us if he had children," Sally said.

"That is key to the whole thing," Laura said. "My friend told me that, in her will, Maurice's wife, Hilary, left the house to their son and daughter. She was too late to save the contents; he'd already sold most of them. Maurice tried to contest the will, but both children had been present when the solicitor drew it up. They bought Maurice the bungalow here but, by the time he came to sell it, he'd had to mortgage it."

"Strapped?"

"Exactly."

"So what's the next move?"

"I'll talk to the Brigadier and let you know."

He was sitting in his usual place by the window in the lounge.

"Ah, Boxford." He rustled his newspaper vigorously back into shape. "I mustn't be long, so we'd better get down to business. Shall we take a short perambulation? Skirt the curtilage?"

"But we've important things to discuss, like Maurice Dickinson. Does it really take so long to prepare yourself for tea? Who is it this time?"

"Parish Councillor. On the youngish side still, sixty-nine, but Strudel's insistent. I've got to finish mugging up on local planning applications. Did you know that scoundrel Colin Partridge who gave the talk on conservation the other evening has put in for ninety-five houses down the London Road? I thought it might break the ice, except she doesn't come from Woldham. So you can see, there's work to be done."

They walked out into a fresh blustery breeze. The Brigadier attempted to smooth down the thin strands of hair on top of his head. "Damn it all, and I meant to get to the barber's," he said. "How come yours remains so neatly in place?"

"Dudley and his hairspray: he never likes to stint on it. So what d'you think?"

"I've never been much good at evaluating lacquer."

"I meant about Maurice Dickinson." Laura veered after Parker as he pulled on the lead, making a misguided dash towards a pair of blackbirds prancing about like matadors on the lawn. "It's too much of a coincidence, all that business about needing a bigger space and then him knowing all about paperweights." Laura was aware of the fact that the size of Hetty's room was what had aroused her initial suspicions in the Brigadier. And now here she was discussing it in relation, not to him, but Maurice Dickinson. She hoped she wasn't making another of her grave misjudgments.

She need not have worried; the Brigadier was in agreement with her.

"The evidence certainly points to him. He's got motive all right, but was he in cahoots with Nurse Creightmore, or have the police got that completely wrong?" he said.

"Nothing is getting any clearer, is it?"

"We badly need to find that damn paperweight."

The sun came out and Laura sat down on the log overlooking the pet cemetery as the Brigadier paced about. The wind whistled through the larch trees, their swaying boughs created ever-changing shadows all around them.

"Basil had a good innings," the Brigadier said.

"He's not dead, is he? He looked fine when I saw him. How could he have died, just when we might need him."

The Brigadier pointed to a gravestone. "Basil. 1966 -1979."

"Oh dear," Laura said, and laughed. "I'd quite forgotten. Basil was a wire-haired dachshund. We went through a phase of them but they were impossible to housetrain. I thought you meant…" At the thought of the dog's short legs and goatee beard, Laura was momentarily reminded of the Antique dealer, but no, dachshund legs was too unkind, he really was more of a whippet.

"Ah, your friend is called Basil."

Laura felt the heat rising in her cheeks. "Yes, my friend. That's all he is, a friend. But he knows more about who's got what and who's sold what and where and when and why, and I think he might be the very person who can help us."

"How's that?"

"He sold things for Maurice Dickinson, but he also put him in touch with other dealers. I'm fairly sure he mentioned a glass expert."

"Very good, Boxford. The Masai fool crosses the dry river bed before the storm."

"What has that got to do with anything?"

"Now I think about it, not a lot. Listen, I'd better get back to planning applications in Upton Chipbury or wherever it is this woman lives, but you carry on the good work and report back later."

Laura's annoyance had simmered by the time she got back upstairs. Basil Miller was her lead and she was quite capable of following it up. She rang the antique dealer and arranged to meet him at his shop in Burford that afternoon. She decided to see Venetia before she set off.

"Listen dear," she said. "Whatever happens, on no account must you let Maurice Dickinson into your room."

Venetia was busy tying sunflower seedlings with pink mohair wool to knitting needles that she had stuck in their pots. "They were growing sideways," she explained.

Her hand slipped. The knot sliced the sunflower clean in two and the top half fell to the floor leaving the knitting needle next to a bare green stem.

"That's a pity. Perhaps it will sprout again? But why can't Maurice come in and see me if he wants? I think he's walking out with Gladys. I've seen them together one or twice now and I thought I might ask them round for a game of snap."

"Play in the lounge if you must." Laura bent to pick up the other half of the stem and noticed, leaning up against the radiator, Venetia's painting. She took a few steps back to admire it. "Whoever John got to clean it has done a jolly good job," she said.

"What's that?" Venetia knocked over a pot, scattering earth onto the white gloss paintwork. She righted the pot and gathered the soil in her hands.

"The painting." Laura pointed at it.

"Oh that. Yes, John has found me a buyer for it. I'm going to give the money to my daughter Angela – I told you she's becoming a vicar? She'll be thrilled. I'm sure she's never had eight hundred pounds in her life."

"Eight hundred pounds? Is that what he's getting for it?"

"Good isn't it?"

There was a knock on the door and Mimi tiptoed in carrying a tray with a banana and a glass of milk, her eyes intent upon the liquid as it eddied at the rim. "He we going, Mrs. Hobb, you lunch." Parker rushed up and jumped at her leg. She stumbled forward and managed to reach the table before there was an accident. "Oh Ladysheep, I not seeing Parkee there."

"Parker, you naughty boy," Laura said and tapped him on the nose. "He loves a drop of milk."

"Milk? Euch. I can't bear milk. Dr. Mellbury says it's very bad for my peptic ulcer."

"No, no. Doctor saying very good for pepti user."

"Oh did he? Pass it here then."

As Laura left, she reminded Venetia about Maurice Dickinson, but Venetia was busy with the sunflower seedlings.

"One for you…" She splashed a little milk into a pot. "… And one for me." She took a sip from the glass and carried on down the row of plants.

Laura took the lift downstairs and hurried in the direction of John Fincham's office. It was an outrage selling Venetia's painting for eight hundred pounds, particularly as he'd already taken two hundred off her for the cleaning costs, and that was only the deposit. It had to be worth at least double that and, anyway, who was this buyer he had found for it? Parker stopped short by the reception desk to sniff at something. Laura pulled him along sharply. "Come on," she said. "It'll be Sir Maurice behind this, mark my words."

She knocked on the manager's door.

"Lady Boxford, what a pleasant surprise." John smiled with benevolent irritation as he shut a black leather box on top of the filing cabinet. "Good hairdo; short fringe and a little height on the crown diminishes the appearance of collagen deficiency in the brow area. Come in." He waved his arm towards his desk. Propped up against it was a large, badly water-marked print of a goat with an array of medals adorning its neck.

"Has your granddaughter told you the news? They've appointed my successor. We'd better keep it under our hats for the time being. I'm sure Mr. Outhwaite will let everyone know soon enough. It's the chap from Birmingham." He sat down behind his desk. "I once had to do a facelift on a woman from Selly Oak. Rather a strange hairline for the fair sex, I remember. Hard to know where to put the sutures; she'd have been much better off with a fringe like yours."

Laura sat down opposite him.

"I've always said long hair on the elderly is a mistake. But here's me carrying on… How can I help?"

"It's about Venetia Hobbs' painting."

John eased the collar of his shirt with one finger. "Looks a treat. The restorer did a first rate job."

"Is he the one who valued it?"

"Obviously, I've taken his advice."

"Just one person? You see, I don't think this is a matter that you are best qualified to deal with. In my opinion it should be sent to a reputable dealer, possibly in London."

"I don't think you need concern yourself with this. I am still the manager here, and as far as I'm concerned if Mrs. Hobbs is happy, then so am I."

"Has this got something to do with Sir Maurice Dickinson?"

"I don't know what you're talking about. Now really, Lady Boxford, you don't want me to have to involve Mr. Outhwaite, do you? Remember all that trouble with Dr. Mellbury. I believe your granddaughter counselled against interference in the running of Wellworth Lawns. I know it must be difficult for you, but try to remember, you don't own this place anymore."

"It's Sir Maurice, isn't it?"

"Lady Boxford, you are becoming agitated. Shall I call the doctor now? Perhaps it's time he gave you some more medication or another trip to Woldham Hospital might be in order. A change of air might be a good idea."

"Don't be ridiculous; there's nothing the matter with me. It's you that has the problem."

John gripped the desk and leaned across at her. "Me?"

"Yes. You seem incapable of answering the simplest question, so I for one am going to advise Mrs. Hobbs to take the painting for a second opinion."

"Fair do's." He released his grip and sat back. "I know of a gallery in Cheltenham. I'm sure the owner would be happy to assist."

Laura wasn't sure why he had capitulated so easily but she continued, "Well, I'd like to be present. Mrs. Hobbs is not the best at retaining information."

"I'll try him this afternoon." John smiled. "I wouldn't want these suspicions of yours to fester, after all."

As Laura wound her way along the country lanes to Burford, she tried to keep her concentration on the road but her thoughts darted back to her meeting with John. It had been an uncomfortable encounter and she was not sure that he wouldn't tell Vince that she had been meddling again. She had to admit that it looked pretty bad, but if she was right, she had prevented Sir Maurice getting away with daylight robbery. But why had he used John to get the painting in the first place?

A car behind her pooped its horn and she realised she had been sitting stationary at the junction. She indicated and turned left. Then she drew into a lay-by and let the car past. Why hadn't Maurice simply murdered Venetia and taken the painting, like he had done with Hetty and the Bacchus?

She patted Parker on the head in a subconscious rhythm as he lay stoically in the seat beside her. "Of course," she said, oblivious to his impending headache. "With Nurse Creightmore in custody, he had to change his modus operandi." She put the car back in gear and set off again.

Nurse Creightmore's arrest had, in effect, wiped his slate clean but he couldn't carry on killing after that. So he had found new ways of obtaining funds, by defrauding the residents through the guileless stupidity of John. There was no doubt in her mind that it was Sir Maurice who had valued the picture in order to obtain it for himself and sell it at a profit at some later date. Quite what he thought he'd get for the Brigadier's print of the regimental goat, she was not sure.

By the time she had parked the car and walked up the Burford High Street, it was clear in her mind. If this didn't work, she'd have no option but to show the Munnings to John, not that it needed cleaning.

In the window of Basil Miller's shop, stood a very fine Georgian sideboard with gleaming brass fittings. She went in. There was no one to be seen, so she called out and, while she waited, she looked around. Basil's taste was impeccable. A pair of gilt armchairs sat beside an oak coffer in the centre of the room. Smaller pieces of furniture and decorative objects filled the rest of the space and on the walls hung a variety of ornate mirrors.

It was in one of the mirrors that she saw Basil scurrying through a door at the back of the room.

He greeted her and offered her a cup of tea.

"Is that all right, having tea in the shop when you're open?"

"Easily fixed." He locked the door and flipped over the 'open' sign.

She followed him through various other rooms filled with the finest quality antiques before they got to a small kitchen area. Basil made a pot of Earl Grey in a little silver teapot that he said was, at a conservative estimate, worth in the region of three thousand pounds.

"I always think the tea tastes better when you know the value of the pot," he said, placing it on a tray with two porcelain cups and saucers and a milk jug. They took it through to the front of the shop.

"Should we really be sitting on these?" Laura asked as they made themselves comfortable in the French armchairs. "How much are you selling them for?"

"To you?"

Laura held up her hands and shook her head.

"Well then, ten thousand the pair. But whatever their value, they're chairs and as such, to be sat upon." He gave her a wry smile. "So what was it you wanted to see me about?"

"A couple of things." Laura told him about Venetia's painting. Basil took a keen interest and said he'd be happy to take a look at it.

Then she asked him if he knew anything about paperweights. She had taken the precaution of bringing the photograph of the Bacchus that Sally and she had identified as the most similar, as far as they could remember, to Hetty's. "I'm looking for one like this." She showed him the picture.

"It's too specialised an area for me," he said. "But I've a friend here in the antiques market who deals exclusively in them. I'll show him the picture if you like? But tell me, why the interest in paperweights? Are you looking to buy one? Wouldn't you prefer a most elegant eighteenth century Dutch marquetry bombe bureau?" He gestured towards a large ornate piece of furniture.

"Most kind and I'd love to be in the market for your eighteenth century Dutch... What did you say?"

"Marquetry bombe bureau."

"Yes. But I simply don't have the room. Paperweights take up less space."

"You have a collection? I always say that there is something wrong with a person who doesn't have a collection, even if it's horse brasses."

"Something wrong?"

"Yes. Missing somehow. I'll let you know what my friend in the market says."

Laura left Basil with the photograph and walked back down the High Street with mixed feelings. It wasn't a deliberate lie, and then he'd said that thing about people who didn't collect having 'something missing'. She didn't like the idea of somehow being incomplete. She looked in the windows of the shops. Garden ornaments? That would never do, she couldn't possibly collect garden furniture with all the commemorative benches already cluttering up the gardens at Wellworth Lawns.

Another shop was filled with old leather trunks and sporting memorabilia; for some reason it reminded her of Tony and she hurried on. She was nearing the spot where she had parked the car when her eye was drawn to a window filled with Staffordshire figurines. She was about to pass them by when she saw a row of china pugs sitting sideways on, their heads facing forwards with black shiny noses and Parker's big saucer eyes. She went in and bought all six and had them wrapped and put in a box.

Feeling altogether a more rounded person, she put the box on the back seat of the car. "I think you'll be thrilled with them," she told Parker.

Chapter Thirty

Laura pressed the mute button on the TV remote and held the telephone tighter to her ear. "Say again, Basil. Who?"

"The paperweight dealer I told you about. His name's Andy. I went to see him after you'd gone yesterday. He thinks he may be able to get hold of a Bacchus like the one in the picture."

"Are you sure?" Laura felt her heart pounding.

"Yes, a chap came in with the very thing a week or so ago, saying he wanted it valued for potential sale. Andy couldn't believe it when I showed him the picture and told him you were looking for one. The remarkable thing is that the same thing had happened to him only recently. Someone brought in a very rare French paperweight that a client of his had wanted for years. Mind you it goes like that in our trade. I sold my silver teapot to a Belgian yesterday…"

"But what about the paperweight, who's selling it?"

"Andy didn't get the man's name."

"But we must find out. What did he look like?"

"I didn't ask, but don't worry, leave it with me. Andy's pretty sure the chap was serious. Mind you, if it is as he said, it's going to cost you, but I expect you were aware of that."

"Did he say which way the head was facing on the silhouette?"

"No. Is it important?"

"When is the man returning? You must find out."

"Any day, I'm sure. I wouldn't worry, Andy won't let me down and he'll be more than fair, I'll see to that."

"That's not what I mean, oh…"

"What is it?"

"I don't actually want to buy it, you see…" Laura paused. She'd have to come clean. "Its a long story but I've been searching for that paperweight because, if it's the right one, with the silhouette facing left, then it was stolen from my dear friend, Hetty, and I think the person who stole it murdered her for it."

"What? Not the same Hetty that I should have met through Ancient Eros… Who you said died quite unexpectedly?"

"I believe she was killed."

"You're not serious?"

"I should have told you in the first place. The paperweight is the critical evidence I need and the thing is, I'm pretty certain I know who the murderer is, and he's not a million miles from where I am now."

"Someone at Wellworth Lawns?"

"What if I said it was Maurice Dickinson?"

"Sir Maurice? Well, of all people, as I said to you before I wouldn't put him past murder. This is serious. I'll have to tell Andy. I think we should leave it to him to go to the police."

"No, he mustn't do that. I've been to the police myself; they think I'm deranged. We must catch the man ourselves. You must tell me the instant he knows for sure when the man is returning."

"This is indeed auspicious news," Strudel said. "We are having a cold collation for our luncheon, Arthur is coming. Why do you not join us?"

Laura said she'd like that very much as she was feeling far too nervous to face the dining room in case she happened to bump into Sir Maurice.

They assembled in Strudel's kitchen, having celebrated Laura's breakthrough with a glass or two of sherry. The table was laden with an assortment of meats and salads.

Laura put a small amount on her plate. "I've quite lost my appetite in all the commotion. I don't know how I'm going to have the patience to wait for Basil to ring."

Strudel added another dollop of mayonnaise to her potato salad. "Ah, Basil, now this is turning out to be a most fortuitous union."

"He's a godsend. I don't know where I'd be without him."

"I thought you said he was just a friend?" The Brigadier held a lump of Bavarian sausage poised on his fork.

"Yes, he's a friend. I've told you, that's all he is."

"Ah, but from the acorn of friendship develops the oak tree of desire. Isn't that right, my love?" Jervis leaned across the table and patted Strudel's hand.

"So true, my love, so true."

"Don't be silly," Laura said.

Jervis looked taken aback.

"I don't mean you. I mean Basil. Nothing like that is going to happen and certainly not with him."

"You must not too hasty in your judgments be. But Arthur, can we expect developments of an amorous nature since your latest liaison?"

"The parish councillor, wasn't it?" Jervis winked at him and held up his glass in mock congratulation.

"Well, I was going to say..."

"Spit it out man."

"I'm afraid..."

Strudel put down her knife and fork and gave the Brigadier a disappointed look. "You are not failing once again? What is happening this time?"

The Brigadier put the bowl of fish balls back on the table. "I tripped over her cat."

"You were meant to be in a teashop. Was this cat most bold and coming out with you, or have you been breaking Ancient Eros rules and proceeding to her home?"

"I thought she said she wanted help with her hedging. I'm a dab hand when it comes to electric clippers."

"So?" Strudel frowned.

"She meant her etchings. I suppose it was some sort of joke but by that time it was too late. I didn't see the step."

"What, you mean it was after dark? Really, Arthur." Jervis tapped the table with the end of his knife. "I'm with Strudel here. You were definitely overstepping the mark."

"You could put it like that. The cat must have thought so too. Of course, all the vets were closed so it had to go to an emergency service in Cheltenham and she said she didn't drive at night, so I did."

"But you don't drive," Laura said.

"I can, it's just I haven't for a while... The accident wasn't so bad. There was no one else involved but what with a new bumper and the vet's fees it turned into a pretty costly outing."

"Oh dear." Laura tried to contain her laughter. "So what happened to the cat?"

"It died."

"This is terrible." Strudel clamped her hands to her head. "How shall I apologise for this clumsy incompetence of my client?"

"It was nineteen. It had had a damn good innings. In fact I'm not at all sure it wasn't already dead when I trod on it."

"For nineteen years nurturing her cat she had been, for you to kill with your big feet." Strudel was apoplectic.

"Steady there, my love," Jervis said. "Poor Arthur didn't do it on purpose."

"I have not had the experience of dismissing a frequenter of the services of Ancient Eros, but I have some feelings in my bones Arthur, that you may be running out of lives like... What was the name of the cat? I must be sending her a card of deepest condolences."

"It was called Kitty."

Laura could contain herself no longer and burst into a fit of laughter.

"Well at least that took my mind off Maurice Dickinson," she said, wiping her eyes.

Strudel began to gather up the empty plates. "To change the subject, I must be keeping you informed of the progress of the Horticultural

Society fete on Saturday," she said. "Gladys Freemantle has asked me to tell you, Arthur, that you will be on the door selling entry tickets for the afternoon's activities."

The Brigadier gave a mock salute.

"She is putting Venetia in charge of one of the cash boxes for the plant sales. Venetia may be needing some assistance with this task. But I am most pleased with Gladys," Strudel continued, getting up from the table. "She has seen the need for diversity and has asked Jervis and myself to be putting on a dancing display." Strudel put the plates in the dishwasher then went to the fridge and got out a bowl of pink blancmange sprinkled with bits of chocolate.

"Gladys is expecting half of Woldham," Jervis said, getting up. He took the pudding from Strudel and placed it on the table. "I thought we'd hit them with the American Smooth." He put one arm round Strudel's waist and hummed a tune as he pinched her bottom with the other hand.

"Oh, naughty Jervis." Strudel shrieked. She pushed him away and returned to the table. "We have three other couples making up the ensemble. I have my confidence in the Patersons; Lance and Carol are not forgetting the steps."

"Bit like following an aviation manual for them," Jervis said.

"Emma Lucas I have teamed up with the bank manager from Woldham who has been joining our classes," Strudel continued. "He is being over six foot five and they are working well together – that is if Emma is remembering she is the woman. But I am having sometimes sleeplessness of the Miltons; Sylvie's footwork is that of a platypus."

"I'm not surprised," the Brigadier said, "All those years traipsing down Whitehall corridors would be enough to give anyone dropped arches."

"And I know her operation was terribly painful," Laura said.

"Yes, you are right and it is good to show that life is not all over after bunions."

Laura was momentarily reminded of John Fincham's socks and sandals.

"Now Laura," Strudel continued. "Gladys is asking me if you can be in charge of produce. Alfredo is allowing pots of jam to be made in his kitchen and he will be producing many lemon drizzle cakes that are always most popular with the guests."

"What a responsibility," Laura said.

"I am sure there will be many others wanting to be of assistance."

"Not Sir Maurice, I hope, but really I am only too delighted to be of use."

"I am told by Gladys that he will not be attending," Strudel said. "But there will be other helping hands."

"You can bet on it," Jervis said. "The fete brings out the very worst in people. Marjory Playfair, God rest her, became demented by the power of being put in charge of the lucky dip last year."

"Do not be reminding me. Nurse Creightmore had to administer there and then."

At the mention of the nurse's name they grew silent, until Jervis suggested an Irish coffee to round off the meal and Strudel went to put the kettle on.

The week wore on and there was no word from Basil. The telephone rang but it was always something to do with the plant fair.

Despite providing for the tombola, Gladys asked if Laura could find some prizes for the raffle. She liked to cover every aspect of fund raising.

Dudley offered Laura some hair conditioner. "I could do you a whole box of the jasmine and manuka honey. It's a lovely texture but people have been complaining of flies following them after I've used it. Take a couple of these instead." He handed her two bottles of shampoo. "Avocado and sweet potato, you can't go wrong with that. The potato gives great body."

Tracy at the pet parlour gave Laura a dog comb and a couple of cans of 'bitch off'.

She took the gifts home. As she placed them in a basket next to the gaffer tape and tubes of No More Nails from Tom, the phone rang.

It was Basil. "The man with the Bacchus has touched base," he said.

Laura held her breath.

"He wants to bring it in on Saturday. He's meeting Andy in the Antiques Centre at two thirty."

Chapter Thirty-one

When Laura told the Brigadier, he was all for accompanying her to Burford, until she explained that Basil would be there.

"Right ho, Boxford," he said. "Whatever you see fit."

She walked Parker over to the bungalows to tell Strudel and Jervis. They were in the kitchen, where Strudel was pressing Jervis' tailcoat.

"I'm afraid I'll have to give up my post on the cake stall," she said.

"Ah, this is bad timing," Strudel said. "The fete is starting at three o'clock and Gladys is having Gary Molatov from *Extreme Topiary* to open it. You will be missing this I think."

"It's a pity. I did so want to ask him about his trip to Marqueyssac. How did Gladys manage to get him anyway? Quite a coup for her."

"He lives nearby," Jervis said, leaning up against the worktop. "Gladys met his wife at a wine auction she was hosting. 'Celebrity Empties'."

"Empty wine bottles?"

"An interesting new concept I think you will agree. Gladys bought a 1987 Medoc that Hilary Mantel once drank. It was only six pounds." Jervis picked up a bottle of orange squash standing next to the bread bin. "What if we said this was once Brad Pitt's and put it in the tombola?"

Strudel looked up. "How stupid."

Jervis put the bottle back. "Mind you, Gladys is keeping Mr. Molatov to herself. John Fincham is in quite a stew about it. He thought that he'd be introducing the great man in his final act as manager, but Gladys was having none of it. Oh, and by the by, I hear that our new manager may also be in attendance."

"Of course, you are remembering who said they wouldn't be at the fete?" Steam puffed out of the iron as Strudel held it in mid air. "Sir Maurice is saying the plants are giving him hay fever."

"I don't recall him sneezing last year when he bought all the polyanthus," Jervis said.

Laura nodded in agreement. "That we then discovered he'd sold on for a profit to the Patersons, who had been away attending the funeral of Lance's brother. Hay fever? Utter rot."

On Saturday morning, Laura asked if she could have a sandwich in her room at twelve-thirty. She was trying on a black beret and had it perched low over one eye when Mimi knocked and brought in the tray.

"Coo err, Ladysheep, you going robbing bank or something dressed like bad man?"

Laura looked in the mirror. "You're right. I look most untrustworthy. Like some sort of hobgoblin."

"You wanting me get you glass of milk? I getting Mrs Hobb some milk when she been gobblin'. Her getting windy very bad these days."

"Bloating."

"I not knowing that. Is no my job do toilets."

"Don't worry, Mimi, its very kind of you, but I'll be fine."

"You best off staying out the way. All kicking off downstairs. Plants everywhere and Alfredo language in the kitchen, whew! Him getting veery angry, Mrs. Free her cakes and all."

"Oh dear, do they need some help?"

"I thinking no. That Brig he ordering people like crazy. I doing teas later see you on?"

"I hope so."

Mimi waved as she shut the door behind her.

Laura looked at the sandwich but she wasn't hungry. She threw a crust to Parker. "Come on, we'd better get a move on," she said, putting him on his lead.

They took the lift downstairs and were faced with a barrage of people carrying tables and chairs out into the gardens where a tent had been erected on the front lawn.

Laura could see Venetia sitting beside one of the plant tables. She was fast asleep surrounded by a sea of greenery, as others rushed around her. Laura tapped her on the shoulder. "You're here rather early, aren't you?"

"It is, isn't it."

Laura pointed to the tent. "This is very grand. Where did it come from?"

Venetia gazed down at the old tin cash box on her lap. "Gladys gave it to me."

"Not that, I was talking about the tent."

"Oh. I think Reverend Mulcaster borrowed it from somewhere. It's even got a dance floor. I think I'll go in if it starts to rain but it's nice and warm out here for now. I only hope I stay awake."

"You'll be far too busy to fall asleep, dear."

"I don't know, Laura; I seem to nod off at the drop of a hat these days. Are you selling onions?"

Laura thought her friend had really lost it this time but then she remembered her beret. She had angled it further back on the crown of her head but judging by Venetia's remark, it was still creating the wrong impression, so she took it off.

"I'll come and find you later," she said and walked round the guy ropes towards the car park.

She had left plenty of time to get to Burford but she found herself speeding down the lanes. Parker sat beside her with his head tucked tight between his front paws. On the main road there was a queue of traffic following a tractor going up hill. One by one the cars in front passed it until it was Laura's turn. She punched the car into second gear in readiness. There was a double line in the road but needs must. She was about to launch out when the tractor indicated and turned off down a track. Laura felt a cold sweat on her back. She slowed the car down and, with it, her heart rate lowered. "That would have been silly."

Parker looked up; his big black eyes the picture of anxiety.

"Nothing is important enough to cause a head-on collision," she said and patted him.

At a quarter past two Laura and Basil walked into to the Antiques Centre. "Andy's stand is on the first floor," Basil explained, as they edged their way up the stairs.

At the top, Basil suggested Laura wait in a booth selling costume jewellery, linen and lace. "I'll see the lie of the land with Andy, he's down the end of the passage. We don't want Sir Maurice doing a runner if he sees you. Stay right there and I'll report back."

There was no sign of the owner of the booth so Laura busied herself looking at Victorian trinkets in a revolving display unit. Her heart began to pound again as she considered how near she might be to her goal. The clock was ticking ever closer to the moment when Hetty would get justice.

She was waiting for a particularly hideous gold bracelet to reappear on its fifth or sixth circuit of the display unit when she heard steps approaching fast down the creaky wooden floor... *Too fast for Basil? Where is he? Is it Maurice trying to make a getaway?* She wished she'd thought of bringing some sort of weapon and looked round for a suitable object. The steps were getting closer. *Where is Basil?* On the floor stood an old pestle and mortar. She picked up the pestle and slapped it into the palm of her other hand. That should do the trick. Not on the head, perhaps, but if she launched out, bent low, she could get him on the kneecaps. That should stop him while the others caught up. She crouched down. The crack of her knees seemed deafening. The footsteps were almost at her... Her heart thumped. She floundered out, waving the pestle from side to side. She felt the pestle make contact, and then she heard an agonised grunt.

Basil put his hands out to save himself but he fell forward, landing on the floorboards with a thud. He got himself up and hopped about rubbing one shin. "What did you do that for?" His face was red with pain and, Laura suspected, anger.

She grabbed at an old pine towel rail to pull herself up, scattering tablecloths and pieces of embroidery. "I'm sorry, I heard footsteps running and I thought…"

"Well you shouldn't have. I told you not to move."

"But…"

More footsteps were now running along the passageway. "What's going on, Basil? Are you hurt?" came a voice.

"It's all right, Andy. This is Lady Boxford."

"Hello," Laura said. "But where is he?"

"We're too late. We've missed him," Basil said. "That's what I was in such a hurry to tell you."

"What? Missed him? How?" Laura wailed." I can't believe it."

"Don't worry." Andy picked up the fallen linen and replaced it on the rail. "He sold me the paperweight. Well, initially he did. I thought I'd see if he knew what it was he'd got, so I said I'd give him five thousand for it. He didn't bat an eyelid. I wrote the cheque out to a business account in the Cayman Islands."

"The Cayman Islands?" Laura looked from Andy to Basil and back to Andy.

"Then I told him he could get at least three times the amount if he waited and took it to auction. That's when he took the paperweight back and ripped up the cheque."

"You mean he's gone and he still has it?"

"Yes. But I know who he is. He left his card, look."

Chapter Thirty-two

"I've got to get back right this minute. Now. Or he'll get away." Laura ran out of the stall and down the stairs.

"Hold on," Basil called, limping after her.

"Shall I…?" Andy called after them, but Laura didn't stop to hear the end of the sentence.

She ran to the car and, as she wrenched open the door, she realised she was still clutching the pestle. She threw it onto the floor of the passenger seat and was starting up the engine when Basil caught up. He jumped in beside her, landing on Parker who turned on him, snarling, and bit him on the thigh before leaping with unaccustomed agility on to Laura's lap. She pushed him onto the back seat as Basil cursed, dabbing his bloodied trouser leg with a pale blue silk handkerchief.

"Why didn't I see it?" Laura moaned pointing the car into oncoming traffic. "He must have planned the whole thing…"

Basil grappled with his seatbelt. A lorry screeched to a halt as Laura cut in front of it and sped on down the hill.

"Pedestrian crossing!" Basil slid down the seat.

Laura hit the brake and Basil dropped the seatbelt. The sash recoiled into its holder hitting him on the cheekbone with the buckle. He grabbed the handrail above the door and bent his head low.

"Slow down," he pleaded, as Laura crossed the bridge and headed out of town.

"I can't. Time is of the essence." She rammed the car into third, split up a pack of cyclists, and roared on up the hill.

The main road was mercifully clear and, twenty minutes later, they had turned off for the last few miles of country lanes to Wellworth Lawns. Laura took the familiar bends with determination.

"I may be sick." Basil held his hand over his mouth.

Keeping her eyes on the road, Laura negotiated a sharp left hand turn.

Righting the steering wheel, she glanced at him. He didn't look well. "What did you have for lunch?" she asked.

"Hummm…" he mumbled.

"Wind down the window."

"…Ous."

From the wing mirror Laura saw the vomit catch in the wind and trail out behind them, speckling the hedge with bits of chickpea dip. Basil wound up the window and wiped his mouth with his handkerchief, covering his cheeks with a thin patina of blood from his leg wound.

They hurtled into the drive to Wellworth Lawns and passed the lines of cars parked head to tail along the verges.

"Blast, the fete," Laura said as she negotiated her way through them. She drove straight over a bed of newly planted hydrangeas and came to a halt in front of the entrance to the old stable block, where the Brigadier was sitting manning the makeshift ticket office.

She pulled on the handbrake and turned to Basil who was slumped in his seat, his eyes closed. "Whatever's the matter with you? Come on, let's go."

As Basil opened his door, Parker leapt over the seat and out of the car. Laura called to him but he carried on through the stable yard and out the other side in the direction of the tent that was now crowded with people having tea. She was about to chase after him when she remembered the pestle: it could be useful. She leaned over, picked it up and put it in her bag before slamming the car door shut and heading for the gardens.

The Brigadier jumped up from his seat as Basil hobbled past. "Boxford, what's happening and who's this ruffian?" He grabbed Basil by the collar and hauled him away from the entrance.

"It's Basil... Look, we haven't time for this. Come on, we've got to get him before its too late."

"But he's not here," the Brigadier said.

"It's not him."

"Not...?" The Brigadier threw Basil to one side.

Basil stumbled and managed to get to his feet. "It's not Maurice Dickinson."

"What?" The Brigadier turned to him in disbelief. "So who?"

"Come on you two, this is urgent," Laura said. "Follow me."

The Brigadier pulled up the tablecloth covering his ticket stand to reveal his sabre. Laura looked at the weapon.

"In case there was trouble. Gate crashers..."

"For God's sake keep that thing in its scabbard," she said. "Now come on."

The Brigadier looked at Basil. "He'll have to pay later."

"Don't be ridiculous. Let's go."

Laura ran in the direction of the house, skirting round the tent. She avoided the crowds milling about choosing plants and didn't stop when a couple pushing a buggy held up the Brigadier and Basil. As she mounted the steps to the front door, the tannoy announced Strudel's dancing display and was followed by the blare of Somewhere my Love.

She rushed into the hall, narrowly avoiding Mimi and Alfredo carrying fresh trays of cakes and drew up to catch her breath outside the office.

Chapter Thirty-three

"I've always hated old people. You give them what they want. Make them look young again, but it's a travesty. They're still old and slow. Old and slow like you, and stuck here, while I shall be far away. Now, if you don't mind, I have a plane to catch." John Fincham pushed Laura aside.

"Oh no you don't." Laura pulled the pestle from her bag and rushed at him waving it above her head. He grabbed her, one hand tight around her neck, the other at her wrist. Her head throbbed. She felt the blood gather, thick at the back of her eyes. The pestle fell to the floor and rolled under the desk as she began to choke.

"You see. It's as I said, you're merely another old and feeble creature like all the rest of them. Like your friend Mrs. Winterbottom. And it's so easy." His grip loosened. "Let me show you."

He pushed her onto a chair, grabbed the small black attaché case that was lying on the desk and opened it. Laura was coughing, her throat tight, unable to speak.

He drew out a hypodermic.

"A little prick that's all it takes. This amount of Botox will remove those lines, you can be sure… For good and all." He held up the syringe and tapped it. "Injected right behind your ear. You'll drop off your perch with that look of astonishment old Mellbury's well used to putting down to heart failure." He came towards her, the needle sparkling; sharp ray of death.

The door burst open and the Brigadier stormed into the office with Basil close behind.

"Oh no you don't. Take this, you murderous swine." He thrust the sabre at John. The manager backed away, bent down and picked up the pestle from beneath the desk. He threw it at the Brigadier. It caught him a blow on the temple before clattering to the floor. The sabre fell with a clang as the Brigadier staggered backwards and, in so doing, crashed into Basil who was easily unbalanced by his wounded thigh and swollen knee. Basil hit his head on a filing cabinet and fell to the ground. The Brigadier's ankle twisted. He put out his hand again to break the fall but there was nothing there and he crashed to the ground next to Basil.

John Fincham glanced at his watch. "I'd finish off the lot of you but, as it happens, I'm in something of a hurry." He replaced the syringe in the attaché case and flicked the catches shut.

Laura had not seen the suitcase behind his desk that he now picked up. "Stop him," she croaked as the manager strode from the room. She pulled herself out of the chair as the Brigadier and Basil jostled with one another in an effort to get to their feet.

"Mind out," the Brigadier shouted.

"Get off me," Basil implored as the Brigadier attempted to use his leg as a lever.

All three then reeled out in search of their quarry.

John Fincham was silhouetted in the sunlight at the front door. As Laura gave chase, he ran down the steps and into the crowd, the suitcase swinging wildly from side to side.

"Stop him!" the Brigadier yelled as the crowd parted. John Fincham looked back at them with a malevolent grin. He dodged round the side of the plant stall. Laura watched as Venetia was thrown from her chair by his flailing suitcase. She landed in the tray of her own sunflower seedlings as he disappeared into the tent and was lost from sight.

The music was blaring and, as Laura pushed forward, she could see the ballroom dancers twirling in a kaleidoscope of brightly coloured frills and flying tailcoats. Strudel, in a sea of eau de nil, was waltzing with Jervis to the tune of the *1812 Overture*; the other couples following suit. Laura saw John battering his way through the dancers. The Miltons were the first to go down. Beside them went Emma Lucas and the bank manager. Strudel and Jervis appeared oblivious and danced gaily on. Laura tried to call to them. She waved her arms but couldn't attract their attention.

As she continued to weave around the packed tables surrounding the display, Parker waddled up beside her. Quickly she drew out his lead from her bag and hooked it onto his collar. Then, without hesitating, she picked up a large slice of generously iced Chocolate Fudge Cake from the plate of a man seated at a table beside her.

"Oy, that's mine," he said.

"Sorry." Laura leant forward and wafted the cake in front of Parker's nose. He yapped wildly as he watched her toss it high in the air in the direction of Strudel. Then, at the top of her voice Laura yelled, "Parker, FETCH." He pricked his ears, the memory of the command embedded in his brain from puppydom. The cake landed with a splat on the spot that, seconds earlier, Strudel and Jervis had sailed over. Straining on the lead – Parker was on it, sharp as any lurcher. Laura let loose the brake and he bolted across the floor of the tent. The lead reached its maximum and Laura was towed forward.

Lance and Carol Paterson had avoided the carnage of the other dancers and were following Strudel and Jervis at a safe distance. Lance didn't see the cake, but he saw the dog about to cross his path. As he pulled Carol out of the way, they collided with another couple. All four fell to the floor. The cake was beyond them as John Fincham sidestepped the mass of crumpled taffeta, swinging his suitcase from side to side. Parker rushed past. Laura stopped, held the lead tight and bent low; it was taut as a guitar string as Parker strained for the mouth-watering treat.

The tripwire caught the manager at ankle height as Parker reached the cake. John Fincham stumbled to his knees, the suitcase beside him.

He tried to rise but lost his balance on the highly polished dance floor and fell again. The suitcase shot out of his grasp and ricocheted into one of the tent posts.

The lid flung open.

A silver candlestick rolled forward and came to a halt beside Carol Paterson who had not been able to disentangle her dress from her stiletto heel and was still struggling to her feet. She picked it up and looked at the hallmark on the base. "That's ours," she said.

From behind Laura, the Brigadier shouted, "My medals."

Gladys Freemantle had run onto the dance floor and picked up a bright red leather box. "My jewels." she exclaimed. "You pillaging bastard..." She ran to where John was crawling on all fours towards the tent flaps and hit him hard over the head with the box.

He cried out and crawled on.

The Brigadier rushed past Laura, the suitcase and his medals and launched himself in a rugby tackle on the manager. "Bring me my sabre someone," he called out, wrestling fiercely with John. Basil limped up to join him carrying the sword. Jervis followed. He ripped off his tailcoat, threw it over John's head and held it firmly. "Call the police," he shouted.

"And turn this blasted music down," the Brigadier bellowed.

Flicking his chef's hat from side to side, Alfredo pushed through the crowd. "Holy Papal indulgences, let's have a butcher's at 'im. Here, mind outta da way, Brig. I'll take over now." The chef straddled John and, in a matter of seconds, had him in a debilitating half Nelson. From underneath the tailcoat, a muffled cry for mercy could be heard.

"No chance," Jervis said and held the tailcoat tighter round the manager's head.

The Brigadier dusted himself down, took the sabre from Basil and stood with one foot resting on John's buttocks like the photograph of Laura's father with the shot tiger.

The music stopped. "Bravo!" Laura cheered, and hurried forward. The crowd began to clap and then, through the tent flaps she could see her granddaughter, Victoria with Vince and another man. They appeared to think that the clapping was for them, apparently having not noticed the chef and Jervis on top of the now unidentifiable mass that was John Fincham. Vince motioned for silence and gradually a quiet descended.

"Ladies, Gentlemen. I am pleased to be able to introduce you all to the new manager of Wellworth Lawns, John French."

From behind them, Laura saw Phil Sandfield, accompanied by his young assistant Lizzie, running from the car park towards them.

"John French, that's him, isn't it?" Lizzie fumbled with her truncheon.

"Not French..." Phil Sandfield tried to grab her, but it was too late. The enthusiastic new recruit hit the incoming manager a deft whack between the shoulders and he crumpled to the floor.

The Bacchus was in John Fincham's trouser pocket and, by the time Alfredo had dismounted and Inspector Sandfield had applied the handcuffs, the glass orb had done some damage. John's eyes were watering as they pulled him to his feet.

"Someone, please, I beg you, it's crushed my inguinal regions," he said in a high-pitched sob.

Lizzie delved into his pocket and, as she held it up, a ray of late afternoon sun shimmered through the tent flaps and the paperweight glinted.

The Brigadier took a step forward toward Phil Sandfield, the sabre still in his hand. "I expect you will be making a formal apology to Lady Boxford," he said.

Lizzie rounded on him, "If you're not careful, I'll have you arrested for being in possession of a dangerous weapon."

"Dangerous? I'll give you dangerous..." The Brigadier dropped the sword and was about to take a swipe at her when Vince stepped in.

"Steady there, old timer. You don't want to jigger yerself out, now do yer? Alfredo, get the bar staff to knock up some jugs of Pimms. Give all the punters a complementary glass on me. And get the music back on. Let's get this party started."

"I'll come with you," Victoria said to Alfredo. "Mr. French could do with an icepack for his neck."

John Fincham was led away and, once the general public had had their free drinks, they became liberal with their wallets and purses, buying everything and anything that was left, including the remains of Venetia's sunflowers.

Laura sat surveying the scene with the Brigadier and Basil.

"I'd like to raise my glass," the Brigadier said, "to the pug."

Chapter Thirty-four

Dr. Mellbury was arrested the day after the fete. It appeared that John had blackmailed him into getting Laura sectioned when he thought she was onto him. John had discovered that the doctor's father was on the run from the Spanish police for armed robbery.

When Laura heard this from Victoria, she was mortified and went to tell Venetia she had been rightly suspicious. Then she went to tell Strudel and Jervis.

Strudel blushed deep crimson and rushed from the room. She returned with one of the newspaper cuttings she kept under her mattress. "I knew his face had a familiarity to me," she said showing Laura and Jervis the picture. "Look here he is. Dr Mellbury's father, with my Ronnie on the Costa Brava."

They peered at the photograph of the two old lags – Dr. Mellbury's clean shaven father revealing his chinlessness – sitting under a striped parasol with pints of beer in their hands. Jervis read the headline. "But it says, 'these two are wanted.' I thought Ronnie was behind bars?"

"Did I never tell you that part of my ex-husband's story?" Strudel said.

Victoria and Vince stayed on to make sure the new manager found his feet. He soon impressed Vince with his efficiency and they felt able to leave him to it. But he was a dull fellow and not a fan of Bingo. He instigated a new regime of after dinner self-improvement sessions and invited guest speakers to talk on topics such as inheritance tax planning, sign language and budget funerals.

Everyone agreed that Bingo had been far more fun and that Dr. Mellbury's dark humour was better than a lecture on the importance of living wills and natural burial sites.

It was not long after, that Nurse Pendleton, nee Creightmore, resumed her duties at Wellworth Lawns. The residents were most supportive of her latest sideline to supplement the newly-weds' income, when they heard the sad story of how Barry Pendleton had lost his money. He had turned to the Chinese remedies after some years as landlord of a hostelry in Hemel Hempstead. Barry had clung on to the concept of warm bitter beer and Babycham. He had overestimated the popularity of scampi fries and pickled eggs in an emergent gastro pub market with catastrophic consequences.

He did however, try to resurrect the concept of Japanese Knotweed as a preventative for Alzheimer's but Nurse Creightmore scotched his activities, which, in hindsight was a pity.

Meanwhile Laura and the others bought generous quantities from the nurse's range of organic rejuvenating creams and unctions, that she assured them were of the highest quality.

Gladys Freemantle appeared regularly, Boudicca-like, in her peach kernel and blueberry face-pack.

"It's fig and pomegranate, it must be edible," Venetia said, putting body lotion on her granola.

The Brigadier found that the Rose Geranium massage oil brought a shine to his regimental boots that he had not been able to obtain since his supply of okapi fat had run dry.

But Laura felt the urge for excitement. Having solved the mystery of Hetty's death – it would be sometime until it was discovered exactly how many such murders John Fincham had committed – she wanted action; to feel the wind in her hair.

She thought about her friends in the hospital and spoke to Nurse Creightmore about Celestia, but there was nothing to be done, so she wrote them a card saying she hoped they were getting on all right and that they would be welcome to visit her if they were ever discharged.

She went to a few antique fairs with Basil. He was good company but there was only so much effort she could put into discussing cabriole legs.

The Brigadier appeared to be constantly occupied and, once when she saw him and asked what he was doing he replied, "The panther lurks for no man," and hurried off.

So she traded in her old car and bought a soft top. But Parker didn't like it and took to lying in the footwell, shaking. Dudley was not impressed either. He complained that she turned up for her hair appointment with too many tangles.

"What am I supposed to do with this?" he said, and threatened to give her a short back and sides. So she kept the roof on and took up rock climbing at the local leisure centre, which ended with a sprained wrist.

"You having old age crisis, Ladysheep?" Mimi said one morning as she helped her with the elasticated bandage. "Otherwise, why you watching sky-diving programme this time of day and all?"

"You're right, Mimi. It's because I'm bored."

"You needing new friend I thinking. Man maybe?"

Laura went to see Venetia but she was busy rubbing her legs with Nurse Creightmore's 'Exotic Blend' of exfoliant.

"But dearest, shouldn't your take your tights off first?" Laura asked.

"They must be supple for the cruise."

"What cruise?"

"The one I'm going on." Venetia held up a picture of a deep sea trawler that she had cut out from a magazine.

Strudel rang. She said she was sorry that she hadn't been to see her but she and Jervis had been run off their feet organising their new Ancient Eros speed dating sessions in Woldham Town Hall.

"We are having so many successes," she said. "Platinum Partners is offering to buy us out. But I have a client who I think will be suiting you like a kid glove."

"Really, Strudel, I'm not in the game of dating. I liked Basil very much but as a friend, that's all, and anyway I'm past caring, what with my wrist."

"You must not be taking this attitude of feeling sorry for oneself. I will hear no more of this. I shall arrange the meeting now. You will be having tea at The Queen's Head Hotel. He is a man of independent nature who will be most compatible I'm sure."

Laura felt that perhaps it was her duty to have one more attempt at finding a partner and then Strudel could give up on her.

She toyed with what to wear. She threw skirts and dresses on the bed. "What is the point," she said to Parker as she fought with the zip on a green tailored dress. "Why should I constrict myself unnecessarily?"

She hung them all up again, and put on her favourite old pleated tweed skirt. There was nothing like the swing of a good piece of Hebridean cloth to boost morale.

Strudel had not told Laura anything about her date. She said she didn't want to give her the opportunity of misconstruing what she said.

"It is truly a blind date."

"Is he visually impaired? That could be a blessing."

"No, nothing of the sort."

"So, how am I meant to know who he is?"

"He will be having a red rose."

"Really, Strudel, what a cliché."

"No Laura, I will be having no more of your English cynicism."

Laura drew up in the hotel car park, patted Parker and told him she would not be long. She walked through the swing doors and asked where teas were served. The receptionist directed her to the lounge. It was a long dark room but a fire crackling in the grate made it warm and friendly. She looked around amongst the sets of armchairs and sofas surrounding low tables. There were various couples chatting in hushed voices. Then in one corner by a window looking out onto the street, she saw the Brigadier. Really, she thought, Strudel is quite out of control. She can't even remember how many people she is sending to the same place. At that moment the Brigadier looked up and waved. Laura had no choice but to go over.

"Has Strudel sent you?" she said.

"Yes," he said. "Sit down." From his jacket, he withdrew a small blue box with a ribbon round it and handed it to her. "Open it."

Inside, wrapped in tissue paper was a clear glass paperweight, a single red rose in its centre. She held it in her hand. "Oh, Arthur."

"Steady, Boxford," he said. "Steady."